THIS IS MY AMERICA

THIS IS MY AMERICA

KIM JOHNSON

Random House New York

Text copyright © 2020 by Kim Johnson
Jacket art copyright © 2020 by Chuck Styles

All rights reserved. Published in the United States by Random House Children's Books, a division of Penguin Random House LLC, New York.

Random House and the colophon are registered trademarks of Penguin Random House LLC.

Visit us on the Web! GetUnderlined.com

Educators and librarians, for a variety of teaching tools, visit us at RHTeachersLibrarians.com

Library of Congress Cataloging-in-Publication Data
Name: Johnson, Kim, author.
Title: This is my America / Kim Johnson.
Description: New York: Random House Children's Books, [2020] | Summary: While writing letters to Innocence X, a justice-seeking project, asking them to help her father, an innocent black man on death row, teenaged Tracy takes on another case when her brother is accused of killing his white girlfriend.
Identifiers: LCCN 2019024787 (print) | LCCN 2019024788 (ebook) |
ISBN 978-0-593-11876-4 (hardcover) | ISBN 978-0-593-11877-1 (lib. bdg.) |
ISBN 978-0-593-11878-8 (ebook)
Subjects: CYAC: Racism—Fiction. | Judicial error—Fiction. | African Americans—Fiction. | Race relations—Fiction. | Prisoners—Fiction. | Murder—Fiction. | Family problems—Fiction.
Classification: LCC PZ7.1.J623 Th 2020 (print) | LCC PZ7.1.J623 (ebook) | DDC [Fic]—dc23

The text of this book is set in 11.5-point Adobe Garamond Pro.
Interior design by Cathy Bobak

Printed in the United States of America
10 9 8 7 6 5 4 3 2
First Edition

Random House Children's Books supports the First Amendment and celebrates the right to read.

For those seeking justice and rehabilitation,
keep fighting.

Friday, April 23

Stephen Jones, Esq.
Innocence X Headquarters
1111 Justice Road
Birmingham, Alabama 35005
Re: Death Penalty—Intake Department

Dear Mr. Jones,

My dad has precisely 275 days before his execution. You're the only hope we have because every lawyer we've used has failed us. In the last appeal, Judge Williams didn't take more than five minutes to consider.

We mailed a renewed application since it's now been seven years.

Please look into James Beaumont's application (#1756). We have all the court and trial files boxed up and ready to go.

Thank you for your time.
Tracy Beaumont

P.S. Jamal's going to college. Can you believe it? All that running added up to something. If you have those letters where I say he was wasting his time, please destroy them.

P.S.S. Next Saturday at 10:00 a.m. Jamal's doing an interview on The Susan Touric Show. You should check it out.

READY. SET. GO.

Time runs my life. A constant measuring of what's gone and what's to come. Jamal's hundred-meter dash is a blazing 10.06 seconds. That's how my older brother got this monumental interview. I'm not thinking about Jamal's record, though. I'm thinking about Daddy's time. Seven years—2,532 days served, to be exact.

This running clock above my head's been in place since his conviction. That moment branded me. Mama gripped the courtroom bench to keep from collapsing as each juror repeated *guilty.* I looked to Mama for an explanation. The empty look in her eye cried out the answer: death.

Since then, it's ticktock.

Here at the TV station, Jamal rocks steadily in the guest chair, watching highlights of his track career with the producer during a commercial break. He glides his hands over his fresh barber cut, his mind more likely on the camera angles that'll best show his waves.

We're true opposites, despite our one-year difference.

He's patient.

Calm.

Thinking.

Living.

Loving.

He's everything on the outside I wish to be. Bringing people in, when nine out of ten, I'd rather push them out. That's why I hate that my mission crosses paths with the biggest day of Jamal's life.

Five minutes and thirty-seven seconds until showtime.

As the commercial nears its end, I don't have to look up to know Mama's leaving the makeup room. The click of her heels echoes past a crew of engineers and radiates as she circles around Jamal to the guest seating area on the side of the studio stage. She enters like only a proud Black mother can, hair all pressed and curled, with a sharp black skirt suit that fits her curvy figure.

Mama's been name-dropping everywhere she can about the news anchor Susan Touric showcasing Jamal as a top athlete. I expected a live audience, but the set is a small studio and crew. I look out to Susan Touric's interview desk with a backdrop image of Austin, the state capital. They've pulled out a white couch so there's space for my family to join Jamal at the end.

Mama smiles at Jamal, then at my little sister, Corinne, but I swear she throws some silent shade my way. Her not-so-subtle warnings have been going on for the past month. She knows I want Daddy's story to seep out, but Mama has made clear there is no room for Daddy on this occasion. Not because she don't love Daddy, but because she wants Jamal to have a clean slate at college as Jamal, not "Jamal, the son of a murderer."

If it was a few years ago, I'd understand, but Daddy's got less than a year. No extensions. No money for more appeals. While time uncoils itself from Daddy's lifeline, she's forbidden Susan Touric from mentioning him, too. The show agreed not to talk about Daddy in exchange for Jamal showing up; and if Susan tries anything, Mama says we'll straight up leave.

Mama stands by me and leans near my ear. "Tracy, ain't it something to see your big brother's hard work paying off?"

"Mmm-hmm," I say, even though I'm still hoping the journalist in Susan can't help but fling open Pandora's box—on live television.

Mama won't be able to stop it then.

Then our truth can breathe free.

The fight for Daddy's appeal won't be in vain. People will finally hear the truth. Wake up to the fact that Lady Liberty has failed us. Failed so many others.

Angela Herron floats into the room with a twinkle of excitement in her eye. Her long blond hair bounces with an unstoppable future. Angela's a new production intern for *The Susan*

Touric Show, even though she's only a senior in high school, weeks away from graduating with Jamal's class. It's no coincidence that her dad owns Herron Media back in Galveston County, where Jamal's worked the past two years. She'll always have it easy. I've worked my ass off to be in the running for the school newspaper editor next year so just maybe I can get into college internships early. Meanwhile, she's already advanced to a position most college grads can't get.

"Nervous?" Angela asks Jamal.

"Nah." Jamal's foot taps as he tries to play it cool.

"You got this." Angela hands Jamal a sheet of paper. "Here are the questions Susan's asked the other guests."

"Thanks, Ang."

All the other interviews have the common thread of compelling American stories: a boy who battled cancer; an almost career-ending torn ACL; a girl hiding her gender at football tryouts. Each story a tearjerker. I'm hard pressed to believe that they'd leave out what's at the heart of Jamal's dedication. What he's had to overcome.

I glance over Jamal's shoulder and skim the questions, looking for my window of opportunity.

"Tracy," Mama says. "Give your brother space."

Hater. I step closer to Mama.

Angela goes over a few pointers. Before I can ear hustle more, Angela's boyfriend, Chris Brighton, enters with a large box of doughnuts that appear tiny in his hands. Chris is still built out from football season, his strawberry-blond hair tucked under a Texas A&M hat with his jersey number, 27, stitched on the side. He'll be playing there next year. Just like at school, he barely acknowledges us.

"Excuse me." Angela goes to meet Chris, and I catch her mouthing, *What are you doing here?*

Chris places the box of doughnuts on the table. Angela touches his arm, like she's trying to be sweet, but by the way her mouth is turned down, it's obvious that she's irritated at him messing up her work flow.

"Can I have one?" Corinne asks, ogling the doughnuts.

Mama agrees, and Corinne tiptoes past Angela. When she reaches in, the box slips.

"Watch it," Chris snaps, catching the box. His square jaw is tight, like he can flick Corinne away with a nasty glare.

Jamal jumps up. Chris's ears get red as Angela shushes him, pointing to the red flashing ON AIR sign.

Sorry, Corinne mouths, then takes a bite.

Jamal joins us, his arm now around Corinne, who's dressed in a striped yellow church dress. I chose a simple black A-line dress. My hair in an updo, sleek edges, and curls all out like a crown was placed on top of my head.

The camera cuts away from Susan, and they play a video of the four athletes they've spotlighted in May.

"It's starting." Corinne nudges Jamal before clapping like there's a live audience. Crumbs flying everywhere.

Jamal chuckles and joins in with Corinne. I can't help but let a smile slip, and I clap softly because Jamal deserves this.

The last of the footage includes Jamal's records rolling up the screen. He's compared to competitive world athletes with Olympic gold medals. Then they show Jamal's last track meet of the season, where he beat the boys' high school track record, tying the long-standing 1996 college record. I feel like I'm there again. The crowd cheered so loud it shook the bleachers. You knew something special was about to happen. Jamal dropped to his knees when the scoreboard confirmed the new record.

"You know what you gonna say?" Corinne asks.

"Do I know what I'm gonna say?" Jamal bends down to Corinne so he can whisper. "You got advice for me, baby sis?"

"Don't say ummm."

I burst out a laugh, then cover my mouth when Mama nudges me.

"That all you got?"

"You say ummm a lot when you're nervous." Corinne shrugs and takes Mama's hand.

"You hear her, Tracy?" Jamal elbows me. "I don't say ummm a lot."

"You kinda do." I smirk.

"Yoooo. You wrong for saying that right before my interview. You know what's gonna be stuck in my head now, right?"

"Yip," I say. "Ummmm."

"Ummmm," Corinne joins in. We sound like a chorus at the side of the stage.

"Knock it off now, girls." Mama wags her finger at us.

Angela cuts between us, gesturing for Jamal to follow her onto the studio's stage while we take a seat offstage. Jamal gives her a wink when she wishes him good luck. Her cheeks go pink. He can always make someone feel special. Daddy says he's got a heart of gold. I just wish he wouldn't throw it around so easily.

I watch Chris in the shadows. White privilege at its finest. Today he's exhibiting classic toxic masculinity. I can tell Angela doesn't want him here, but he's too arrogant to think different. He acts that way in school, too, like he could get away with anything, since his dad is sheriff.

Poised and ready, Susan Touric faces the camera marked NBS ONE. She looks like all the white newscasters they have at this station except the rotating weather girls of color. Susan's dressed in a white blouse and a gaudy necklace of choice for the day. Her silky black hair is coiffed in a bob around her fake-tanned skin, and pink lipstick matches the color of her glasses.

The crew shifts into movement. The spotlight zooms in. The producer gives her a hand signal near the teleprompter. A green light blinks, and Susan plasters on a smile. On cue, the music begins. My heart now beats at a rapid pace.

"Reporting live here at NBS World News. If you're just tuning in, we've been highlighting top scholar athletes across the country. I have the pleasure of introducing a local star: the number one track athlete in the state of Texas, soon to be high school grad, Jamal Beaumont."

Jamal's dark brown skin shines as he flashes a wide smile. He sits lean and tall in a closely tailored dark blue suit, white shirt, and red tie he saved up for so Mama wouldn't worry about the cost.

The camera loves him. My stomach twists because I need the interview to bring attention to Daddy's case, but it'll take away from Jamal. I hope he'll forgive me once he realizes what I'm trying to do.

Bring Daddy home.

Alive.

"When did you first start running?" Susan leans forward and rests her hand on her chin. The same way she begins every interview.

"You're going to have to ask my mama, because I swear I came out running."

Mama laughs, nudging me, then mouths, *It's true. It's true.*

I chuckle. Mama's loving every second of this.

"When you're not running, you're also working at a local radio station and have your own show Thursday evenings."

"Yes. I love it. I'm planning to major in communications and media."

"One day you could be interviewing me."

"That's my sister's thing. I'm more behind the scenes. Audio engineering."

"Brains and brawn, huh?"

He gives her a modest smile. Susan eats it up.

"Do track stars run in the family? There's usually more than one. Am I right?"

Jamal swallows, stopping for a millisecond, but I'm sure only Mama and I notice.

"The men in the family have those genes for sure."

Jamal's talking about Daddy. Before we moved to Texas, Daddy had his own track glory days in New Orleans. His name kept his hometown business afloat in tough times, with customers wanting to help him out. After the flood, all that was lost. People left, and the local history was forgotten. Life was still hard a decade after Hurricane Katrina, so when Hurricane Veronica hit, we also left for good.

We evacuated to Texas, but Daddy never ran again. During his trial, they said it was his speed that got him all the way across town so quick. Daddy's fast, but he's not Superman fast.

I watch Jamal, nervous with how he'll handle this.

"Well, they must be proud," Susan says.

"He is." Jamal hesitates after he says "he." He looks directly into the camera, and I smile at his secret way of acknowledging Daddy, and his ability to sidestep additional questions is impressive. Jamal's not going to let this interview go down like that.

I'm both proud and nervous. I bite my lip, regretting that I tried all week to persuade him to use this as an opportunity to talk about Daddy's appeal. Now Jamal's guarded, each word carefully crafted to avoid Daddy coming up.

"One thing I love about highlighting you, Jamal, is that you could have chosen to go anywhere in the country, but you chose Baylor. Everyone thought you were going to Track Town, Oregon, or North Carolina. Why Baylor?"

"I'm a mama's boy. Plain and simple. Got my two sisters over there." Jamal points to us. "And I can be home in less than four hours if I need to. What can I say?"

"I'm sure your family loves that you'll be close. Let's bring them out now."

Angela leads Mama to the stage, where she sits next to Jamal. Corinne squishes in, and I end up at the edge of the couch.

The hot lights beam down on me. I'm dizzy now, with one thing on my mind.

The thing everyone here is thinking about, the thing that hasn't been said but that's boiling near the surface.

"Let's meet your sister Corinne."

Corinne's round face immediately goes blank; her eyes bulge, like they're about to pop.

"How old are you, Corinne?"

"Seven."

"You love your brother?"

"Yes, ma'am. I'm gonna be real sad when he goes off to college."

"I bet you are. What's special about your brother?"

"He's fast. And . . . when he packs my lunch, he always leaves me notes. I'm gonna miss that."

"What kind of notes?"

"Nice stuff." Corinne pauses. "Like if he knows I'm worried

about something or trying to be funny. Like, 'Smile. I'm watching you, Bighead.'"

Susan laughs awkwardly.

"It's okay if he says Bighead." Corinne shoots me a warning.
"Only he can say it, though."

I chuckle, because she's told the world her nickname from
Jamal, and now he'll have to triple his notes to her.

"Or on Mondays when I'm real sad, he always leaves me a
note like, 'I love you more than the sun.' I keep all those."

Her voice has a heaviness to it no seven-year-old's should
have. The thing that goes unsaid in our family. That missing
piece of us that keeps us down because we only see Daddy an
hour on Saturday or Monday.

"Tracy." Susan tries to stay upbeat. "You're a year behind
Jamal. Are you also an athlete? College plans?"

"I used to do track." I pause, looking at Corinne, and then go
for it. "I'm a school journalist and organize Know Your Rights
workshops in the community."

Mama digs her finger into my side. I have to grind my jaws
together to keep a smile.

Susan's face is expressionless before she turns to Mama.

"Mrs. Beaumont, what do you think about your son?"

"I'm so proud of Jamal. Anyone would be lucky to have him.
He's respectful. Dedicated. Charming. There's no one like him."

"I've definitely picked that up." Susan rests her hand on her
chin again. "Bet your husband is real proud, too."

"He is." Mama gives a tight smile.

Three minutes left on the show clock. My chest floods like I'm being filled by water. Time's almost up. Susan has opened the door to talk about Daddy. I know that what hurts Jamal will hurt Mama. But we all want Daddy home. I can't let this opportunity pass us by. I speak before Susan asks Mama another question.

"College seems so distant because I've been focused on helping my father's appeal."

Mama parts her lips. A small gasp escapes.

Jamal flinches, and it's like a wave has come crashing down over the entire interview.

"Jamal." Susan turns to my brother. "Is this what influenced your decision to stay close to home?"

Jamal's expression goes blank.

Susan keeps going when Jamal doesn't answer. "Because your father is in Polunsky Prison."

I watch him. Hope this pushes him to speak up on Daddy's innocence. But he's staring past the camera like he wants this to be over.

"Not too long a drive from Baylor to see him or your family." Susan uses her hands like there's an actual map.

Jamal stays composed. "I couldn't find a reason in the world to go somewhere else. I wouldn't want to miss any time with Pops, Moms, Corinne." Jamal gives me a once-over. "My dear sister Tracy."

Shame runs through my veins when Jamal singles me out.

"I can imagine," Susan says. "You don't get that time back. Every week counts."

She's wrong; every second counts.

"Now, your father, how long has he been sitting on death row?"

Sitting? Why do people say *sitting?* Like he's waiting patiently in line with a number in his hand.

"Yes. Ma'am. He's . . . umm." Jamal shoots a look at Mama. He's starting to flounder.

The crew is buzzing, scrambling at the breach of contract.

"He's been, umm . . . on death row nearly seven years since the conviction," Jamal says.

Inside I scream out in joy that he doesn't skirt the issue.

"Must be painful."

"A lot of pain felt from him missing in our lives." Jamal pauses when his gaze is caught on Mama. "I'm sure there's a lot of hurt, of course, from the families who lost the Davidsons that night."

Daddy's innocent. Why did he say it like that?

"But I take all that and train. I run. I care for my family. I work. I live my life freely because my dad can't. I don't need to be at a big track school. Not when the thing that matters is putting in work to help take care of my family. That's something I can control. No one can beat me." Jamal gives a shy smile. Slows down his rapid pace of talking. "In my head, I mean. Everyone has to lose sometime. But in my head, I can't lose. Because I'm growing with each race."

"Your dedication's a rare trait, Jamal."

"Thank you, ma'am. I don't let things get me down. That's why I'm so glad you highlighted me, and we can focus on my accomplishments." Jamal smiles, unaffected by her prodding questions. I almost believe him.

"Must be hard, though." She puts her delicate hand on her chin again. "Your father's death sentence, having to start over from New Orleans, and then . . . the challenges in Texas."

"Texas is home now. I plan to keep it that way." Jamal keeps his fake grin.

It aches to watch Jamal hold his composure. He's avoiding the topic as best he can. Mama's scowl says she'll slam it shut if Susan tries her.

"How long does your father have on death row?" Susan's voice goes low.

"Two hundred and sixty-seven days." I say it because knowing how long Daddy has left is the air I breathe. Time to live. To appeal. To turn back time.

Mama whips her head at me. The camera follows.

"Two hundred and sixty-seven days," Jamal repeats. "That's why we want to keep our family together and focus on the good."

"Yes." Susan touches Jamal's shoulder this time. "I can't imagine how hard it must be having your father in prison. Convicted of a double murder. Unimaginable."

"Our father is innocent," I say. "He's been trying to appeal. But we don't have the financial resources to prove his innocence."

I've been writing to Innocence X to take Daddy's case. They represent people wrongfully convicted and sentenced to death. Especially those in underserved communities. People who can't afford their bail, let alone an attorney with a team of expert witnesses to prove their client's innocence.

After seven years of letters and no response, I'm getting Innocence X's attention. Today.

"If your father is innocent, I'm sure the system will work."

"No," I say. "The system has failed us. Continues to fail us."

"I don't know much about the details of his case, but we can talk after the show, since we've reached the end of the interview time. Jamal, what would you—"

She's cutting me off. I can't let her take this time away from me. I haven't said enough. I stand so the camera is forced to focus on me.

"Do you know how many men have been put to death who were later exonerated postmortem?" I point to the camera. "What about conviction rates by race and class? The system works if you have the money to defend yourself."

Backstage, the crew creeps to the edge of the stage. My legs are Jell-O underneath me. I'm close to collapsing right here, so I form a fist that fills me with courage.

"My father is innocent, and we have the evidence, but not the legal support to appeal his case. There are hundreds, thousands, of cases like his. Innocent people sentenced all the time."

Susan's spiderlike eyelashes blink rapidly. Her legs point

toward Jamal because she knows this should be his interview, but the journalist in her focuses on me.

"What evidence do you have proving your father's innocence?"

The producer throws his arms up in frustration.

"He was home all evening," I say.

"You were young then. I'm sure it's hard to remember. I barely remember what I had for lunch."

"That's not something you forget, ma'am. A small town with a double murder, everyone locked in the memories of where they were that day."

"He was home," Mama interjects, even though I know she's angry at me. "This interview today is about Jamal, but I can't sit here and not defend my husband. He. Is. Innocent."

"Then who do you suspect killed the Galveston couple?"

"Mark and Cathy Davidson were murdered, but not by my father or his business partner, Jackson Ridges. Other suspects have been recently identified," I say.

Mama's and Jamal's expressions turn hard.

I know Mama doesn't like when I lie, but we need to catch Innocence X's attention.

"Unfortunately, the Galveston Police Department refuses to look into them, but we will find a legal team to represent my father's case. When they study what we have, we'll prove his innocence and the real killer will be arrested."

As soon as the interview is over, Jamal jumps out of his seat.

"Tracy." Mama's got her hand on her hip. Susan Touric steps between us. Along with the producer, she blocks my view of Mama, but not before I witness how upset she is.

"This is unacceptable," Mama says. "We had an agreement."

"I stayed within my parameters," Susan says. "Your daughter—"

Mama puts her hand up to me as I draw in closer to join the conversation. Her gesture is instantly sobering. This won't be the time or place to talk to Mama. She won't listen to a word I say. I want this to be a moment to celebrate because I did what I'd planned, but to everyone else around me this isn't a celebration. I'm standing in the rubble of a building I blew up.

I follow Jamal, who is now in the hallway with Angela. Jamal's shaking his head, and Angela is tearing up. Her boyfriend, Chris, paces as he waits for Angela on the other side of the studio.

"Jamal." I reach for his shoulder, but he brushes me away. My cheeks are hot. "Jamal, I'm sorry."

"Forget it. Go to Ma." His voice is expressionless.

"I mean it. I'm sorry."

"I knew you'd make it go the way you wanted to. Just wish you wouldn't have done it like that."

His response isn't what I expected. I wanted him to be upset with me. Shout. Yell. Anything to help me figure out how to approach him, but he doesn't budge.

"Give me a second, please," I start.

"I don't wanna hear it." Jamal walks back to the studio.

I turn my head to find Mama. Angela stands in my way.

"You're so selfish. You think you know everything, but you don't," she says.

"My father's innocent." I turn away from her.

"It's not just this. It's the same thing with the school paper, always about you and what you want to do. Think about how Jamal must feel." Angela shakes her head, then storms out the exit doors. The Texas heat sucks the air out of my lungs until the door shuts behind her.

Mama's no longer on the stage. The only person left is Corinne. She hasn't moved from the interview couch. She's crying. Jamal gets to her first; a sob builds in my throat watching them. Jamal sinks down to his knees and wraps his arms around her waist. I stand awkwardly behind him, wanting to help but knowing I did this. Corinne puts her arms around Jamal's neck, her tears wetting his collar. The hurt I've forced onto my family knocks me backward as I look down at Corinne's searching eyes.

"Everyone is angry," Corinne says.

Jamal brushes her hair back. "Sometimes people do things that hurt because they think they're helping."

I shut my eyes and hope it's not a lie.

WHAT HAD HAPPENED WAS . . .

Mama's silence is worse than being scolded. I can't take it anymore, so I text my homegirl Tasha for a ride to Polunsky Prison. Maybe this way I can smooth things over with Daddy before Mama and Jamal get to him on Monday.

Tasha's twenty minutes away on foot if I cut across the field from my house. She lives on an old historic block that seems to be forgotten. The rows of shotgun homes perch up close to the sidewalk along dusty potholed roads. I swiftly approach her dull-green-colored house.

Tasha's already out front. "You know I'm not one to judge, but damn, why'd you go off like that?"

My face droops. "Nice to see you, too."

"I'm surprised your mama didn't skin you alive on television."

"It wasn't that bad, was it?"

"Train wreck." Tasha slams her palm and fist together. "Full-on collision."

Damn.

"If I take you to Polunsky, I'm not aiding and abetting, am I?"

"She didn't answer when I asked." I shake my head. "I didn't want to stick around for her to stop me."

"Come here." Tasha leans in to give me a hug. "Are you grounded?"

"Probably."

"Jamal pissed?"

"He won't talk to me." I put my head down. "Didn't even come home with us, so I haven't seen him since this morning."

"Jamal's not the type to hold grudges." Tasha lets me in, and I enter her living room. "Remember when you washed his white jersey with your red pants?"

"Yeah," I say, and chuckle. "He rocked that pink for weeks."

"He'll forgive you. Just don't hold your breath if he ever gets another interview. No way he'll let you in the building."

"I know." I let out a small smile that hurts, holding on to hope that Jamal won't be mad forever.

I follow her down the hallway, passing two tiny bedrooms on the way to the kitchen that's placed in the back of the house. Tasha only has two window units for air-conditioning, but the long shotgun shape of the house lets cool air flow throughout.

When we get to the kitchen, Tasha's sister, Monica, is

practicing on her keyboard while her mom washes dishes. They all have the same long, thin braids, same flawless dark brown skin and high cheekbones. Folks easily confuse mother and daughters for sisters when they're out shopping. Only thing her mom's missing is the large gold hoop earrings.

"Need any help?" I ask Tasha's mom, Ms. Candice.

"Hey, Tracy." She gives me a hug. "I'm good. I know you rushing. Tasha, get your daddy's keys."

"Daddy Greg! Tracy's here." She yells out the kitchen window instead of going out back.

She calls him Daddy Greg because she grew up not knowing what to call him, since he was in prison. She wanted to call him Greg, but calling him Daddy was a requirement. *Say it with respect,* her mama always said to her. So Tasha did what she do, calling him *Daddy,* but making it a point to add in *Greg.*

We used to be on the same page about getting our dads back. The first time Daddy Greg was out, Tasha was excited, but he barely stayed in the house and disappeared days at a time. He had a hard time adjusting, especially when he couldn't land a job, part of his parole. So back in jail he went. Three more years. Now he's done all his time, and Tasha don't trust he won't mess it all up again. Her tone stays sharp with him. Unyielding. Unforgiving. He spent his time in prison only to come home to a new prison, where he's free, but serving his own penance through harsh glances and judging looks.

Tasha pounces on Monica's keyboard and starts singing off-key.

"Stop." Monica pulls it back toward her, then gives me a nod. "Hey, Tracy."

I nod back.

"Tasha, quit playing around," Ms. Candice says. "You know you can't hold no tune, so just leave it for your sister."

"Damn, Mama, why you gotta say it with your chest like that? Can't a girl dream? Be the next superstar. Try out for one of those talent shows."

"You love to sing, baby. Got a real nice voice."

Tasha smiles.

"But you ain't no Whitney Houston."

"Ain't nobody trying to be Whitney, Mama."

"What you want me to say. Beyoncé? Come on now. You best focus on school. Be a business major. Accountant, I say, because you always up in my business. Checking my wallet."

I let out my first hearty laugh since before the Susan Touric interview. Glad I chose to come see Tasha and not lock myself in my room, holding my breath every time someone comes up the stairs.

"That's the problem with this generation, going on these reality shows because someone didn't knock some sense into them before they get on the screen and have their dream snatched on live television."

"That's cold, Ma." Tasha crosses her arms. Then scowls at

Daddy Greg as he enters, joining in naming all the careers she should try that require no musical talent.

When things finally die down, Daddy Greg hands over his keys and turns to me. "How's 'Tracy's Corner'?"

"Good," I say. "The column is getting popular. Readers are up."

"Most popular with Black folks," Tasha says. "The rest hate-read. You know them white kids don't like hearing about Black Lives Matter each week."

"That's their problem. And they're about to be big mad next year when I'm setting up feature stories."

"Let me guess," Tasha says. "Court cases and police brutality on every page?"

"Don't let Tasha give you a hard time," her mom says. "She stays reading 'Tracy's Corner.'"

"The editor position is a lock." Tasha gives a wicked smile because she was just messing with me.

"Better be. I put in as many hours as the editor this year." I glance at my watch. I want a lot of time with Daddy.

"You got this, Tracy," Daddy Greg says. "Speak your truth."

"So, whose fault is it you broke parole again?" Tasha rolls her eyes at Daddy Greg.

"Don't you start." Her mom's tone is icy.

"It ain't easy getting out and finding work. I'm lucky I did this time. You don't know what serving six years can do. I was out early, thinking about who's protecting my peeps. Are they gon' feel some type a way I'm out?"

"That's your problem," Tasha says. "You were thinking about them and not us."

"Tasha." I touch her hand. We can't understand what that life is like. Every moment of your day controlled. The people in there were his family for six years.

"The last three years I was thinking about what kind of man I was gonna be when I got out. An end date became real after messing up. I wasn't going to spend the rest of my life in there. I was caught up on that before."

I gulp hard, look away. He's talking about people like my daddy who aren't ever getting out.

"I'm sorry, Tracy. I didn't mean it like that," Daddy Greg says. "I feel your daddy coming home. I didn't mean to put you out like that. I'm just saying, I was gonna be ready this time."

Ms. Candice hands a glass of sweet tea to Daddy Greg. I look at them with envy that they're back together, but Tasha's not looking like she's happy. She's looking at them like she's lost. Been betrayed.

"We gotta go." Tasha spins, grimace on her face. Not even realizing while she's mad at her dad, mine's still in a cell block.

Tasha storms off without me.

"All right, I'll be seeing ya." I lean back awkwardly with my hands shoved in my shorts pockets.

"Don't worry about all this," Daddy Greg says. "I gotta prove myself. She'll come around."

We look at each other, nodding. But Tasha's gone hard; her

walls have climbed so high that I don't know if she can break them down and let anyone in.

The car is silent, so I pull out my notepad and start a letter to Innocence X.

"Damn, you stay writing letters." Tasha breaks the silence. "I've only written letters to Daddy Greg. Never even knew what to say then."

"Gotta reach them somehow."

"Why don't you call them?" Tasha says, backing up her car. "Just call until they answer. Email."

"They don't take email or phone calls for cases. Only letters and applications to their intake department."

"It sucks your dad's locked up, but at least he's still a good dad. Hell, he could trade places with Daddy Greg. I wouldn't mind."

"Tasha." I put my pen down. Jokes about death row I don't take lightly.

"Sorry." Tasha taps my leg. "I didn't mean you better off than me. Just having Daddy Greg home isn't all it's cracked up to be. He's trying to fold into our lives, and he just don't fit, you know."

"He's been gone," I say, then pause. "Time stopped for him but kept moving for y'all. You guys will figure it out. Even if he was here all that time, you're seventeen—you were gonna give him hell anyways." I bump her shoulder and she only gives me a sliver of a smile.

I bite my tongue to keep from saying how easy it is for her to think that. She had a clock to work with. Mine is different. Mine is a countdown.

"Can't change the past, Tasha." My voice is strained from irritation.

Tasha huffs but keeps her thoughts to herself.

We keep our chitchat light for the next hour, knowing we've touched nerves. I count down signs until we reach Livingston, a small town where Polunsky Prison is located.

Silence completely takes us over again. Everything else washes away except the fast beat of my heart as we take the long road past acres filled with grass and farmland. Then we see the fenced-in wall of the maximum-security prison. It's twenty feet tall along rows of cinder-block towers with razor wire atop it. From a distance, you can see the guards standing on top and the surveillance cameras lined up around the perimeter. As usual, an uneasy feeling swirls in my stomach. But this time is different—I defied Mama during Jamal's interview. Lied about new suspects, and I'm certain Daddy's heard all about it by now.

THE APPLE OF OUR EYE

We turn into the prison's parking lot. A roar of laughter escapes a group of boys perched outside. They circle around one guy who's trying to play it low-key. His eyes shift, watching the parking lot. A black garbage bag is sprawled on the ground in front of his feet, confirming he's the one just released. Also by how his boys are all hype. They punch playful fists at each other, rapidly spitting out catch-up stories to him. I think they might be so into themselves they'll ignore us parking, but the second we drive toward the visitor lot, I hear their chatter.

"There you go, man." I'm not sure who says it.

A whistle blows out long and low.

"Not a chance," Tasha says out the window.

His boys huddle, laughing, saying "oooh." Their voices eventually fade as she pulls into the lot farther away from releases.

I give a grateful smile to Tasha for driving me the two hours to visit Daddy. Knowing she'll be out here waiting for me when I'm done.

I enter the first small building and join a short line, dump my things in a yellow bin. The security woman smooths her hands down my arms, up my waist, across my bra line, then down my legs.

Then I go to the next building and wait until I'm called over the loudspeaker. I sit by a small round-table bench as the prisoners line up behind the glass. I'm grateful they changed the rule to visit death-row inmates, and I don't have to come all this way to pick up a phone to talk to Daddy through a glass window.

There's a buzz, then a clank as the locks release and the door is propped open by an officer. Rushing in to see their visitors, a few guys bump into one another.

My heart stops, hoping this doesn't turn into some altercation that'll shut down visiting hour while they go into lockdown. Or worse, I witness Daddy getting into it with someone. I shut my eyes for a moment, thinking about the first time I saw him with injuries. I blink the memory away.

It takes so much out of me and the family getting ready for a visit, hiding our own troubles. Always finding a way to ball it up during our visits so we don't put that stress on Daddy.

The men size one another up until one's distracted by his son yelling, "Daddy! I see Daddy!" He turns to mush, then gives the guy a dap.

A grin takes over my face when I finally spot Daddy in line.

He's tall, with broad shoulders that are covered by his white jumper. His beard is grown in a bit, and he's kept his Afro about two inches. He used to keep his hair lined up before prison. Considering everything, he still looks the same to me, which gives me comfort.

Daddy scans from corner to corner until he finds me at the table. I warm over at his matching grin. I tap my fingers nervously until Daddy takes a seat in front of me.

"You came," Daddy says.

"What do you mean?"

"I thought your mama might've locked you up after that stunt you pulled. What were you thinking?"

I put my head down.

Daddy flicks at my hair, then shoots out a bellowing laugh.

"You should've seen your mama's face on television. Eyes all bugged out. It's probably the one time in my life I was glad to be locked up, so I wouldn't be on that car ride home or have to stay up listening to your mama talk my ear off all night about you, girl."

I laugh with relief. "I'm sorry. I know you said not to."

"You wrong. This was Jamal's day today. My baggage don't need to follow him to college."

"I know, but we gotta catch Innocence X's attention."

"You're a fighter. I love that about you." Daddy brushes my hair back. "But you need to start preparing yourself—"

"Never." I glance away.

A bald-headed, muscular white guard watches us; the way he's looking at us bothers me. Daddy follows my gaze.

"Don't pay them no mind."

Daddy rubs his hands together, callused from the three-hour daily work outside. He gets one hour in the library, another break from his concrete sixty-square-foot cell. In his cell, he reads five hours a day. That's where Daddy picked up studying the law, after being filled with disappointment with each appeal. This is what we share between us on visits. Our ability to swap facts back and forth and all my letters to Innocence X. Mama tells him everything going on with us kids. Jamal fills the visit with things Daddy likes. Like his working hard, his track practice, Mama, and all the notes Jamal's left for Corinne that week. Daddy loves that the most.

When I talk to Daddy about his case and get too hopeful, he makes me promise not to be upset if an appeal doesn't happen. Because getting one grows more unlikely with each day. But Daddy's also not the type to give up. He could've accepted a plea deal, but he said he wouldn't admit to something he didn't do. God would be watching over him and set him free. He believed there'd already been tragedy enough with the Davidson couple being murdered, and him and his best friend, Jackson Ridges, being blamed. Mr. Ridges was killed by the police as they tried to take him from his home. Daddy thought God wouldn't let more pain come from that tragedy. So he pled innocent, and life without parole was off the table. It would be a death sentence if found guilty.

I used to believe that what Daddy said about no more pain was true. Like the Messiah himself would walk right through the courtroom and carry my daddy out. Now I know it's up to us.

"I didn't mean to ruin Jamal's moment." I watch him with hopeful eyes.

"I see no one else came to make this visit." Daddy squeezes my hand. "I need you to stay close, not pull apart."

"I just wish Jamal'd understand what I was trying to do. I couldn't not talk about you."

"I knew you wouldn't be able to control yourself if you had the chance. I had a bet out here when we watched it, but I didn't expect you to lie. You don't know what that does in here."

I look away. I know I shouldn't have lied about possible suspects. I only wanted to attract Innocence X's attention.

"Someone got away with murder, and it's never been right I had to do the time. Trust me, no one knows that injustice more than me. I feel it every day. But you can't make stuff up."

"But if we get someone to look into your trial, they could see they didn't have any evidence to convict you in the first place. Then they'd find new suspects."

Daddy pats my hand. I try to let the topic go. We've talked about this too many times. I'm preaching to the choir. The fact is, the gun that killed the Davidsons was never found. Daddy never owned a gun. They arrested him anyway.

Next, they went after Mr. Ridges. He paid with his life when he refused to open the doors for the police. Mama had called to warn him that Daddy'd been taken in. Mr. Ridges didn't want to go out like that. Not in front of his kids. But it was too late. The police shot up the house, hitting Quincy, who was my age, and killing Mr. Ridges with shots through the window. They didn't wait for a negotiator like they do on TV. They straight-up started shooting.

After he was dead, it was easy to put blame on Mr. Ridges. They *needed* him to be guilty. Especially when they could've killed Quincy. I've always believed the police and prosecution were willing to do anything they could to justify killing Mr. Ridges and shooting a ten-year-old. Regardless of whether Mr. Ridges or Daddy owned a gun, they both had alibis. Their fingerprints were found in the office meeting room, along with the prints of multiple other people who'd met with the Davidsons, but it didn't seem to matter that their prints weren't found in the back, where the bodies were discovered.

"Don't think I haven't thought this through a million times. Sometimes these things happen. Everything kept boiling down to the fact I was about to do business with Mr. Davidson."

We both look down.

They'd questioned other suspects. Rumors flew around town that Daddy was upset with Mark Davidson. It's true Daddy and Mark Davidson had gotten into an argument the day before, but it was because Mark didn't want to join their business venture with Jackson Ridges, just with Daddy.

That's not worth killing someone over.

Daddy changes subjects, tells me a story about when I was a baby and he'd knew I'd be trouble, but I've heard this story a million times. The only thing in my head is what I can do in the next nine months to bring Daddy home. A chance to stall his sentence. Save him before it's too late.

When I get back in Tasha's car, I can't hold in all the disappointment from *The Susan Touric Show* and the helplessness from seeing Daddy. Each moment replays in my mind. I hold my mouth closed to stop a cry from escaping.

"Let it out, girl." Tasha rubs my back. "Don't hold that shit in."

"I just don't know what to do," I say between cries. "I've tried everything."

"Not everything. You still got something left. I don't know you to give up. What you did today could've worked. You don't know yet." Tasha hands me my notepad to finish my letter to Innocence X.

Blurry-eyed, I take the notepad from her, the pain still sitting in me. Tasha drives away as I finish my letter.

I used to plan the letters out more, writing pages and pages on why Innocence X needed to help Daddy, but time is running out. The climate's changed with a new governor who's stricter on sentences, filling up for-profit prisons with minor convictions. Increased visibility of racial injustice in policing adds more pressure for Innocence X to respond to cases hitting the media. My fear is they'll forget the old cases—unplug the chance for those, letting the clock wind down. Because I know the truth is, no one's excited to look into a seven-year-old case. Attention spans are reserved for big stories and hashtags following the next news cycle.

Innocence X knows who I am, and now it's the principle of writing. There's nothing I've been able to control about what happened to Daddy. I'm broke. Can't vote. Can't afford a lawyer. But I've got control of my voice and my mind, and that means I can do at least one thing: write a letter.

Saturday, May 1

Stephen Jones, Esq.
Innocence X Headquarters
1111 Justice Road
Birmingham, Alabama 35005
Re: Death Penalty—Intake Department

Dear Mr. Jones,

Congratulations on the Donovan case out in California. I've been watching it progress this last year. Every time I see good news, I think you might be ready to take on our case, but then you don't. Will you do it this time? Everyone in my family has given up. They want me to accept that my daddy will be killed in less than nine months.

My friend Tasha got her dad back, but she acts like he's still locked up. When he's around her, she acts like he's got the plague or something. Is it like that for any of the families you work with, or is it different for the ones not innocent? Seems to me it's harder to adjust to life when you're innocent. Because you think you're losing your mind trying to prove the truth. But when you're guilty, you accept it. Not happy about it, but there's time to learn. Rehabilitation. I tried to tell Tasha this, but she's still holding on to being mad. I know it's not fair to compare. I guess I'm just looking for answers.

Did you watch the Susan Touric interview of my brother, Jamal Beaumont? It aired today (on Saturday).

Please review James Beaumont's application (#1756).

Thank you for your time.

Tracy Beaumont

MISSION (UN)ACCOMPLISHED

Usually I roll to school with Jamal, but Monday he dipped out of the house before I could ride with him, and then he crept in close to curfew. Skipped a visit with Daddy. Again. I shouldn't have expected different just one day later; now it's Tuesday and I have to go with Mama to Galveston so I can catch a ride with my best friend, Dean, at his parents' antique store, where she works.

I usher Corinne into the car and frantically roll down the windows to let the heat out, wishing we could take Daddy's old Buick. It stays hitched under a tree and tarped away with layers of filth—seven years deep.

I wipe my brow from the morning heat. The humidity is the worst, though, the way dust particles stick to my skin like it has a natural adhesive. Another shower is useless, since the sweat will build right back up. Part of me knows the same feeling from stained memories. They never disappear. Just dormant, till they awake in full force during summers in Texas.

Mama joins us, taking the passenger seat so she can finish getting ready. We swerve onto the dirt road, leaving a billowing trail of dust behind us. I cough and hack, then frantically roll up my window before jabbing my fist onto the front dash in three quick pops, hoping the AC will kick in faster.

"We can't survive without AC this summer," I say. "It's already hotter than usual."

"Hush and be patient while it cools." Her voice has a sharp edge she hasn't let go of since the interview.

"We could always sell our car and the Bu, then get a new one."

The words come out before I can stop them. I know we'd never sell the Bu. Even when money's tight. Because selling it means giving up on Daddy ever coming home. And if he ever does, Mama wants one thing that hasn't changed, so he won't have a constant reminder of the years taken away from him.

"We're not touching—"

"It stinks." Corinne pinches her nose at the stale air pumping out of the vents.

"You stink." I give Corinne a wink in the rearview mirror. Even she knows not to go there with Daddy's car. She must've been born with that gift, 'cause I sure don't have it.

We take the exit to Galveston Bay, leaving Crowning Heights behind us. Within ten miles, the difference between the cities is glaring. Crowning is basically the no-man's-land part of Galveston County. We're more inland, closer to Houston, but poor and rural. The homes in Crowning Heights are shoddily put together, unlike the resort living you see the closer you get to the bay.

All talk of developments stopped in my area after the Davidsons were murdered. Daddy and Mark Davidson had plans to build out here, but after the trial, no one's touched it. This left Crowning with a long stretch of gravel roads, one rickety gas station, a market owned by a Vietnamese family, and the few migrant workers who stuck around after the farms dried out. We stayed out here because we can't afford to move closer.

Forty minutes later, we park in front of Corinne's school. She takes her sweet time getting out. She's a mini version of Mama when it comes to being on her own schedule.

"Need help?" I motion so Corinne can see how easy it would be for me to unbuckle her jammed-up seat belt.

"I don't need your help." Corinne squints at me before fiddling her fingers so the latch releases and she can jump out of the car.

As she gets out, Mama gives her a once-over, studying her heart-shaped brown face before kissing her cheeks. Mama leaves a big red smudge of her lipstick. Corinne scrunches her face, acting like she don't love the attention.

I should be more like them, enjoying these little moments. I can't help myself. The pull of being on the move takes over. That rush to hurry, even if it's to wait and do nothing. Jamal always walks Corinne to class if he's dropping off, no matter how late we're running.

Mama wraps her arms around us for a daily prayer. I bow my head. When she's done, Mama takes off her hair wrap and presses her hands around her edges before checking for stray hairs as she smooths out her thick black hair. She steps into the sunlight, and her long dark brown legs send a shadow climbing up the sidewalk as she walks Corinne to the entrance. You can hear the screams of kids rushing to beat the bell.

"Can't I go with you guys?" Corinne asks.

"Tracy's going to school. You want to switch and have her homework?"

Mama's threat works. Corinne throws her backpack over her shoulder and turns to school, but not before waving good-bye. I love her smile. My heart twinges at how much different her life is at that age from mine. When I was her age, Daddy took Jamal and me to the park down the street from our house every weekend. We used to earn points during the week so we could pick out ice cream when the truck would ride by in the afternoon. We never asked for money 'cause he didn't have much to spare, so those times were everything to us. I even miss those empty threats of spankings when we were awful. Corinne will never know what it was like to have Daddy home. All she's known is Daddy locked up.

Mama and I get back into the car to head to Evans Antiques.

"Can Jamal give me a ride home, or is he working tonight?"

"Don't be fishing for information about your brother from me. If he wants his space, you're giving it to him. He'll forgive you when he's ready."

Mama's words fill me with the hope that I haven't forever changed my relationship with Jamal before he goes off to college.

"Me, on the other hand," Mama says, and tsks, "you've got a long way to go. I don't know what you were thinking."

"I was only trying to help—"

"I don't want to hear it now. You're gonna make me late."

With Mama, it's different. She can forgive, but I know she won't forget. This is on my permanent record, even if Mama wants Daddy home as bad as I do—if not more. My mind searches for ways to get Mama to forgive me. I look away, thinking of everyone's disappointment at the studio, and my eyes cloud with tears.

We arrive at the downtown complex that's filled with small businesses and a variety of local grocers and stores. Herron Media, where Jamal works, is three blocks away.

At the antique store, Mama's the bookkeeper and online consignment sales rep. They gave her a job after Daddy's trial.

When I park, Mama nudges me. "Don't get used to riding with him to school now. Friends are good things, but you don't need to get caught up with him just 'cause y'all get along . . ."

Mama doesn't finish her thought. Instead, her mouth is in a firm line that says that's all Dean and I should ever be. She's never straight-up said I couldn't date Dean because he's white. She's never had to.

It wasn't always like this. Going with Mama to Evans Antiques was the best part about her job. It had a place for me to study with a view of antique knickknacks, jewelry, and furniture, along with somewhere to kick it in the back with Dean, the Evanses' son. She didn't have to worry if I was running out in the streets or getting in trouble, since I was only twenty yards away from her office. It was also a place I didn't need to think about being teased, like I was in school after Daddy's trial. And when I got a little older, Dean was the one who gave me the paper and stamp to mail off my first letter to Innocence X.

Dean's and my friendship began days after Jackson Ridges was killed by the cops and Quincy was hit by a stray bullet. While Quincy recovered at the hospital, Dean took his place as a friend who looked out for me.

I was devastated by the arrest, but Dean stuck on so much during Daddy's trial, you wouldn't see me without seeing Dean. The more he latched on, the more it made me normal again. We've stayed tight—even as our crowds segregated more with age, not less. I will always love Dean for that.

Track also kept us close until I was forced to quit two years ago because I wouldn't stand during the national anthem in protest for Black Lives Matter. Coach Curry said I could always come back, as long as I knew I gotta stand.

Sports is our normalizer for crossing racial groups. There are Black, brown, and white, and there are athletes. In season, I had competition to hang out with my best friend because it gave Jamal a chance to hang with Dean.

What's been killing me lately is I can't tell if Mama's more against Dean and me being together, or if she's protecting me from Dean's mom's watchful eyes. Puberty's hit, and the rules have switched up on us, making me hesitant to drop in on Dean last minute because I don't know if Mrs. Evans is there.

To be honest, I'm feeling some type of way about this. We've always played on the lines of friendship and relationship. I thought I'd have more time to sort things out. Now I can't tell if we're pushing each other away because of how his mom acts around me.

I want to ask Dean what he feels, but I've spent too many years joking around about why we couldn't be together. It's always been my fear of what the world was telling me more than what I've felt about Dean. It's hard to believe we'd be right for each other, when everywhere I look is a hidden reminder. Magazines, television, everyday micro-aggressions. Beaten down with the backhanded compliments I've heard all my life, like "You real pretty for a dark-skinned girl."

I push my thoughts aside, opening the door to Evans Antiques. The gold script glints a bit as the sun hits it just right, and the familiar ring of the bell above the door doesn't hide my entrance—it announces I'm home.

THE ODD COUPLE

Dean stands at the counter, his hazel eyes staring at me as he runs his hands through his sun-kissed brown hair. Perfect teeth, perfect smile. I hate that I notice this about him now. Because I've grown up with him in all our awkwardness, when he used to be filthy or goofy or unassuming. The easygoing way about him that didn't make me act too proud when he split his lunches with me. He's never made me feel less than, when everyone else around me so easily could.

My grin drops as Dean's mom joins him at the register.

Mrs. Evans seems perfectly happy anytime she's talking to Mama, but she's never given me much love.

"Hi, Mrs. Evans." I give her a half-ass wave.

She gives me a half-ass smile. "Tracy."

Dean's eyes widen, and that little dimple I always stick my

pinkie in to tease him reminds me how our friendship is so con-trolled by who's around us.

Dean moves away from the counter, toward what has always been our corner. Together. For, like, ever. Most of my letters crafted right there. His mom doesn't move, blocking me from our nook, while he grabs his things.

I should've just stayed outside and waited for Dean to come out, but he's always trying to get me and his mom to interact. It never works out right. I swear, since I turned sixteen last year, Mrs. Evans has acted like we'd never met before. Cold. Always asking if I came by to get my mama when she knows darn well I'm here for Dean. She also loves name-dropping girls who come by for Dean. Lately I've been avoiding the store when Mama tells me Mrs. Evans is around.

I want to say I'm being ridiculous. Snap out of it. The truth is, I don't know how to be around Dean anymore.

"Ready?" Dean slings his backpack over his shoulder.

I nod, sensing Mrs. Evans's judging eyes on me. So strange how a replica of Dean's eyes can give me such an opposite feeling. It's not in the way she acts about Daddy being gone; it's just I know she don't want to know me. The truth is, I don't want her to know my story, either.

As soon as we step outside the store, I can breathe again.

Dean loosely places his hand on my shoulder as we walk toward his truck. When we arrive at school, we hop out and take the steps up to the front doors side by side.

"I'm working after school. Want to do some homework in the back?" Dean asks.

There's nothing I'd rather do than stay at the store and hide behind a good book in the corner while Dean works. Watch him jump to help a customer, then slide right back to me and read over my shoulder. And on busy days, sneak up to the empty loft upstairs and play music, since his parents have never been able to rent it out.

"I need a ride back, but I can't stick around," I say.

Dean looks down. "She doesn't mean to be like that, you know."

"It doesn't bother me," I lie.

"You sure you won't come, though?" Dean asks. "I can take you to where you need to go and wait."

"Maybe tomorrow."

I know he thinks I've been avoiding him lately, but it's just that being at the store's not the same with his mom watching me all the time. And I've got some making up to do.

"I was gonna try to catch Jamal off guard," I explain. "You know, hold him hostage until he talks to me."

"Smart." Dean's face brightens. "I still don't get why you did it, though."

"Not you, too?" I look away. I was hoping to skip this conversation with Dean.

"I got your back, but the way your family looked on TV. They were shocked. My stomach was churning watching it go down. It was like a car accident, and I couldn't look away."

Dean's always on my side. The fact he was hit hard by what I did really seals the deal. I messed up. He's supported me through all the letters I've written to Innocence X and helped strategize ways to get their attention. He knows how much this means to me. The guilt twists in my stomach. I've gotta fix things with Jamal.

"I don't know what I was thinking. I thought I'd immediately get a call from Innocence X, and then all would be forgiven, but nothing. Like usual." I shake my head.

Dean slings his arm around my shoulders. "You'll fix it. You always do. Come on, grab your books, bell's gonna ring soon."

We head to my locker, where Tasha's lingering, grinning as she watches Dean and me head her way.

"Hey, Dean."

"What's up, Tasha?"

"Waiting on this girl. But now I know why Tracy is so late."

"Yeah," I say, "because Jamal ditched me again. You seen him?"

"Nah. Not yet. I heard something, though." Tasha shakes her head but keeps her mouth shut in front of Dean.

"All right, Tracy." Dean backs up, catching a clue. "I'll see you later."

I give him a thankful grin as he walks away. I mouth, *Maybe I'll stop by,* and he flashes me a smile.

"Cuteness." Tasha clicks her tongue as she hands me my books. "I don't know why y'all don't just bite the bullet and date. He gets a pass, you know."

"Oh yeah, why?" I shut the locker and flick her hair.

"Because he's the finest white boy I've ever seen. People would understand."

"Oh, that's how that works, huh? You know I'd have every white girl in school thinking they could get with Dean because they'd be mad he's with me."

"Please. Those heffas still wouldn't even think in their wildest dreams y'all was together. You wasting time playing friends. You know that's why nobody asks you out, anyways. That and Quincy."

"You stay on that Quincy tip. He don't want me; I told you to go after him already."

"Don't think I didn't try. He got eyes for everybody but me. And I know it's because of you. He's just waiting for his moment to edge right on in between you and Dean."

"Okay, enough. What was that look you were giving Dean, anyways? Why you want him rushing off?"

"I was in the bathroom and overheard Natalie Hanes is vying for your editor spot."

"What? She barely has a feature. What makes her think she's even got a chance?"

"Girl, I don't know. She was talking about you not being a team player. She's going to talk to Mr. Kaine, then work them votes against you. She feel she's got Angela in the bag because you hijacked *The Susan Touric Show,* and Angela's pissed."

"Damn! Angela shouldn't even get a vote, since she's graduating. It should be up to this year's juniors." Angela will have influence, though; I've got to talk to her. She works with Mr. Kaine in the morning for internship credit. He's the one who wrote her letter of recommendation to Susan Touric. I'm hoping to get one from him, too.

"Thanks, Tasha. I gotta talk to Angela."

I weave my way down the hall, skipping my own class and going straight to the newsroom, which is just a repurposed classroom with desks set up into stations.

Angela and Chris are in heated debate. His boys, Scott and Justin, are crowded together watching them argue. I know Scott from the track team; he's a long-distance runner. Used to be a sprinter but wasn't fast enough. He's tall and lanky with light brown hair; his neck would blanch in pink-and-white blotches when he'd run. I couldn't stand him because he was always whining about Coach not being fair by taking him off sprinting and putting him on long distance. Said Coach was being racist against him. Never mind Dean runs the four hundred. But Texas be like that. Chris, Scott, and Justin, always a trio sticking together and not having any nonwhite friends.

I wait until they stop arguing. Chris hugs and kisses Angela. Her response is blank. Like she didn't want him touching her. Chris doesn't seem to notice, just takes off with the guys as the bell rings.

I step into the classroom, catching Angela by surprise.

"Mr. Kaine's out this morning." Angela shoves her heart-covered cell phone into her bag.

"I came to talk to you."

"Listen, whatever happened is over. You should talk to your brother about the interview."

"He won't talk to me."

"Well, I can see why. You ruined his interview." She loops her blond hair behind her ear. "Your approach needs work. I tried to tell you, but you blew me off last staff meeting."

"You wouldn't get it." I shake my head. "No one listens to me. You're all a clique on the newspaper."

"We're not a clique. You just don't try hard enough to get along."

"I don't try hard enough?" I put my hand up. "What can I talk about when bonding time equals talking about lavish vacations, brand-new cars for birthday gifts, all things Starbucks? And music? Have we ever tried to listen to a Black radio station? Don't even get me started on television references to reruns of *Friends* and *Gossip Girl*."

What I don't say is it's the talk about the weekends that shuts me out. Mine are filled with prison visits, church, and me babysitting Corinne while Mama and Jamal work.

Angela's face softens, but she says, "And that has what to do with Jamal's interview?"

"I work just as hard as everyone does."

"I never said you don't work hard," Angela says. "I said adjust your approach."

"That's why I came to talk to you." I'm tired of explaining to her, so I switch subjects. "I want to be editor next year so I can change things. Make it more inclusive. There's nobody of color who works on the paper except me and Rosa. That's a problem."

"What can *I* do about you getting the editor role?"

"I've worked hard for this. It hasn't been easy. I'm trying to make the paper something that matters, make an impact. Be real journalists. If Natalie gets the position as editor, we'll go backward, and I'll lose 'Tracy's Corner.' Stuck writing about graffiti behind the school or cafeteria exposés. I want to write about real stuff."

I play up the fact that Angela takes her work seriously. She has always pushed Mr. Kaine to have our stories be meaningful. When "Tracy's Corner" was up for debate, I wanted to solidify it as a social justice corner, and Angela gave me a vote. Even said my articles about my dad's case were important. That she learned about her rights with police through my write-ups.

Angela sits down, runs her hands through her blond curls, then ties them up and puts on her glasses. She never wears them outside the newsroom.

"I'm not going to block you, Tracy. But Natalie has some truth to what she's saying. You aren't a team player."

"That's not—"

"I get why you don't fit in. Everyone's got their own interests. But you don't even give people a chance to try it their own way, because you can't trust them. If you want to be editor, you have to work with everybody—even if you don't like them."

"They don't like me."

"Not everyone likes me."

I scowl. Everybody on the paper likes Angela. Hell, she was homecoming queen.

"What about Jamal?" she says. "He told me he didn't want to talk about his dad. That your mom wouldn't allow it. You did it anyway."

"Because I've tried everything else to help my dad. What do I have left to lose? I thought I could get Jamal to talk about it, but he wouldn't." I don't know why I'm telling her all this. Maybe because Jamal won't talk to me. Maybe because Angela knows how to woo people with her reporter skills to get answers. She set me up for that one.

"Do you really have evidence for your dad? Jamal said it's bullshit."

"They never found the murder weapon, and there were no witnesses. There should have been reasonable doubt, but the all-white jury felt otherwise."

"Do you know much about the missing gun?"

"No." I pause at the way she asked the question. Like she's setting me up to give her more information than I planned. I shake off overthinking things. "But I know my dad is innocent. I'm a team player, I swear, and I've worked hard to be in the running for editor. But my dad's in the last year of his life—I was desperate."

Angela pauses. Her shoulders settle and she lowers her voice. "You think you're a team player?"

"I am." I put my hands down in front of me. "I earned the right to be editor. Giving it to anyone else would be wrong, and you know it."

"Prove it. Prove you can work with me on something, and you won't go off on your own. You think you can do it, without telling anyone?"

"Of course. I'm loyal." I know if I work well with Angela, she'll put in a good word with Mr. Kaine, then secure more votes.

"All right. I've got an exposé that's good for 'Tracy's Corner.'" Angela sticks her hand out. "Meet me here tomorrow at eight a.m."

I agree. Then turn to see if I can catch the last half of my first-period class. Angela calls out when I reach the door.

"Don't tell Jamal we talked."

I nod, even though her request seems strange. Angela's always been a straight shooter, so why do I get the sense she might need me as much as I need her?

FLESH AND BLOOD

After school, I walk alone to Herron Media, avoiding eye contact with everyone I pass. Still, I can't help but notice an older white lady pull her purse closer as I walk by her on the sidewalk. Her action sends my mind spiraling on high alert to the people around me. Every time there's a whisper in the ear, a stare in my direction, a flinch from someone passing me. A million subtleties that let me know my place. Branded as an outsider more than seven years ago, like each member of my family. We don't belong. The Davidsons' office was in this same business complex, and although Mama and Jamal kept ties, I've never felt we were accepted back in the community. Each visit is a reminder that life changed for us.

I snake through the crowd of passersby, turning my head, hoping their focus will be on my big black natural curls that take up their own space, rather than on my face. I used to love having Daddy's uncharacteristically slender nose, full lips, bright white teeth, and wide smile that used to draw people in, always catching attention. But now when people see me, they perceive something different. Something appalling. Layered with their unforgiving small-town judgment about the family of someone on death row.

If Daddy were here, he'd say, *Chin up. Nothing to be ashamed of.* His words fill my head like music as I enter the administrative building for Herron Media and wave to Valerie at the reception desk before heading to the staircase.

I make my way upstairs to the third door on the right, the production room. It's always mesmerizing stepping into the audio room where the commercials and voice-overs are made. The buttons and displays blink like flashing lights in the sky. When the door swings open, my mouth drops.

Jamal freezes, stopping his rubbing all up on Angela, who's sitting on top of the audio table. Her blond waves are all mussed up, the audio control's surface out of place, tucked to the side. Although Mr. Herron's cool for white folk in Texas, he ain't *that* cool.

"Tracy." Angela pushes away from Jamal, fixing her skirt and wiping her lips.

This has to be Jamal's greatest flaw: a girlfriend for every day of the week and of every race. He doesn't think twice about who he's talking to. Society's double standard. Jamal knows he'd give me a hard time if things were turned around.

"Hmm." I scowl and raise an eyebrow. "How long's this been going on?"

Jamal doesn't answer, so I turn to Angela. "And shouldn't you be at work?"

"Call me when you're off." Angela touches Jamal's neck, and he covers her hand with his. It's intimate. I want them to be embarrassed they were caught. Just earlier today she proposed we work on some exposé. Her last words were *don't tell Jamal.* What is she up to?

Angela walks past me, all carefree, acting like she doesn't hold my future as an editor in her hands. Is she playing games with me? And the way she was all up in Chris's face at school— arguing over something, then making up with him—only to mess with Jamal hours later? She's got no concern for what kind of harm she could do to my family if Jamal lost his job. This is probably some kind of thrilling dare for her, seeing how far she can take things without getting caught. Then she'll joke and tell her friends as they laugh at how brave she was for hooking up with Jamal, the son of a killer. How stupid was I to think I could trust her to help me lock down my editor position for next year.

"Really, Jamal?" I punch Jamal's arm for taking such a chance with Angela, messing around at work. He's never held the reserved shame like I do, so I'm hoping he'll feel some kind of semblance of pain this way.

"Why you gotta be like that?" Jamal flinches, blocking my hand before I land another punch.

"If you get caught, you could lose your job."

"I know. I know. But I'm too quick, though. Fastest feet in Texas."

"Well, you're not that quick, 'cause I could straight see you as soon as I walked in. What if Mr. Herron came in?"

He should know more than anyone, one slipup and your life can change.

"Here's some dinner." I throw the bag on the table, and he starts unwrapping it. "It's only four o'clock!"

"Gotta keep my energy up." He scarfs his meal within minutes.

I watch him eat, reminding myself why I'm here.

"I saw Daddy on Saturday." I pause and run my fingers across the flickering lights on the production board. "I told him about the interview, how it was my fault. He watched. Said we should talk it out. Wants us to stick together."

"No time to go over spilled milk. I'm working, and it'll be a late one." Jamal doesn't hesitate.

"I can come back after."

"No. I mean, it'll be a laaate one tonight."

Jamal brushes his shoulder to emphasize how fly he thinks he is, then leans at the edge of his stool, putting his hand on my shoulder. "You must be desperate to want to hang out with me when you know you owe me big-time for what you did. I don't know if I'll ever forgive you."

"Jamal!" I cry out his name. "I'm sorry. I mean it."

"You don't wanna hang out with me anyway. Probably saw Mrs. Evans's car at the store and turned around like a sucka."

"For a second you had me feeling bad."

59

"Please, you ain't thinking about me. Dean's mama has you shook, and you don't know what to do about it."

"It's not my fault she acts the way she do. She don't bother me, though. Dean's my best friend. Not my boyfriend."

"Good. Dean's cool, but you know it'd never work out."

Inside, I cringe.

"Not that I'm interested, but it doesn't seem to stop you from messing with Angela." I force a smirk.

"Not the same, but okay, playa'."

"Stop." I wave him off.

"Breaking hearts wherever she goes." Jamal hits his fist playfully.

"I know what you're trying to do." I turn our conversation back. "I know you don't believe it, but I wasn't trying to hurt you."

The door opens; on the other side is Jamal's best friend, Quincy. Jamal got him a part-time job helping in the mix room.

"What up, T?" Quincy runs his hand along his chin and touches his locs framed around his ears.

I can never tell if Quincy flirts with me only to anger Jamal. I give a shy smile back. We used to be cool before he was shot. Before his dad was killed. That was a long time ago.

"Watch out. Jamal's on one today." I pass Quincy.

Quincy follows after me, the hem of his jeans hanging over his shoes, so he drags his leg real smooth and slow. His limp came after the shooting, but it's now all part of his swagger.

"Where we going?" Quincy asks.

"*We* are going nowhere." I smile. "Unless you wanna go through Jamal first?"

"You don't think I would?" He sidles up next to me. "I'm waiting for my chance."

Quincy's got so many girls, I can't take him seriously.

"Q, I'm right here, dude." Jamal puffs out, ready to pounce on Quincy from the studio.

He switches back and forth, looking at me, then Jamal.

"Bye, Quincy." I nudge him gently.

"Tracy." He touches my arm. "Forget Jamal. He knows you were badass in that interview."

My cheeks turn hot as I fumble, passing Quincy, who's holding open the audio room door.

"Hold up, Tracy," Jamal says. "I'll be right back, Quincy."

"A'ight." Quincy takes a seat in the studio.

Jamal catches up to me and follows me downstairs. When we reach the lobby, Jamal gets serious. He's done with the jokes.

"How was Pops?" Jamal asks.

The tension building in my chest loosens.

"He was good." I touch Jamal's shoulder. We both know Daddy hides things from each of us, and I'm usually the one who gets the real story. "Daddy knows you'd visit every day if you could. He knew why y'all didn't come on Saturday. He was surprised to even see me that late."

"Once college starts, I can't manage every week."

"He knows," I say. "Daddy would be disappointed if you did. You need to take care of your business at Baylor."

"Still . . . All right, then." Jamal turns, taking the stairs two steps at a time.

"See you at the house."

Jamal stops at the top of the stairs, pausing. I wait for him to speak.

"What's up, Jamal?"

"I'll be late. I gotta take care of some things. Cover for me with Mama."

"Yeah." I pause. "Okay."

I stop to watch Jamal leave. Puzzled by his response. The first time he said he would be late, he was joking around, but this time there's a heaviness to his words. Like something else is on his mind, but he just don't trust me enough to not mess it up.

THE FAST AND
THE FURIOUS

I'm jolted awake by the shuffle of someone in the hallway. I rub my eyes, then realize what it is. Our upstairs toilet runs, especially at night when someone doesn't give it a good flush. The sound won't stop, so I force myself up.

I can't help but run my fingers along the grooves of the walls, knowing Daddy's the one who put them up. Every ding or repair is unchanged, like he left it. The only thing different in the house is my room. I've painted my walls a rotation of colors, hoping one of them would soothe away my bad dreams. Shake up the house enough to look different, but in the dark, I can see it like it was before.

"Hurry up," I whisper at the bathroom door, so I don't wake Mama.

Corinne doesn't answer. When I notice the door is open a

sliver, I push it, blink with the bright light blinding me for a second.

Jamal's splashing water on his face. His eyes are shut as he wrings his hands together over the sink. I rub my eyes because it looks like red water swirling down the drain.

"Damn, Jamal. What happened to you?"

"Shit." Jamal jumps back, grabbing a towel. His hands are all jittery as he cleans up his face, then bunches the towel into a ball.

I watch the last bit of pink-colored water disappear down the drain.

"Why you always in my business?" Jamal pushes past me, and I'm taken aback at his response. He sounds like he got caught, but I'd already known he'd be in late.

"What'd I catch you doing?" I hit his shoulder, playing around, and he flinches. He's scared. But of what?

"Jamal. You okay?"

I touch his neck to get the rest of what's on him off, then I make a face when I realize it's blood. There's a long scratch across his neck.

"What happened?" I flick the water on and wash up. "You okay?"

I watch him hard because nothing about this fits his late-night routine. I can't tell if he's coming or going. I move to ask another question, but Jamal's already heading off to his room. He gives me a look like I better keep my promise and not dare wake Mama, then shuts his door.

I lie restless in bed and listen for movement. The air is thick and hot. There's heaviness in the atmosphere, like so many nights when the past takes over the present. I try and tell my brain it's just the wave of an old smell, a phrase someone says that can put me on high alert. I've never been able to get over what happened enough to live fully in the now, always rush back to the night Daddy was taken from us. A moment that won't erase.

My sense of déjà vu is heightened by the sound of a vehicle riding down our quarter-mile gravel driveway. I listen more closely, and my heartbeat picks up, throbbing when I recognize there must be two or three cars driving way too fast for our road. A minute later, a knock at the door jolts me.

I run down the hallway to the stairs.

"Get back to your room." Mama's already at the front door. She waves me away.

"Who is it?" I mean to whisper, but I'm yelling.

She looks through the peephole and rests her face on the door. I see the lights flash blue and red before she confirms it.

"Police," Mama whispers.

She doesn't need to say more. Something awful has happened.

Corinne meets me at the stairs in her rainbow pajamas. She clutches her thin arms around me.

"What is it, Tracy?"

"Everything is fine. Go back to bed," I say, although I'm holding her as tight as she is me.

I want to let her go, but I'm frozen. My heart is beating in my throat, pounding, thrumming out through my ears.

Over my shoulder, I glance at Jamal's room. There's no way he's asleep so fast.

Inside I'm tangled up, searching for a reason why they're here. If I was standing by Jamal, we could look at each other without saying a word. Just know it's them that's wrong, not us. But something went down with Jamal, and whatever it was, I sense I should let him be.

I leave Corinne and make my way downstairs, my Know Your Rights training kicking in.

Mama waves me back, but I don't stop. I'm concerned it's gotta be about Daddy.

He's hurt.

Worse.

"What's happening?" Corinne calls from the stairs. Her eyes scrunch up like if she thinks real hard, she'll figure out what's going on all by herself without having to ask.

I look up one more time at Jamal's door, but it stays shut. Doubt hits me. He must've been on his way out when I saw him. He's going to trip when he gets home.

"Things are fine," I say. "I'm sure of it."

I take deep breaths, swallowing up the panic that's racing to my brain. I try and push down the memories of the time they came for Daddy. Thank God Corinne wasn't born yet. She didn't have to see him dragged by his neck through the house by police. I screamed nonstop when Jamal opened the door and the cops pushed him aside. They rushed Daddy, threw him on the ground, and shoved a knee in his back.

Daddy told me he wanted to lie still, but your body does the opposite. Survival. Someone's holding you down, you want to ask why, yell out in pain. They beat his head down, expecting with each punch he was supposed to take it in silence. Each cry he made, they hit him harder until he shut his mouth and they cuffed him.

Mama was stuck between fighting for Daddy, holding on to her pregnant belly, and keeping me calm. My scream ricocheted in the background as they read his rights, accusing him of murdering Mr. and Mrs. Davidson.

Corinne never held that memory, but I know she feels it in everything we breathe. It's in the polite nods across the street we have to make, the way our family turns down our music when there are others around. Say *yes ma'am* and *no sir.* Leave our jackets and backpacks in the car when we go shopping.

It's in the way I carry myself that tells our story now. I can't risk being accused of anything. Because if something goes wrong or missing, I know it's in the back of someone's mind that maybe I had something to do with it. And it's in the way that the voice of the strongest woman I know stumbles when saying, "Hello, Officer" as she walks through the visitation gates to see Daddy.

Only recently has it been cemented in my mind and made clear that acting civil, being deferential, doesn't matter. It's like

Mama has always said: *Black lives don't matter enough to them.* That evidence is live and in color, on every news channel in America.

I'm snapped back to the present as they yell, "Police! Open up!"

Mama goes for the door.

"Mama, no," I say. "Not until we see they have a warrant."

"Baby, no. This ain't a workshop. This is real life. Look at Corinne."

Corinne is shaking, terrified on the steps.

Mama pushes me behind her, then cinches her robe's belt and loosens the chain lock, before cracking the door open. A flood of blue and red lights streams through the house, and then a bright light flashes in Mama's face. She steps back and blocks it with her hand. When she does this, she's shoved back by the sheriff, John Brighton, pushing the door open more, gun drawn. His face is stern, red-fleshed around his neck. He has the same strawberry-blond hair, like an older version of his son, Chris—shorter, but with a matching body type, more fluff than muscle. If I didn't know better, I'd think he was frightened.

We should be the ones who are afraid, not him.

"We're here to take in Jamal Beaumont, ma'am." He shoves a warrant in front of us.

I suck in my teeth. All my training to review the warrant slips my mind as fear snakes up my legs and freezes me from moving. I look up to Jamal's room. Behind my shoulder, his door slowly opens to a crack. I'm reminded of his odd behavior. Jamal must've gotten into a fight. I look to Corinne, praying she won't cry out for Jamal on the stairs.

With my arms folded, I finally settle my list of what I should be doing as I make eye contact with Jamal. I only see a sliver of him, but it's like I can read his mind. That thing that siblings always have ingrained in their DNA—never rat on each other—lips sealed. The blood I saw tonight will never be mentioned. They wouldn't wait for his side of the story.

I step in front of Mama, making sure to only keep the door ajar. Mama digs her nails into my skin accidentally. It helps me focus on staying silent. If I'm calm, Mama will be, too.

"Let me review the warrant, please." I take the warrant from Sheriff Brighton's hand, but I'm not fully reading it. I'm stalling.

The house creaks as Jamal scuffles around in his room. The rusty glide of his bedroom window opening sends prickles down my spine. Mostly sounds I've gotten used to when he comes home by curfew, only to scoot out the window to stay out later. I'm not sure if I'm thinking it, but I swear there's another thump outside.

In my head, I imagine Jamal jumping off the roof and sprinting away. I keep my face stone-cold. Because no matter what my brother might've done, I'm not gonna let them take him away from us.

With every delay, it's another second for Jamal to escape. I will him to get to the river trail and up through the hills, running the route he takes every day to train during track season. He knows every nook and cranny in the dark because we've played hide-and-seek in the woods for years, and my brother is a master at it. I pray the sheriff doesn't have tracking dogs and Jamal can cut through the woods to the other side of the highway and catch a bus.

"It's late, Sheriff," Mama says behind me. "Come back tomorrow."

"Get your boy." Sheriff Brighton's voice has the same sharp bite to it as his son's.

Behind the sheriff, a squadful of cars are parked outside our house. Some cops are posted by the cars, others putting protective gear on.

"What the hell," I whisper under my breath.

Mama's back is as rigid as a board as Corinne joins us in the entryway. I don't know what to do, because the warrant looks legit. I want to run to Corinne, to be by her side and block them from Jamal, but I know it won't make a difference. Corinne's weight pulls on me. I know it's more important to keep her away. Keep her safe.

"I said, get your boy," the sheriff says.

A few more officers draw in closer to the door, like they're about to rush our entryway.

"Almost done," I say. "It's our right to verify a warrant."

I wonder what it's like to be someone who'd feel safe in their presence. I try to trick my mind, pretend we called them. It helps me settle more, and I give Mama a squeeze, hoping I can do the same for her. But it doesn't last long, because the word *boy* keeps running in my head. A bitter taste flushes in my mouth, the way that word drawls out like just another slur in coded language.

The officers, guns drawn, spread to each entrance of the house.

Mama's struck with fear, with grief, and it's like she gave them permission from that moment and it didn't matter I was planning on reading this warrant over a thousand times. Mama removes the chain lock and opens the door wider. They flood past us, scattering through the house and up the stairs before she can say she'll bring Jamal down.

As they make their way upstairs, I pray that God led Jamal into the woods and he is doing what he knows best, using his God-given legs to run.

RIGHT TO REMAIN SILENT

Mama wraps her arms around us as they search our home. Sheriff Brighton stays back, making sure we don't touch anything.

"Where is he?" the sheriff asks.

"I have no idea," Mama says. "I'd be able to help if I knew why you're here."

"If you know anything about his whereabouts, you should get him in here before—"

"Before what?" I breathe out heavy, angry.

"What exactly do you want my son for?" Mama tugs my arm back to take over the conversation.

"You'll hear soon enough, but right now I'm going to ask you to get your daughter in line and bring your boy in."

"I'll bring my son in. Don't worry about that."

A Black officer tentatively steps inside. Relief shoots through me. It's Beverly Ridges, Quincy's older sister. Right after playing college basketball, she went to the police academy. Since joining the force, she's kept her hair cropped short, so it takes me a second to recognize her. But everything else is the same, tall and fit.

Beverly looks at us, then up the stairs to Jamal's room. She's been in our house a dozen other times with Quincy. She's Jamal's oldest crush. Her senior year, she took Jamal to a dance because her date flaked on her. It was totally innocent, but as a freshman, Jamal couldn't hide his crush on her. He's always tried to play it off, but he loses all swagger around her.

"I came as soon as I heard," Beverly says.

I can't tell if she's talking to Sheriff Brighton or us.

"We're done here," Sheriff Brighton answers. "Going to place an officer on-site in case he comes home."

"I can take a shift," Beverly says. "My mother's house is on this side of town. Should be convenient enough."

"I'm aware." Sheriff Brighton quickly dismisses her.

He leaves the house, officers trailing behind. My shoulders settle once they're finally gone.

"Mrs. Beaumont." Beverly's hands are clasped loosely behind her back.

Mama releases a soft smile before her eyes go dull again.

I know Jamal would feel some type of way that Bev is out here looking for him. We were all shocked when we heard Bev wanted to be on the same force that ruined our lives. Killed her dad.

"Why don'tcha put Corinne to bed, Tracy?" Mama asks.

"I wanna wait up for Jamal." Corinne rubs at her eyes.

"He won't be coming back tonight." I put my arm around her, directing her to bed.

When I come downstairs, I catch Beverly telling Mama why they're after Jamal.

"They found Angela Herron." Beverly has a grim twist to her mouth. "Dead by the Pike."

Nausea rolls through my body.

"Did you say dead?" I have to confirm.

Beverly nods, and my hand cups my mouth in shock. I'm stuck for a moment, eyes welling—I just saw Angela earlier today. Then I recall the blood on Jamal and the scratch on his neck. Fear wraps itself around my body because I don't know what this means for Jamal.

"Oh my God." Mama's posture stiffens. "What happened?"

"She was murdered."

My throat begins to ache. How is it possible Angela is gone?

"That's terrible," Mama says. "But what's that got to do with my Jamal?"

"Before she died, she called 911. The operator heard Angela cry out Jamal's name."

The pieces start pulling together, and I have to hold my thoughts back to keep from screaming them out loud. Jamal and Angela were hooking up today, and before I left him at Herron

Media, he wanted me to cover for his late night, something out of the ordinary. Then I think about the blood swirling down the drain, and it hits me. Angela's been dating Chris, but she was cheating on him with Jamal. Sheriff Brighton brought a whole crew of police to search for his son's girlfriend's supposed killer.

"There's no way Jamal had anything to do with this," Mama says. "We have to fix this."

"Where could Jamal be?" Beverly asks.

"This isn't like Jamal to be out this late without letting me know," Mama says.

I hold my tongue, wanting to trust Beverly with how strange Jamal was acting tonight. But then I'd have to admit that maybe he was involved, that I caught Jamal and Angela together. That Angela told me this morning she had an exposé she wanted to work on, and not to tell Jamal.

"Have you tried to reach him?" Beverly asks.

"No." Mama looks away. "Not with all them police here."

"Try his friends." Beverly's voice shakes. "It's better you reach Jamal first and get him to turn himself in."

I run up to grab my phone from my room and dial Jamal's number. It rings and rings, then goes straight to voice mail after the third attempt. I send him frantic texts about what's happening before I go back downstairs. Mama's doing the same, so I step to the window to make a call.

I dial Quincy's number. It goes to voice mail. He answers after my second attempt. "What's the emergency?"

"Why didn't you answer the first time?"

"I'm busy. You know how it is."

A long pause sits between us as I wait to hear anything in the background. But there's nothing.

"Tell me if you've heard from Jamal."

"Jamal . . . Nah, I ain't heard from him."

"Quincy, I'm serious. The cops were all over the house." I walk closer to the window so Beverly and Mama won't hear. "Beverly's here. I know Jamal was messing with Angela. The cops didn't tell us, but Beverly told us they found Angela dead by the Pike."

Quincy's silent. He already knows.

"Quincy."

"I heard you. I'll tell him you called."

The click of Quincy's phone rings in my ear. Either he knows something, or he's going to do his best to get ahold of Jamal.

If anyone would be sympathetic about why Jamal would want to run . . . it would be Quincy.

After the cops went to arrest Jackson Ridges for the Davidsons' murder, there was a lot of talk about whether the cops had to kill him. They went in like they had no other option. I saw the way they approached our house with Jamal, with Daddy; it didn't need to be like that. They didn't have to kill Mr. Ridges.

My throat tightens, thinking about that time. The news coverage, the rallies. The things people said at school. Everyone in town talked about the shooting. The white community was quick to blame Daddy and Jackson for the Davidsons' murders.

At school, kids were cruel. Recess was Justin Draper's favorite time to corner me. Back then he was a pudgy white kid with a mullet. He's outgrown the mullet now but still has the same jackass attitude and thick, square head. I used to find excuses to help the teachers so I wouldn't have to go outside, but it didn't always work. The trial was public, and everyone was talking about it. We got death threats at home, so Mama thought school was the safest place for us.

One day Justin circled me, calling me the N-word. He'd never get away with that if Quincy wasn't still healing. If Quincy would've been there, he'd have handled it. Justin yelled at me and punched me in the stomach. I was down on the ground, my heart hurting more than anything else, and Dean came running at Justin like a linebacker. A fight broke out. That was the incident that pulled Dean and me closer with each day of Quincy's absence. Quincy and I've been distant ever since the shooting. Jamal was able to hold on to him, but my path went elsewhere. I feel our old history in this call. Knowing he'd be the only one to get what this means, but also knowing we aren't close no more.

When I turn around, Mama's shaking. She can't reach anyone who's seen Jamal, either.

"How did Angela die?" I ask Beverly.

"Autopsy won't be in yet, but it looks like a blunt force trauma to the head. She was found out on the Pike by the dried-up dock, near the old seafood-packing place."

"The call doesn't mean anything," I say. "She could've been asking for help. That doesn't prove Jamal was there."

"He was there tonight. And . . ." Beverly pauses.

"And what?"

"I shouldn't say. It might not be public."

"Beverly, you know Jamal—could you see him do anything like this? You've seen him at his worst. Nothing riles him up. He's never hurt me, even when I'd pick fights with him."

"Jamal was seen fleeing the scene . . . and his letterman jacket was found by her body."

My vision goes blurry, and I blink hard until it comes back. This can't be happening to us again.

"Someone else could've been out there with them. What if Jamal's injured, too?" There has to be a reason. He wouldn't leave his jacket, and it could explain the blood. Was Jamal attacked? Did someone try to kill him?

"Witnesses identified your vehicle, Mrs. Beaumont. He made it back here. We haven't been able to locate Angela's phone yet, but that could help."

"But if the 911 operator heard her call out for Jamal—"

"Y'all get some sleep. I'm sure we'll know more tomorrow," Beverly says. "Tomorrow I'll do what I can to find Jamal; you do the same. Mrs. Beaumont, try to get more information from Sheriff Brighton so you'll have legal counsel ready."

"I'm gonna finish making calls upstairs," Mama says.

I give her a kiss good night before she takes her time walking upstairs. Slow. Disoriented. She'll break down when no one's watching. Then I close the door behind Beverly.

I watch Beverly set up to guard the house, regardless of what the sheriff said. She must have persuaded the other officers to leave, because they drive away, and she takes their post. My heart soars; we have her on our side.

I take this moment to sneak out the back door. Barefoot, I run toward the grass. Warm air whipping around me, I ignore that it's pitch-black, and chase the path Jamal would've taken without being seen. I stop midway into the woods, cup my hands, and yell.

"Jamal!"

I wait for a response. Keep focused on the woods for the slight chance to spot him running back home. I wait and wait. Then yell again.

"Jamal! Jamal!"

I yell until I'm so hoarse it rips my throat to call out again.

I hear my name.

"Jamal." My voice is strangled. "Come back. Don't leave us."

I hear my name again. Turn when I realize it's coming from behind me, toward the house. Beverly's arms are wrapped around Mama, watching me cry out for my brother.

I drop to my knees because it wasn't him. Painful tears spill out my eyes, down onto my chin.

When I'm all dried up with nothing to give, I pick myself up. Prepare myself for the fight.

Wednesday, May 5

Stephen Jones, Esq.
Innocence X Headquarters
1111 Justice Road
Birmingham, Alabama 35005
Re: Death Penalty—Intake Department

Dear Mr. Jones,

My brother, Jamal Beaumont, is on the run. The Galveston County police think he killed a girl at my school. He didn't. He couldn't. They're blaming him because of who his dad is. The cycle won't stop. I need your help more than ever. We have to help Jamal, take every last drop of money we have—which is almost nothing, so maybe our house—to help defend Jamal. That means nothing left to help with my dad's appeal.

I can't have my father and my brother be in prison in a death penalty state. You are the only one who can help us. There's no hope if you don't take his case. Help us, so we can help my brother.

Please review James Beaumont's application (#1756).

Thank you for your time.

Tracy Beaumont

GUILTY . . . UNTIL PROVEN INNOCENT

Wednesday morning Jamal's still missing. That's how Mama sees it, but I know the truth. He's running. Each call to his friends was a dead end, all denying they know anything about where Jamal is. He was home. I locked eyes with him, and now he's out of touch. Suspected of killing Angela—the girl he's been secretly seeing. His boss's daughter.

Mama moves gingerly down the hall, stopping at my door to wake me, but I've been up for hours, waiting to hear from Jamal and writing a letter to Innocence X to let them know about Jamal's situation. As much as I want Jamal home, I'm also hoping he ain't stupid enough to come back, at least not until we know it's safe for him. Deep down I know it won't be easy. We've never had it easy.

"You up?" Mama asks.

"Yeah. You heard from him?"

"Grab that legal-help handout from your workshops for me. Gonna make a few calls before we head to the police station." Mama's hair is haggard, sticking up. I don't think I've ever seen her without her hair wrap on in the morning.

I go through my drawer and hand the paper to her, then help Mama by checking on Corinne, who will be going to school. She's in her bed, folded into a small ball with her arms wrapped around her legs, fully dressed, knowing we'd need to be ready in the morning. It's a routine of urgency we've all mastered. Usually, we can brush away the fear. Today feels different. Today, we don't know the rules we're supposed to follow.

"Morning." I rub my hand on Corinne's back, then kiss her hair that's sticking in all directions.

"Jamal back?" Corinne asks.

I shake my head.

"Maybe he's at work," Corinne says, getting up.

I run my fingers across the hash marks on her doorway that track her height. When I've capped the top of her most recent smudge, I glance out the window.

The road that leads to our house is a quarter mile long, but you can see the unmarked police car parked down by our mailboxes. Beverly no longer there.

The image of blood swirling down the drain comes back to me. Worry fills me that Jamal is hurt, or worse: he did something horrific on accident and he's too scared to ask for help.

The cops left last night with Jamal's toothbrush and clippers, but no towel. I have to confirm if it was blood or if my mind was messing with me so late into the night. I search the bathroom for the towel Jamal used. The rack is empty. Then I remember he balled it up before going to bed.

I rummage through every crevice and corner of his room.

"What's with you?" Mama stops at Jamal's door.

"I was looking for the bathroom hand towel. You seen it?" My gut churns with dread.

Mama pushes her lips out like it means nothing to her, but then she looks down, which makes it harder to study her for the truth. I wait until Mama goes back downstairs, and then I search Jamal's nightstand.

All he's got in here are college acceptance letters, a Bible, Chapstick, and a handful of pencils. I flip through a small notebook filled with scribbles of reminders to himself, like school application dates and deadlines. A date: July 14, with Angela's name, circled. I pause at the writing near her name, then make my way to his window. He rarely lets me in his room, but sometimes when we're both up on a sleepless night, I get the chance to join him when he climbs out on the roof. I've always been a captive audience when he allows me into the world inside his head. We'd talk for hours.

I want to be closer to Jamal, so I push up his window to go out on the roof. It creaks like when Jamal left last night. I extend my leg out, pull my body through, and settle on the roof. Sit in

Jamal's spot. I angle enough, though, so that the cops who are posted on the side of the road can't see me.

In my head, I sort through what Jamal might be doing. He might not feel safe to come home, but Jamal wouldn't just run. He'd keep watching out for us. Work on clearing his name. He should also know I'm the best one to help. If I hear from him, I'll need to persuade him to tell me what happened. For Daddy, for Mama. For me.

Back inside, I go through Jamal's things one more time. Except this time, it's to get supplies and clothes for Jamal. Make it easy if he ever decides to come home quick. On my way back downstairs, the television catches my attention when BREAKING NEWS flashes at the bottom of *The Wendy Williams Show*. Susan Touric comes on the screen. I step closer to study her reaction. She'll influence the media coverage of Angela, and if she does, Jamal could feel safe enough to come home and tell his story.

We interrupt this program to share a breaking news development in the case of our production assistant, eighteen-year-old Angela Herron, who was murdered last night. The Galveston County sheriff's office has identified a suspect.

Angela's homecoming photo flashes on the screen. She's smiling bright, her hair in those rolling blond waves. They do a close-up on her face, angelic precision, the way they highlight the photo with doctored light around her face.

I'm jarred into reality when Jamal's picture flashes on the screen. The word *suspect* stamped under his name. They didn't use his footage from her show last week. Not his homecoming picture, a school photo, or a picture from the countless track meets and fund-raising banquet dinners.

Instead, they use a photo of Jamal with a red cup in his hand, middle finger up, a big grin on his face. I remember it from his Instagram. They have it cropped close around him, but if you saw the rest of the photo, you'd see the entire track team. A unity shot of everyone flipping off Coach Curry for scheduling an early-morning run the day after homecoming.

They've got Jamal painted like a *thug*, standing between two other Black team members with blurred-out headshots, Dean and the other white teammates conveniently cropped out of the original photo. All Jamal was doing was being a teenager at a party, no harm. He was the designated driver that night, but the red cup sticks out. Now it don't matter he was hydrating with water before the early-morning run.

My breath catches when Angela's photo lines up next to Jamal's. The words *suspect, on the run, last seen* flash in front of me. I'm sick, wanting to heave. They can't set him up like this. We can't go through this again.

My phone pings and I get a text from Tasha.

You see this! The news is a mess. Jamal had no business with Angela. This is stupid.

I know. I'm watching Susan Touric.

Turn it off, it's trash!!

I can't help it. I need to know more.

You going to school?

No. Heading to the police station with Mama.
Let me know if you hear anything at school.

I'm on it . . . Jamal still gone?

Yip . . . See if you can corner Quincy.
He was real short with me on the phone.

Oh, I'd be happy to corner Quincy.

Ummm . . . Never mind. I'll call him again.

Hater. Let me know if you want me to come through.

K. Love you.

♡

I should turn the TV off, but I can't help myself. I turn up the volume. Susan plays footage of Jamal's interview. They replay Mama saying Daddy is innocent, then Jamal smiling onstage. The words *The calculated act of a killer?* flash up on the screen.

The news continues, except this time Susan's talking about

Daddy. His mug shot goes up with sketches from the courtroom. It's been so long since I've seen his story on the news. Flashes of old memories run through my mind. Déjà vu.

Jamal Beaumont is the son of convicted killer James Beaumont. Cathy and Mark Davidson were killed by gunshot in their downtown Galveston County office. A second suspected shooter, Jackson Ridges, barricaded himself in his home and died when police attempted to bring him in for questioning. James Beaumont stood trial. Upon conviction, he was the only one to pay for the crime in the Davidson family massacre.

"Jackson was murdered, too," I say to the television.

The district attorney wanted Daddy to take a plea deal, say it was self-defense, anything to get the death penalty off the table. Daddy's attorney thought he should take the deal because of the way the case was building against them. But Daddy wouldn't do it. Not when he was innocent. He also believed if he took a deal, then he wouldn't just be pleading guilty for himself; he'd be claiming that for Jackson, too. He couldn't help justify Jackson's murder, so Daddy didn't take a plea deal.

We lost.

Even with the gun missing . . . even though there was no blood or marks on Daddy . . . even though he had multiple people who could confirm his alibi . . . we lost.

My father's alibi was trumped by white witnesses in the neighborhood who swore they saw Daddy's Buick, with two Black men inside, leaving the Davidson office late that afternoon, not at noon like Daddy said. I used to ask Daddy if he thought things would be different if he'd had a Black attorney, that maybe his attorney would have understood the bias in the trial more. Daddy squashed that. It wasn't about the race of his attorney, but about being a Black man on trial in a town that never accepted us. Everyone wanted an answer to a heinous crime, and it was easier to think it was an outsider—someone "not like them."

I won't let Jamal go down like that. Not this time. Not if I can help it.

We can't lose again.

POLICE STATE

Mama's waiting on the porch with Corinne. She meets me outside, the ends of her hair hastily bumped in a curl. She's so shell-shocked she's not tracking things well. Like she knows she needs to be strong, but inside she is cracking. Scared to death.

"Anything on the news?"

"Just local weather," I lie. Mama knows how bad it can get. I don't need to add to her concern. "Tasha's gonna ask around at school. See if anybody's heard from Jamal."

"Good." Mama's eyes are glazed.

"He didn't do it. We'll get Jamal back."

We both know Jamal could never, but when has that mattered? It sure didn't when Mama kept saying Daddy was coming home.

As we leave, we're forced to pass the police car staking out our house. I square my shoulders and narrow my eyes while I reach for Corinne's hand to pull her close to me. Beneath our anger, there's hidden shame and embarrassment that's similar to what we felt the first time we left the house after Daddy was arrested.

Ten minutes on the road and I let my mind wander. Every small town looks the same, all rolling into each other. Except, of course, when we reach the WELCOME TO GALVESTON COUNTY sign. Whenever we pass it, I have the same visceral reaction.

The first time I saw the sign, I was riding a bus from New Orleans. Daddy tried to hide that he was just as frightened about evacuating as we were. The way his eyes skittered around, though, I knew he was questioning if we should've waited out the storm. I didn't know the answer then, but I know now that it wasn't the levee failures in New Orleans that wiped my family's life away. It was moving to Texas.

Not returning was Daddy's idea. Daddy partnered with Jackson Ridges, who'd gotten him his first contractor job when we evacuated to Texas. Later, Mark Davidson hired Daddy by himself for renovation work. After a few jobs, he said Daddy could get a loan if he wanted to expand his business to land development. Mark trusted Daddy. He knew he did good work. He didn't know Jackson Ridges, and so he tried to edge him out of the development deal. I think he just didn't like what part of town he was from, but Daddy was always loyal and was ready to pull out unless Mark agreed to include Jackson in the new business venture.

Daddy being charged with the Davidsons' murder was unbelievable for anyone who knew their relationship. There was no bad blood. Just a disagreement.

I lean my head against the window, let those memories wash away as the signs turn into a blur. Then distract myself with Mama's voice that rises and belts as she ups the volume on the radio. She points her finger to the ceiling of the car, humming along at the notes that are too high to hit.

The gospel music baptizing her the way it can rear inside your veins and cleanse your entire body, giving you goose bumps, making you raise your hands high. Probably the thing that gives Mama hope and the strength to rise and fight whatever the battle is for the day. And for today, we need all the help we can get.

After we drop off Corinne at school, we pull up to the police station. The first person I recognize isn't a police officer. It's Dean.

"You call him to meet you here?" Mama points at him.

"No," I say. "You know Dean, though."

"Well, tell him to go to school. The last thing I need is his mama giving me grief we got her boy caught up in our mess and skipping school."

"Mrs. Beaumont," Dean says, approaching our parked car.

"Morning." Mama and I both get out of the car. "You shouldn't be here, Dean. You got school."

"Where else would I be?" Dean runs his hands through his hair. "Y'all are like family to me. My dad knows I'm here."

"Go back to your mama, then. You know she won't like you here." Mama purses her lips.

Dean doesn't budge, and the truth is, I'm not ready for him to leave. He's always been someone I can rely on, and I need him more than ever. School won't be easy. We lost a classmate in a horrific way. Today will be a shock for everyone, and then all that anger will be directed at Jamal as a suspect. Someone to blame so people can move on, because it hurts too much not knowing who could do something like that to Angela. I've seen this all before.

"Were you always this stubborn, or is my daughter to blame?"

"Definitely your daughter."

I sock Dean lightly on the arm.

"After we done, get back to school. I don't want you missing a whole day. Get Tracy's work from teachers. She'll be out of school the rest of the week."

"I'm not going back until Jamal gets help," I say. "He needs a lawyer."

"You need to be in school." Mama rests her hand on her hip.

I swallow hard. Being at school won't be easy. It took years to get people to stop talking about my father's trial, and even now my circle is still small. I'd rather be absent the last month of school and do my work from home, but Mama won't have it. I know.

"Stay out here with Dean."

"I thought I was going with you," I say.

Mama knows I can help. I might not have been able to help when Daddy was arrested, but I've made up for it in working with the lawyers and running Know Your Rights campaigns in the community. I pull out my rights crib sheet from my back pocket.

Mama studies me, then closes her eyes in agreement. As soon as Mama turns toward the station, her face goes stern, like she's going to put a hurting on anyone who gives her the runaround.

I show a grateful smile as Dean waits by the stairs. I know he'd be out here all day if he needed to, and that helps take away the feeling we're alone in this.

Following Mama, I clutch my phone before sending another text to Jamal that'll probably go unanswered. I look back one more time at Dean, then suck in a breath to prepare myself.

This time has to be different. We trusted that the truth would come out in the Davidson murder investigation, but we should've known. Daddy was the number one suspect, and nothing else mattered. I won't forget that. All we've been through with Daddy has to have been preparation for fighting for Jamal.

Goose bumps pucker my skin from the cold air in the police station compared with the heat outside. There's a long hallway to the back, where three offices stand to the right of a small holding cell. A few deputies from last night shuffle back and forth with paperwork. I search for someone who'll listen. Who'll want to help. The room is empty of that care. They know who we are and have already made a judgment.

"Sheriff Brighton, please," Mama says to the desk officer. "You can tell him it's Mrs. Lillian Beaumont."

Mama doesn't wait for a response. She whips around and takes a seat at the bench.

"Let's do this," I say under my breath.

"If Jamal don't come home, we're going to need to get word to your dad."

I gulp hard. I know this truth. Daddy's already been pulling away, pushing me to get prepared for when he's gone.

Mama closes her eyes and lays her hand over her purse. They must not realize Mama can wait them out all day.

I look past the officer, over at the deputies stopping to talk to each other. Standing with them is Chris Brighton, wearing his orange Texas A&M hat. My heart squeezes; Chris just lost his girlfriend.

The sheriff rests his hand on Chris's shoulder and says, "It's gonna be all right, son."

He gently grabs the back of Chris's neck. My eyes well at the sweet gesture between father and son. Then I begin to wonder how much it'll hurt when Chris learns Angela'd been spending time with Jamal. That kind of secret comes out at trials, and I hope it doesn't make Jamal seem more of a suspect. When Chris turns, his piercing blue eyes are hidden behind a black right eye, his face all splotchy and red.

I squint at him.

The sheriff goes back to his office, and Chris is joined by a guy who looks to be in his forties. He's wearing a USA hat and a collared shirt with nice dress pants. He makes the hairs on the back of my neck stand up. He puts his arm around Chris, waves at the sheriff, and whispers something to Chris. I see a resemblance between this man and Chris and the sheriff, the same broad build and strawberry-blond hair. Definitely related.

The guy leads Chris down the hallway, without letting go of him. Chris is shook. Part of me is angry with Jamal for messing with Chris's girlfriend. How stupid do you have to be to run around with someone who's dating the sheriff's son? This might be what got the cops after Jamal for Angela's murder. An easy suspect. That's the fastest way to jail—don't stop at go, don't collect two hundred dollars.

Theories flood my mind: Chris killed Angela. Jamal and Chris got into a fight; Angela died by accident. Whatever the case, it'll be Chris's word against Jamal's. I don't care about the blood; Jamal couldn't have killed her. Whatever happened, though, I need to hear it from Jamal.

Chris passes without even noticing me. I can't say the same for Mr. USA, who stops dead in his tracks by Mama. She must feel his scrutiny, because she opens her eyes. She folds her arms tighter around herself, like she wants to disappear. I've never seen Mama show her fear in public. Chris watches Mr. USA, and then he finally recognizes me.

"Your brother's not getting away with this," he says.

I tighten my fists at my sides, ready for an altercation with Chris. "He didn't do this. He could never—"

"Chris! You don't say a word to anyone," Sheriff Brighton calls out, then charges toward the front desk.

"Let's go." Chris gives me a glare before he exits, breaking out of the hold of the guy with him.

As soon as the door closes behind them, Mama pulls at the cross on her necklace.

"Mrs. Beaumont." Sheriff Brighton approaches Mama. "I hope you're here with word about your son."

Mama goes to answer him, but not before I step in front of her.

"Is focusing on Jamal a personal vendetta on behalf of your son, or do you have any evidence?"

"Excuse me?" Sheriff Brighton's jaw goes tight.

"You bring the entire force to our home looking for Jamal, holding a warrant. What evidence do you have on Jamal?"

"Tracy." Mama pulls me closer.

"This is abuse of power," I say. "You should know this won't stand in a courtroom, especially the way you barged into the house. When we hear Jamal's side of things, you're going to regret—"

"What exactly are you charging my son with?" Mama asks.

"Murder."

I gasp and Mama rocks back. We heard about Angela from Beverly, knew it was leading up to this, but hearing it from the sheriff makes it more real.

"We have a witness at the crime scene. A 911 call placing him near the victim, and your son's letterman jacket covering her body. The sooner he comes in, the better chance he has of getting the DA to give him life rather than a death sentence."

My fingers touch my parted lips. He knows what that threat means to our family.

"Have you heard different from Jamal?" Sheriff Brighton asks. "Seen him at all since the murder?"

I gulp hard because I don't have an answer about the blood on Jamal. I can't deny he was jumpy last night.

"Jamal could be injured," I say. "Have you thought for one second that maybe his life is also in danger? Someone could be after my brother."

"The facts aren't adding up that way."

"Next time you come barging into my home, you better expect our lawyer will be ready to make charges of excessive force," Mama says as she shifts her purse around. She doesn't wait for him to respond; instead, she stands and steadily walks out the front door.

Outside, Chris's red truck drives past with him in the passenger seat; he must trust Mr. USA to drive his car. Hitched to the back of the truck is an American flag that flies in the wind. Something tells me that to him the Stars and Stripes represents the good old days when the American Dream was narrowly defined. Our nightmare.

"I'm sorry, Mama." I touch her shoulder. "We're going to find Jamal."

Mama wraps her arms around me, shaking.

"What should we do about Jamal?" I ask.

"I'm worried we haven't heard from him yet. I wish—"

Mama doesn't finish her thought, but I know what she's thinking. *I wish Daddy was home.* Having his son be a suspect in the murder of a young white girl isn't going to help his appeal. I gotta see Daddy. Gotta find Jamal. Before I lose them both. Before I lose Mama.

I know Jamal would be mad, but Mama can't be engulfed in worry over his disappearance. She needs to know he chose to leave.

"Jamal came home last night." I pause before telling her what I know about Jamal and Angela, and how I heard him last night. Everything . . . but the blood I saw. That could be the stake that nails the coffin.

Mama sweeps her trembling hand across her forehand. Her voice catches, and she's unable to speak.

"He's safe, Mama." I stare up at her with hopeful eyes.

"Do we tell someone?"

We both know the answer. Not yet. At least not until we know more.

"Jamal needs a lawyer," Mama says. "We can't wait until they find him." Mama smooths her clothes as Dean approaches us. Like she's trying to get the wrinkles out to convince herself things are fine.

"I've got some things I need to take care of. You gonna be okay with Dean? Let him take you back, so if Jamal comes home, we got someone who can watch out for him."

"I'll keep her out of trouble," Dean says.

"I'm counting on it. I don't need more on my plate than I already have."

I nod. Give her a kiss.

When Mama drives away, the tears build, and I can't stop them. I let them run down my cheeks, biting my bottom lip to keep any sound from escaping. The only thing I can think about is wanting to see Daddy. Like he might have some answer, something he's learned over time that'll fix everything. Stop this cycle from repeating itself.

"Why would Angela be with Jamal by the Pike?" Dean asks.

I blink. Stuck on this question and so many others. Angela was alive less than twenty-four hours ago, and now she's gone. Jamal would never hurt anyone. Couldn't hurt anyone. I force myself to ignore the blood I saw on Jamal last night, the thing I can't explain away.

"You don't—"

"Absolutely not," Dean says. "It'll clear itself."

"Like my daddy?" My eyes get blurry.

"It's not the same," Dean says.

His voice is firm. I agree, even though on the inside I feel different. I can't trust that things will get better.

"Chris looked like he got into a fight, but he walked out, so they weren't arresting him. Not like the sheriff would do that to his own son."

My phone vibrates, and I pull it out.

Jamal.

How is Ma?

> This looks bad. Jamal, what happened to Angela?

I didn't do it.

> What should we do?

DON'T tell Mama you heard from me.

> Meet me?

I can't. Gotta keep moving.

> Do you have enough to get by?

A few days. Don't worry about me.

> What can I do?

Take care of Mama. Corinne.

> Who killed Angela?

I wait for a second longer, but he doesn't text again.

I want Jamal to come home. But if he doesn't, the cops are taking him in. When they took Daddy from our house, that was the last time we saw him not behind bars. Except in the courtroom. I used to pretend he was the lawyer, all suited up, trying someone's case. I couldn't pretend that any longer when the decision *guilty* crossed the lips of every juror.

Jamal is in the same boat now, and things don't look good. But I have to believe I know my brother better than anyone. Then prove it to the world before it swallows him whole.

Friday, May 7

Stephen Jones, Esq.

Innocence X Headquarters

1111 Justice Road

Birmingham, Alabama 35005

Re: Death Penalty——Intake Department

Dear Mr. Jones,

"Let us realize the arc of the moral universe is long, but it bends toward justice."

This saying is etched outside your main office. I saw it in all your photos. I got a question: Dr. King wrote this and Obama believed it, but how can it be true if it seems like everything is going backward? Does it mean a hundred years from now someone else won't go through the same pain that my family's been through? Because if that's what you believe, then what about me? What about my family? Do I have to lose my daddy? My brother? Because if people just wait enough years, laws will change. I'm not trying to be funny. I really want to know. Because right now I'm looking for something to make me feel hopeful, and I've got nothing.

Please review James Beaumont's application (#1756).

Thank you for your time.

Tracy Beaumont

FAMILY MATTERS

On Saturday morning, I visit Tasha's to catch up on school the past few days, but when I enter her house, I can feel the tension. I don't know what I walked into, but they act like I'm not even here. Everyone is gathered in the kitchen.

"You can't tell me what to do," Tasha says.

"We'll see about what I can and can't do," Daddy Greg says.

"You gonna be around long enough to make sure I don't?"

"I'm not taking this shit from you. You might have got away with this before, but I'm not letting you talk like this in my house."

"Your house? Ha! I've paid as much of the bills as you, more even."

"Tasha, you stop this right now," Tasha's mom says. "The both of you. I won't have this talk in *my* house. Let's be clear.

This is *my* house. Besides, we got guests. Tracy don't wanna hear this bickering when she got bigger things to think about."

She wraps her arms around me, holding me tight. "Excuse their manners, Tracy."

"Sorry, I just came in," I say.

"Girl, you family. No need to apologize. I just wish they'd both act civil around here. I can't take it."

"I'm sorry." Daddy Greg kisses Ms. Candice's forehead.

She shoos him to the front of the house, and I follow Tasha to her room.

I was trying to get away by coming here. Jamal is hurt, gone. Mama is lost, stressed. But I'm now consoling Tasha. We have so much in common, except she's turned to stone. I know I'm the only one who can bring her back. I touch Tasha's hand to warm her and pretend it doesn't hurt when she flinches.

"What was that all about?"

"He thinks he can come back and tell me what to do," Tasha says. "Like I gotta ask him for permission. Where the hell's he been if he wanted to play daddy so much?"

I rub Tasha's back to comfort her.

"I'm annoying. Sorry." Finally, she smiles. "I'm glad you came by. I was gonna head to you."

"I had to get out, too. It's suffocating being home."

"I know the feeling." She squeezes my hand.

"You hear anything at school?" I ask, studying Tasha.

"Nah. Bunch of rumors." Tasha's eyes cut away. "You know how school gets. Things were crazy, though. We barely had class.

First period, people were just crying, and then they had an assembly to share the news. Grief counselors came, and they'll be there next week, too."

"They say anything about Jamal?" I hold my breath. I know it's bad. That's why I came by today, because Tasha wasn't saying much on the phone, trying to protect me.

"A little on Jamal, but mostly everyone feeling sad about Angela. The school is split. You know how it goes."

"Black and white?"

"Pretty much everybody Black's got Jamal on their mind. They better find Jamal and clear things up soon, or by the end of the year there's gonna be a riot."

"Anyone seen Jamal? Know what he was doing out by the Pike?"

"Last people saw him at school was Tuesday. Rumors are flying, though, that he looked upset, but people thought it was because of the Susan Touric interview."

"Great." I shake my head.

"I did hear it going around Jamal was talking to Angela Tuesday morning."

"I skipped class and spoke with Angela that morning, too." I flash to our conversation. "Angela wanted me to work with her on some exposé. I was supposed to meet her first thing Wednesday."

"Damn. Really? Maybe she got herself killed."

"Over what, a school scandal? Rigged student council elections?" I tighten my face after I say it. Reality sets in. She's gone now.

"I don't know," Tasha says. "It's messed up."

"Really messed up, and to make it worse, the cops believe Jamal did it, but he's running, can't defend himself."

"Somebody knows something," Tasha says. "If she was out by the Pike, there's gotta be witnesses."

"On a Tuesday night? Who knows what they were doing out there?"

I hold in my worry that Jamal and Angela chose that night because it'd be isolated and they could hook up. Jamal's only witness could be whoever killed Angela. Him admitting to messing around with a white girl in the middle of nowhere isn't going to be much of a defense. The Pike has the reputation for being the underage party spot on weekends, but Black and Latinx folks don't hang out there. Lots of drinking and white boys with big trucks off-roading in the dried-out marshes. I can't imagine Jamal even being caught out there. I just can't see it.

"What about Quincy?" I ask. "You see him?"

"His fine ass wasn't at school."

"Wait, he was out?"

"Trust, I looked."

"I saw Chris at the police station, too, so he was out of school on Wednesday. What about the rest of the week, or his boys?"

"Haven't seen him. I heard people talking about how he was all sad. That he witnessed what happened. Scott and Justin were at school, mourning Angela like everybody else. I'll admit, school's been depressing as hell."

"The news hasn't said anything about Chris. I wonder what that's all about."

"Maybe they think he'd be in danger. If he said he was a witness and all."

I shake my head. I have no idea.

"What the police been saying?"

I go over everything I know. But I hold my tongue about the blood and the fact that Jamal was messing with Angela. I love Tasha, but sometimes she can slice you with her words. Cut people off without giving them the benefit of the doubt. She's already hot with her dad; I don't know if she'll give Jamal the grace. So I keep it to myself for now.

PAST IS ALWAYS PRESENT

Quincy knows something. That'd explain why Quincy was short with me on the phone, and why he didn't go to school the rest of the week. If Jamal was in trouble, Quincy wouldn't turn him away. Any other situation, Quincy'd be hollering back real quick. My cheeks blush at the thought. He'd hit me with his usual jokes about if I'm finally giving in or that he knew I wanted him all these years. I'd hide a change in expression, but inside I'd be squirming because Quincy is easy on the eyes.

When I pull up to Quincy's place, his Impala is nowhere in sight. I pause, unsure if I should get out. Quincy's mama opens the door, hand on her hip. Her lips sealed tight. I want to vanish, but I make my way to her.

"For a second I thought Jamal was driving with you." Mrs. Ridges's expression relaxes, her hair with purple tips framing her face.

"Is . . ." I pause. Unsure what exactly I'm supposed to say to her. "Quincy home?"

"He gone. What you need with my boy?"

She's lost a lot. I know she blames Daddy for mixing up Jackson in his business. We hadn't lived in Crowning Heights long before we met the Ridges family. She can't blame us for what happened to the Davidsons. And Jamal's been a good influence on Quincy; that's why Mrs. Ridges took to him. But by the way she's staring at me, all that's lost. Every time Mama sees her, hurt floats in Mama's eyes. There's a longing for a friendship that ended the day the police killed Jackson. I don't think Mama and Mrs. Ridges stopped caring for each other. But when you lose someone, and an entire town thinks your spouses were guilty, it does something to your friendship. Being close reminds you what's missing.

"Jamal, that you?" Malcolm, Quincy's younger brother, comes strolling to the door, disappointed when he sees it's just me.

I'm taken aback—Malcolm's about my height now. He's wearing a washed-out track shirt that used to be Jamal's. My throat closes because Jamal was always hooking up Malcolm with gear. Jamal wasn't just watching out for Corinne and me.

"You coming in?" Malcolm asks.

"She was looking for Quincy, but I told her he ain't here. I got to get to work, so come on now."

Malcolm's eyebrows raise. "You heard from him?"

"Malcolm." Her voice is biting.

"No." I smile. "But I'm sure we will. It's all—"

"Bev will find him. She'll clear things up." Malcolm's all puffed out.

I hope that's true. Hope that Beverly won't forget where she came from.

I look past Mrs. Ridges to the inside of her house. It has remnants of our home. Jamal's old bike hanging in the entryway catches my eye. My coat hangs on a hook. I purposefully tore it so I could beg Mama for a new one and keep up with my classmates. The rip is sewn, barely noticeable; it must belong to Quincy's sister CeCe now. Being here is like seeing my family echoed in someone else's.

"I should go," I croak out.

"I'll tell Quincy you came by." Mrs. Ridges grabs her keys and walks to her car, Malcolm trailing behind. She stops. "I'm sorry to hear about Jamal, but don't come 'round here bringing trouble. If they looking for Jamal, I know they gon' be bugging my boy about this. Already been here once."

"I'm sorry, ma'am." I slump my shoulders. She's right. I wanted to find Jamal.

"Don't be like that now, Tracy. Hold your head up. I still love you. Still love your mama, Jamal, too. But I can't lose one of my boys. They all I got."

"I know." I turn back to the car.

"How your daddy doing?" Mrs. Ridges yells after me.

I put my hand up to block the sun and see if she really wants to know.

"He's okay." My voice cracks. "He got less than a year, you

know." I stand there, waiting for her to say more. She almost seems like she's done with me, but then she speaks again.

"I be praying for him, you know. Every day. Always in my prayers. We lost Jackson. We don't need to lose nobody else. So, you tell him I say hi. You tell him . . ." Her voice stops, choking on her words. "I hope God'll answer y'all's prayers. Bring him and Jamal home."

She steps into her car, waving at Malcolm to hurry up and get inside. Malcolm catches my attention, pointing to the garage before he waves goodbye. That's when I notice Quincy's Impala hidden behind Mrs. Ridges's car. That garage never could close all the way.

Quincy's home.

GOTCHA!

I walk around the porch to the back window and spot Quincy watching TV. I tap on the glass and give him a winning smile.

I read Quincy's lips: *Shit.*

When I come around, Quincy's already by the door, leaning on the frame. Even though he is lounging around the house, he never looks unkempt. Locs twisted tight, clean-shaven, and crisp white shirt and blue jeans.

"What's the occasion?" Quincy's locs sway as he checks me up and down. His soft brown eyes perk up, curious.

"What's up with having your mom cover for you?"

"That was all her."

I study him. He looks like he's telling the truth, and Malcolm acted surprised when she mentioned Quincy wasn't home.

"Can I come in?" I step closer, foot in the doorway and hand on my hips.

"A'ight." Quincy towers over me as he leads me to his family room. Stacked up along the wall is his DVD master collection of *The Wire*. He binge-watches like new episodes are still coming out. He turns the volume down on the television.

"You talk to Jamal?" I ask.

"Your brother?"

"Of course, fool."

"Damn, Tracy." Quincy cocks his head to the side. "Why you always gotta run that mouth of yours?"

"You like it," I say. "When was the last time you talked to my brother?"

"Why? You ratting him out or something?" Quincy points for me to sit right next to him. Normally, I'd choose the opposite seat to get under his skin, but I don't.

"Does that mean you're finally going to admit you're happy to see me?" Quincy loosens a grin when I sit next to him.

"I'm looking for Jamal. I'm worried. The whole family is."

Quincy's face gets serious. He sits up, and his broad shoulders stand out as he pulls himself up from slouching on the couch, dragging his left leg in so it's even with his right. He's always kept his athletic, muscular build, training and working out, even though he never had a chance to compete much in sports.

"I know you've heard from him." I don't know if it's true, but

I'm betting something is up, since he didn't want to answer the door.

I reach for Quincy's hand. It's rough but soft at the same time.

"I'd tell you if I could," he says.

I drop his hand.

"Damn, T. Why you gotta be so disappointed in me? That shit kills me. I promised your bro I wouldn't get you caught up. You feel me?"

"You admit you've seen him." I flick my hand at his leg. "C'mon, where is he? Is he safe?"

"Slow down. I saw him yesterday. He needed to get cleaned up and clear his head, pick up a few supplies. Ma spotted Jamal hiding out in my room after the police came by, and she flipped her lid. She covered for him, since they weren't searching the house, but made me promise not to see him again or she'd tell Beverly."

"What do you know about that night, and where is he?" My voice rises in excitement. I should've come here Friday. Tasha should've sent me a text to let me know Quincy was out yesterday, not waited until today to say something.

"This ain't CNN, Don Lemon."

"Quincy." I play-punch his arm. "This is my brother."

"Damn. He's safe. I mean, I don't know exactly, but he ain't in jail. Shit." Quincy pauses. "That's all I can say. You know I got a soft spot for you, but you gotta trust your brother. I can't get in the middle of this." Quincy reaches for my arm but then pulls his hand back. "He's already gonna kick my ass for talking to you."

"You promised me you'd always look out for me."

That was years ago, when Daddy was in jail awaiting trial. We went by to visit Quincy. Mama made his favorite pie. He suffered through the pain and acted like he was fine, even when I could see a grimace on his face with each move. The next day he forced his mama to visit us. He'd heard I'd locked myself in the closet because I was afraid of getting shot like him. Nightmares filling me each night, that the police would storm through our house. I got over it; never dreamed it would happen again with Jamal. When Quincy came to visit me back then, he stayed by my closet for hours. We talked about our favorite shows. Things we liked to do. How much he missed school. When he left, he promised he'd always look out for me. Sealed it by kissing my cheek before hobbling down the stairs, our mamas yelling at him to be careful.

I can tell Quincy's thinking about that day. He drops his head and runs his fingers around his locs.

"Jamal's took care of you pretty much your whole damn life. You think he'd run so far he couldn't get to y'all if he needed to?"

"He's close, then?" I grip Quincy's arm, my heart hanging on every word.

"Nuh-uh. Don't be using your flirtish ways unless you mean it. I'm not playing these games with you."

"Quincy," I say, "tell me where my brother is and what you know about Angela."

"All I know is he was messing with someone else's girl on and off since right after homecoming. A white girl at that. Fast-forward six months and she ends up dead. That's why I stick to sistas." Quincy gives me a lazy smile. "They were supposed to hook up that night. Then I get a text that plans changed. So he met me here. Whoop-whoop, she didn't show. Typical. That's it. Then when Jamal was here, he got a text, said he had to bounce. Whoop-whoop."

I pause, make sure I should admit this out loud. "I saw Jamal at home before the cops came, and he was cleaning up blood."

Quincy glances up at the ceiling as he grips the chair, then makes eye contact. "Jamal wasn't messed up the first time he came over. But . . . when he came back, he said he found her, tried to save her, but she was pretty much dead in his arms, bleeding from her head. Like someone banged a rock on her head. He got there and found her like that."

"Why didn't he call 911?" My heart aches at what Jamal must've been feeling, finding Angela like that.

"What you think was going to happen in this town if your brother called 911 and he got blood on him out at the Pike, hanging over a dead white girl's body?"

I rub my hands over my face. I get it, but I wish he did something different. "Who does he think did it?"

"I don't know. You gotta talk to him, because as far as the

po-po is concerned, the common denominator is your brother. You notice how these jokers ain't doing much investigating. They came around here, but all they were asking about was your brother."

"What did you say to the cops?"

"Shiiiit. I didn't tell them nothing. And Jamal damn sure wasn't about to give me no details so I could get hung up by this. I'm lucky Beverly had some pull, or you know they'd drag me into a room until I said something."

"You didn't want to know what happened to Jamal?"

"What for? If I know, they got me ratting on my boy. If I don't know, it don't make a difference. Jamal's my boy, and I know he didn't put no hands on no girl. I'd whip his ass on principle."

Everything he's saying is the truth I've known for Jamal. It makes more sense why he didn't call the cops. I wish he hadn't touched her and just called the cops, but Jamal wouldn't be the type to not try and help her. He'd go to see if she was alive. If he could save her. Quincy doesn't have more to say, so I stand. He walks me to the door. When Quincy opens it, I scoot through, but he stops me.

"For your brother, me, whoever will get you to listen, please watch out." Quincy brushes my hair back, then cups my chin. It's intimate. I go still, mesmerized, wanting to see what happens.

"I will," I whisper.

Quincy's leg is pressed up on me, and his fingers touch my

hair. God, it's weird, I want him to kiss me. He's looking into my eyes, and I feel like he can hear inside my head. He leans in. I blink, breaking our eye contact. He tenses up, like he's expecting me to shove him, but I don't. Quincy grazes his lips past mine without touching them, skimming my cheek and kissing me by my ear. He releases me, opening the door wider. I almost say, *That's it?* Because if he kissed me right now, I would definitely kiss him back. He doesn't do anything more, though, so I try not to stumble down his porch to my car.

At the bottom of the last step, I hear Quincy call out to me, "Think if I didn't get shot, I'd be your ride-or-die and not Dean?"

I try not to think about how that moment changed our paths. I can't say I'd be friends with Dean if Quincy hadn't gotten shot. Not with how black and white school is. Dean filled Quincy's absence, and I never let Quincy back in. I don't know what to say.

He waits for an answer. I want to say something smart about all his girlfriends, but Quincy's move literally did catch my feelings by surprise. I turn to answer.

"I've never forgotten how good you were to me." I pause. "Are still. Thanks for helping me today."

Quincy gives a shy smile. "Jamal's gonna be okay," he says.

My throat closes at how sure he is.

If only I was that certain.

LIKE FATHER, LIKE SON

Mama fidgets as we sit in the prison visiting room. Last Saturday I was asking for forgiveness, and now, a week later, Jamal is gone. Daddy's gonna see how we're holding up for real. How Mama's doing without her boy, who Daddy made promise to take care of us while he was away.

My stomach lurches. I'll have to lie to him for the first time and pretend we're okay.

We're not okay.

There's a stall in the line after we're searched. Up ahead you can see it's a correction officer who's the holdup. The same hard-ass from last time who was looking at me and Daddy.

"Back in line." He points at us.

I turn my head. I know better than to argue with him. Finally, we're at the front.

"Tracy, Lillian, and Corinne Beaumont," I say. "Visiting James Beaumont."

"I didn't ask for your names yet."

I shut my mouth and wait for direction, even though we're following exactly what the family in front of us did.

"Who are you visiting?"

"James Beaumont."

He scans the visitor roster. He passes Daddy's name, but I don't say anything. Being a smart-ass won't help me. He takes another minute before he speaks.

"You've already made a Saturday visit for the week."

Mama's eyebrows knit together, but she doesn't speak.

"I'm sorry," I say. "You must be mistaken. Can you please check again?"

"No exceptions."

"I . . . Please check again. I promise you there's a mistake."

Mama taps at my arm to take a breath and calm down. Arguing with COs never helps, but I want to see Daddy tonight.

"No, see right here." He points to my time log. "Next in line."

Twenty-five minutes. He's stopping me from visiting my father because last Saturday I checked in twenty-five minutes later, so we're technically still in the same week. This is absurd. He knows it's absurd. They've never gone by the hour here. It's always the date. Saturday or Monday. Never the time stamp.

"No. It's my visit day. The rules are the day, not the time. Right?" I look at the people behind me. "Right, the day?"

There are a few concerned looks, but no one is willing to back me up. Mama takes Corinne to sit without arguing. I study him: I'm not going to win.

More rumblings behind me. A little boy asks, "When did we visit last Saturday? Are we going to have to wait, too?"

I start the waiting process over and join Mama so I can follow these new rules.

Corinne grabs my hand. I hold it fiercely until she smiles. Her eyes soften.

"Tell me how he was last time," Corinne asks, since she didn't go with Mama on Monday after the interview incident.

"Tired," I say.

Corinne's neck tightens.

"But good. He was strong, said he missed you the most."

"He did not." Corinne rolls her eyes, then studies me for the truth.

"He did. He said you grow up the fastest."

A smile creeps across Corinne's face. Mama winks, then puts her arms around Corinne.

"Well, I sure don't look a day over thirty," Mama says.

"Thirty?" I smirk.

"Yes. I hear it every day at work." Mama rocks in her seat, all black-don't-crack proud.

"You think he'll notice I'm taller?" Corinne scoots up in her seat and stretches her neck up.

"Definitely," I say.

"Yeah, he'll notice," Corinne says softly.

I glance at Mama, and her eyes are misty. Like me, she knows Corinne's been marking off her height for a long time, and for her sake I hope she never has to worry about Daddy missing her grow up much more than he has already.

"Don't talk your daddy's ear off about Jamal," Mama says. "He wants to hear how you're doing."

I nod, but it's a promise I won't be able to keep.

"Lillian, Corinne, and Tracy Beaumont." The CO finally calls us when he's ready, waving us through to the visitation room. When I pass him, he grips my arm and leans in. "Disruptions get visitation revoked. Remember that next time you wanna show off on TV."

I take a hushed breath as I pull my arm back. He made a lesson of me because of *The Susan Touric Show*.

The crank of a door pops, red lights flashing, then the sounds of the buzz. The men are all lined up, Daddy in the middle. He's clean-shaven, Afro combed out but freshly cut with sharp edges that frame his face. His face lights up when he sees us, and we let out a resounding breath as we wait for him to greet us.

Corinne jumps up. I hold her back by the shirt so she doesn't wrap her arms around him. Against the rules. She taps her thumbs on the table instead until Daddy sits down. He grins before folding his hands over ours that are now in the middle of the table.

There's nothing that fills me more than seeing how bright his eyes are lit with us here. Today is different because of Jamal's absence. Daddy's eyes are dark today, like he's had no sleep. Like the light of hope has flicked off after hearing about Jamal.

Mama's face falls when she sees him. She's carrying the weight of the world right now. She doesn't think I know she's been crying in her room, stuck staring at photos of Jamal as a baby.

"I drew you a picture." Corinne points at her drawing, all of us in front of our house, Daddy leaning on his Buick. Daddy smiles, then leaves it on the table for approval from the CO so he can take it back with him.

"How's school going?" he asks.

That makes Corinne perk up. "Good. There's this one kid . . ."

Corinne tells random stories that trail off before she picks up another thread. When she runs out of steam, I pull her arm so she knows it's time for us to leave Mama alone with Daddy before it's my turn.

Corinne and I walk back to the window and watch them.

I read Mama's lips and think she says, "Jamal." She lowers her head. Daddy kisses the top of it, touching along her face. It's so intimate I want to look away. Put a wall around them so they're alone. No one else should share in their moment, but I can't help watching, because it's the only time I see my parents together.

Usually when they're close like this, hands clasped tight, it makes me cry with joy. Daddy talking away at Mama, and the way she flicks her eyes at him. Her hardness she's always cracking like a whip becomes as soft as can be. Melting with Daddy.

You can't tell them they weren't transported to another place for this moment. Their ability to block out the guards, inmates, noises in the background, even us. It's only them. Until the time passes and they have to travel back to reality. Back to thinking about another long drive home without his heavy laugh.

This time when they talk, it's different. This time Mama is telling Daddy about Jamal, and he's hanging on to every word. They look over at us, force a smile. They talk some more, serious looks. I want to lean in closer, catch what they're saying.

"I miss Jamal," Corinne says.

I pull myself away from staring at our parents, but not before locking their image in my mind. Make up a background where they're swinging out on the porch.

"Me too."

"You think he's okay?"

"Yeah," I say, even though I don't know.

"I hope he never comes back."

"Corinne." I grip her chin, so she doesn't turn away. "Why would you say that? Jamal's coming back. He has to come back."

"They'll take him away."

I meet her worried eyes, pause before speaking. "Jamal is coming home, and he's going to be fine."

She gives me a smile, but the rest of her expression is empty. I hug her close, and she stays limp. A tear escapes down my cheek, and I wipe it away with my sleeve so she doesn't see. I don't want her to lose hope.

Daddy sits up when it's my turn. I can barely exhale until I sit down. His eyes are red. I want to give him a hug, but it's against the rules, so I hold tight to his palms, bending my head onto them, an old habit from when I was little. I look at him.

"Baby girl. How you been?" He rubs his hands together. They're dry and cracked. An aching regret builds. We've neglected him by not adding money to his account this month. My eyes well for not making life a little bit easier. A little more comfortable for him. By the roughness, I can tell he's out of Vaseline. A necessity for those long days working outside in the heat.

"We'll leave you something." My voice cracks. "For your account today."

"Don't worry about me. Your daddy's fine." He rubs between his fingers and makes it worse, so he hides them below the table.

My chest aches from being so close but so far away. Although I want to be strong, hold back my fear, I let out a slow sob when he holds my cheeks in his palms.

"Ahh," Daddy says. "Baby girl, don't let me see you like that."

It's like we're back home again before his trial. Mama cooking after a long day at church. Trying to fill us up so we start our Monday right. I don't see the gray-painted brick walls or the white uniforms around the room. Just home, like it was.

I want to tell him we had trouble seeing him today. But that could make things worse. I'm not the one who would have to face repercussions on the inside. Daddy is.

Daddy doesn't say it, but the stress is all over him.

"Jamal says he didn't do it," I whisper. Desperate to give him some sense of relief.

"Have they picked him up?"

"No. We don't know where he is, but they're convinced Jamal killed Angela out by the Pike. But how, Daddy? Why?"

Daddy's searching for answers, too. I don't want to tell him more because I don't want it to end up hurting Jamal. Not until I know what happened. His eyes are weighted with worry. Silent. He's never been shy about giving advice. Rather than speak, he slumps his shoulders. He doesn't know what to do.

Neither do I. A sinking, hopeless feeling presses heavily in the pit of my stomach.

Daddy grabs my hand. "Hire a lawyer."

"Mama's looking, also fund-raising through the church. I don't know how we're going to pay. We'll have to get free legal counsel, but they won't be assigned until he's arrested."

I wish I didn't have to be the one to put it out there on the table that we can't afford a good defense lawyer. We're barely hanging on as it is.

Daddy rubs his chin. "You have that list of the lawyers I've worked with?"

All of them were useless. A lump grows in my throat. To trust the lawyers that failed my daddy? I don't know if I can.

"Give 'em to your mama. One of them might help," Daddy says.

"Daddy, what if—"

"Call them." His face goes stern.

"I will. Beverly said the same thing. Do you think she can help?"

"She's brand-new to the force. I doubt she has any pull. She has to prove herself, too." Daddy squeezes my hand again to get me to focus. "Get ahold of Jamal. Find him. The longer he waits, the worse it's gonna get."

"I don't know where he is. What am I supposed to do if I can't find him?"

"If anyone can find him, you can. And what do you mean, what you gonna do? You gonna do what you were born to do. You a fighter. Chase down his friends until they tell you something. Make sure the police don't run down my boy, do one of your rights workshops, a community gathering. Keep yourself busy—but outta trouble."

"I went by Mrs. Ridges', and she told me to tell you she was praying for you."

"Tell her I said I'm doing fine. I be praying for her, too."

"Do you think Jamal will be like Jackson? Fight being taken in?" My biggest fear is things will go down like that with Jamal.

"Jackson had his own history with the police. He thought he was protecting his family. He had a big heart and didn't think about consequences. All he ever wanted was to build something for his family in Crowning." Daddy frowns. "I don't know why he thought he could barricade himself like that . . ."

Daddy stops. Grimaces. Swallowing up that pain before he speaks. There have been so many reasons I thought Jackson locked himself in his house. The guilt because he'd gotten Daddy to take one more meeting with Mark. Maybe that decision brought them to the wrong place at the wrong time. How he couldn't face my daddy knowing they were getting pinned as the murderers. Jackson might've convicted himself for that reason alone.

"Promise me." His voice shakes. "You'll forget about helping me and just find Jamal. Keep praying that things end up better for him. I need you to keep him strong."

I hang on to each word, nod at promises I want to keep, so he can let go when it's time. But when I look at him, I can't convince myself it'll be his time in less than nine months now. I shake my head. I smile, tell him I'll be somebody.

But inside I know I can't let Daddy give up. Every person who was against his partnership with Mr. Davidson is a suspect, and that history Daddy keeps trying to make me forget might be what I need to hold on to.

"What were you doing over there at Mrs. Ridges'?" Daddy gives me a mischievous grin. I know what he's going to say next. He always has a way of turning my questions back on to me. "You know, Quincy has to ask me for permission if he's going to date my daughter."

"Daddy." I tap him playfully. "That's not happening."

"I remember you two as kids, right when we moved here."

I smile shyly. We were kids. Daddy knows how Quincy was my first crush—before Dean—one of those mysteries he knows about. He used to know everything about me. Before the shooting, before all our lives turned upside down. He's always been observant.

"Quincy's not the same boy you knew, Daddy. He has a million girlfriends."

"I know Quincy. He comes here with Jamal sometimes. He ain't forgot me, and I ain't forgot him."

I didn't know this. I wonder how often he comes to visit, but I know if I ask more, Daddy will think I care too much and prove him right.

"I guess since you and Dean are dating now, that won't work out. Maybe when you get a bit older."

Daddy loves acting like he can see everything I do from his prison cell. I have to chuckle.

"I'm not dating Dean, either. Who has time to date? I'm a lawyer in training now."

"Well, I'd like to see that. My daughter a lawyer."

"What, you don't think I can?"

"You can do anything. I've never heard you talk about college, let alone a profession. I'm glad you're starting to listen to us."

I let myself think about the future for a moment, then pause. The urgency of here and now brings me back down.

"First I need to help Jamal. Whoever got to Angela could be after him," I choke out.

"My story won't be Jamal's."

"Jamal will come home if you're free."

"Their minds are already made up about me. Help your brother. Get him to come home. He can win if he speaks out. They already filled their heads about me from the moment we moved into town. Watching us, being outsiders. Convincing themselves of whatever fit their narrative. So, when the David-sons ended up . . ." He looks away, and I know he's had this thought a thousand times. "Ended up dead. Town already upset we're taking some of their jobs. Who's easier to believe, some-one who'd been a part of that community for years, or me? So, it ain't that complicated, girl. But that don't mean that Jamal's roots to the city can't be planted. He's no outsider. He can do different than me."

I can see the weight of not being home, able to help us, pulls on Daddy. I stay with him another twenty minutes, finding any-thing else to talk about. Daddy holds on to my hand like he wants to drain every last second he can with me, slowing down the clock that's running out on him. The same clock I live and breathe by.

When our visit ends, I expect him to get up and leave right away, but this time when we both stand, he gives me a long hug, even though we both know he shouldn't. It takes everything in me to not break down and cry. I'm so focused on him I barely hear the guards yelling, "That's enough!"

He doesn't seem to hear them or care that they're approaching us. We only let go when the two men are within steps of us. The COs rush him along, but all I see is Daddy, everything else grainy and blurry as I watch him line back up and blend in with the rest of the inmates.

RUBY BRIDGES BRAVE

Mama didn't force me to go to school when Daddy was arrested. Jamal and I stopped during the trial and didn't return until a few weeks after. She tried to shelter us from the news, but every channel covered the murder trial. You'd either have to choose to tune it out or completely shut it off. I didn't want to go to school anyway. Quincy was still recovering; it put him a year behind so he's in my grade because of it. Without him, I thought I'd be bullied forever before Dean stepped in. Eventually I knew we had to go.

To give me courage that morning of the first day back, Mama told me about Ruby Bridges, a little girl from my hometown in New Orleans. How brave she was as a first grader going to school with guards because white folks didn't want her integrating school. Mama talked to us about being brave, the same talk she gave Corinne last Wednesday when she left for school. Mama had me imagine how hard that must've been. That anything I was going through would pale in comparison. Then she dug around and found a Ruby Tuesday pin from the restaurant, so I'd think about her when I was at school.

I hadn't touched that pin in years, but on Wednesday I gave it to Corinne. Now with Monday rolling around, I wish I had it for myself. I dress baggy so I'm swallowed up by my oversize tank top and black yoga pants.

Mama doesn't care I only have a few weeks left of school. She doesn't trust Jamal's teachers will be fair. He'll go from As to Cs, since his missing assignments will turn to zeros, but she's hoping it'll at least be a passing average so he can graduate. I need to be there so they don't forget that we're real people—"good kids."

In fifth grade, when I went back to school, I wore earbuds on the bus to drown out the chatter about Daddy. There were snickers, taunting, jokes, but never a crowd.

Today is different.

Media outlets are parked on school property, roaming the lawn. Lights hover over classmates being interviewed. Mama took Jamal's car to work so I can drive her car and lay low at school. I fling on my backpack and baseball cap. With the media outside, it's chaotic enough that I think I'll go unnoticed, as long as I put my head down and skirt to the front doors of the school.

Justin Draper doesn't let that happen, though. He stops the camera operator from NBS and points to me with his booming voice. "That's Jamal Beaumont's sister."

My mouth opens; I look to my left and right, unsure of the best escape route, the camera moving closer to me as other media outlets pick up on who I am. Each one angling to get their exclusive. If this wasn't about Jamal, I'd embrace it, use it as an opportunity to talk about Daddy.

They get closer, and I feel the blood rushing from my face.

I'm frozen, until a hand swoops under my arm and steps in front of me, blocking the cameras.

Quincy.

"We're going to the west gate out by the track. Ready?" Quincy says with a rushed, heavy breath.

I nod, his arm securing me, and we go on the move. I follow his body, weaving in and out of crowds that haven't caught on that the cameras are after me.

The west gate is usually locked in the morning unless there's an early track practice. I pray Quincy knows what he's doing.

There's a buzz behind me, cameras clicking. People talking, coming after us. I block it out, listening to Quincy tell me to duck my head and he'll take care of the rest. He takes off ahead of me; even with his limp, he's still fast as hell. He races toward the door, then skips, leaning heavily on his left leg. It doesn't stop him from hopping and gliding to the door.

Quincy enters in a code, the gate unlocks, and I race through it.

He slams it shut, then takes my hand and leads me behind the school through the path toward the senior lockers. There's a buzz behind us, followed by a series of camera clicks, but we're beyond their reach.

Panting, I touch Quincy's shoulder as he grips his hands on his knee. He bites on his lip; pain must be shooting through his body. This is what made track impossible for him, even if the coach said he could still train but not compete. The steel bolts keeping his left leg together just make it too hard.

"You okay?" I calm my breath, the fear fading away with him being here, even if he's in pain.

"I'm good." Quincy rubs his knee and walks back and forth, shaking his leg. "Just got locked up running. Haven't moved that fast in a long time."

"That was out of control. Thank you for helping. I wouldn't be able to handle the cameras like that. I told Mama it's too soon to go to school."

"Come on. They can still see you." Quincy takes my hand again, and my heart flutters. I look at him, shake my head because I didn't expect that.

We walk past the lockers into a breezeway.

"If you go out that way, and back through those doors, you'll find your way to your locker."

"How do you even know this?" I ask, when our view is blocked from the corner.

"Skipping class. Gotta know the best route to move unseen." Quincy turns to leave.

"Wait."

Quincy pauses, and I hug him before he slips away. I fight back the ache in my body. I just needed to get into school today, and Quincy made that happen.

"Remember when this was my job? I forgot how physical it could get helping fight your battles." Quincy chuckles, covering up the awkwardness.

"Justin's always been an asshole, huh?" I say.

"You gonna be all right?" Quincy asks.

"I can't do this every day. What am I supposed to do?" I let go of him.

"Don't trip on the news. The kids at school. None of that matters. I stopped caring a long time ago."

"What about Jamal?" Quincy's guard is down. I can't help but use this. "You heard from him again?"

"Nah. He's a ghost now." Quincy looks away. "Too dangerous. Jamal's tough; he'll figure it out."

"If you see him . . . talk to him . . . tell him I get why he doesn't talk to Mama, Corinne. But he's gotta know I got his back. That I will fight to the death to free him."

"He knows. He also knows you gotta keep your family together. You're gonna be the key."

"Right," I say. "How am I supposed to do that?"

Quincy rubs his hands over his head, considering, then reaches into his backpack. He puts a small phone in my hand.

"Once a day he turns his burner on. Won't answer a call, only text. Whatever you get, you delete. Whatever you send, you delete."

I shuffle back a step, surprised. Quincy and Jamal have been in touch.

"Don't make me regret giving that up."

"When did you—"

"Jamal will seriously be pissed. Please do what I say."

"How will you reach him? Get another phone?"

"Can't risk it. Shoot, after this, I think your brother might write me off. Anyway, you know how to help him more than I do. Don't waste his minutes. He can't get a replacement or charge often. He turns it on at ten each morning."

"Thank you for trusting me."

Quincy turns back around.

"Wait, where you going? Bell's about to ring."

"I'm not going. Came to make sure you got in safely. See, this knee be acting up, so I'm gonna need to make up my work at home." Quincy grins.

"Two weeks, Quincy. Summer will be here soon enough. You can do it."

Quincy steps back and points at me. "Stay in school, Tracy." Then he jogs off toward the west gate.

When I reach my locker, I find Tasha waiting at hers for me.

"Where you coming from?" Tasha asks. "It's a madhouse out there."

"I came from the west gate, cut through the back hall. Media after me." I keep to myself that I've got a way to reach Jamal.

"Damn," Tasha says. "They should just close school for the rest of the year."

"I wish," I say. "I thought today would be hard, but not like this. All this media, you'd think they'd respect minors' privacy."

"You didn't hear?" Tasha pauses. "There's gonna be an assembly first and second period to memorialize Angela. They're doing attendance in homeroom, then heading out in groups by class."

My jaw drops. If I knew, I wouldn't have come today. Maybe that's what had Quincy ready to bounce; he was too loyal to want to hear slander about Jamal. He faced the same with his dad.

"I'm sure you can skip out. The office is open, and counselors are making themselves available."

"All right." I shut my locker. Tasha looks at her watch and I wave her off. She's been struggling in science, and late attendance will knock her grade more.

I look around the school as I walk through the hallway, deciding between going to class and lining up for assembly or hiding out in a classroom.

Hard stares meet me as I walk. Inside, I'm regretting I didn't push back with Mama more.

There's a fissure in the school, and you can feel the divide. I'm clearly on one side, so I know I have my answer about the assembly. I drop into the newspaper room to escape.

It's only been a few days since I've been here; usually there's a buzz of energy that the room always gives me. But the last time I was here was with Angela. Sadness takes up the space. I'm expecting her to be working away at the student assistant desk next to Mr. Kaine's. I've barely had time to mourn for her, to feel the shock and pain of losing someone so suddenly. Being here, I can't hide from that. Angela is gone forever. I know the paper will memorialize her, so I want to take a look at what they've done. Sad I couldn't be a part of helping tell how much she meant to our team, but also knowing there's no way I could be included in that discussion. Not with my brother as the number one suspect.

I weave my way to where we last spoke. Usually Monday mornings I come in early, get a sneak peek at the layout, and see how "Tracy's Corner" looks in print.

The front page has one large photo of Angela, her name, birth and death years below the picture. I flip through the print layout, page after page, looking for her write-up. Then I note that "Tracy's Corner" is missing. The heading was supposed to be "Social Justice's New Generation." I spent hours on interviews and turned it in early.

"Tracy." Mr. Kaine steps into the classroom. He's always been one of the cooler white teachers at school. He makes the newsroom come alive. Walls plastered with blown-up photos of banned books and iconic images like the Tiananmen Square protester facing off tanks and the 1968 Black Power salute at the Olympics.

"What are you doing in here? The assembly is about to begin."

I give him a blank stare, until he can put two and two together and realize what a ridiculous statement that is for the sister of Jamal Beaumont.

"My piece is gone. I met the deadline." I touch the paper and lift it up. I don't know how to say what I really want to ask. Was it intentional to place Angela's story instead of mine as a way to shame me and my brother? It aches that anyone could think Jamal killed Angela. That they might have decided on the placement of the article because it would show what side they're on.

"The editorial board decided to go with a different feature."

I look closer at the article.

Tragic Loss of One of Our Own:
Saying Goodbye to Angela
By Natalie Haynes

One of their own.

As strange as this might sound, I think Angela was probably the closest to understanding me. I should be allowed to mourn for her, too.

This was the one place that kept me surviving in school. A place I could use my voice. Maybe one that everyone didn't agree with, but I had a space for it, and Angela always advocated for me. She had my back.

"The last paper of the year is designed by the new editor," Mr. Kaine says. "There's been a shift."

I shake my head. New editor? The vote is supposed to be this coming Wednesday.

"When was the vote?"

"Friday." Mr. Kaine looks down, avoiding my gaze. He could have stopped it if he thought things were unfair, but he didn't.

"You allowed this? What about my vote?" This is unbelievable. I thought next year would be different. I could play a more prominent role. Now that hope is gone.

"If there had been a tie, I would have let you vote."

"What was the vote?"

He doesn't answer.

"What was the vote?" My heart beats fast.

"Unanimous. I'm sorry. You'll have to pitch 'Tracy's Corner' to Natalie and the executive board next year."

In one breath, he confirms that Natalie will be editor and I didn't even get enough votes to be on the executive board, after three years of putting in the work.

"We should go." Mr. Kaine says. "I'm speaking about Angela."

"I just need a moment."

Mr. Kaine looks like he's about to ask me to leave, but instead he closes the door behind him. I'm conflicted with thoughts. Loss is all I can form. Loss of Jamal. Loss of Angela. Loss of my dream to become editor. Each has a different impact, but they each mean so much to me.

My head is spinning. I loved my corner. The newsroom. And it's gone. I take a seat, head down, crying.

Seconds later, the door opens. Mandy Peters enters with a backpack gripped in her hand. She jumps at the sight of me; she is Angela's best friend, after all. My throat constricts. What can I say? I haven't thought this through, hadn't pushed Mama enough about all the reasons why I shouldn't come back this week.

Mandy seems shell-shocked. Her face is pale white, eyes puffy, and brown hair tumbled into one large messy bun. She stands in the doorway, not speaking. She almost backs up, eyes skirting around the room.

"I'm sorry," I whisper. "I won't be here long."

Mandy steps into the classroom, hesitant. "Angela's desk? Where she kept her things, do you know?"

I point toward the student assistant desk.

"Anywhere else she used . . . stored things?" Mandy pauses, her hands shaking. "I told her parents I'd pick up her things." She doesn't move, just stares at me. I can't tell if she's another person who blames Jamal or if she's just in a state of grieving disbelief. I know I should get up and go, that maybe she's waiting for me to leave, but I don't have anywhere else to go. Nowhere else has been a place of comfort for me at school.

I shake my head, then look away, out the windows, to give her privacy. I can hear Mandy finally move to Angela's desk. I sneak a peek. She carefully places Angela's things in a backpack. First a book, some notebooks, photos, then she throws away some papers. My eyes well.

As Mandy goes through Angela's things, I think about the exposé Angela wanted to include me in. I wish I could go back and ask her more about it.

The announcement speaker comes on to say the assembly is

beginning. Mandy jumps and then leaves without a backward glance.

I stand, praying no one else enters. A few minutes go by and I make my way to Angela's desk. I don't know what I'm looking for, just something to help me sort out what could've happened to Angela. Out of the corner of my eye, I see the garbage bin where Mandy tossed some of her crumpled papers. I pull the bin out and grab the papers. Most are draft copies of older articles, but mixed among them are a few pages from Angela's calendar. Last Tuesday is circled.

Tuesday: PIKE—underground rally
Wednesday: Meet w/ Tracy: Exposé!!!

Underground rally? There's something here. At ten, I'll try to reach Jamal and ask him about this. Something had to be going down at the Pike related to her exposé. This might be something the police are keeping from the public, because the news stories are portraying Jamal as having lured Angela there and attacked her. But this shows she already had it on her calendar.

I have to go to the Pike. See it for myself.

Monday, May 10

Stephen Jones, Esq.
Innocence X Headquarters
1111 Justice Road
Birmingham, Alabama 35005
Re: Death Penalty—Intake Department

Dear Mr. Jones,

Four percent of defendants sent to death row are supposedly innocent. Do you think my daddy could be among them? What are the chances for my brother?

It doesn't look like I'm going to get any help from you. I'm going to keep taking things into my own hands, looking for my brother, searching for Angela's killer. I can keep sitting around waiting and writing letters, but that hasn't done much. I've got to do this myself. Prove my brother didn't do it and find out what happened to Angela. I'm going to start my own investigation and I'll start at the location she was found.

The day she died, she wanted me to work on an exposé with her. Now I'm not on the newspaper anymore, but I'm going to find out what she was working on. Maybe it's nothing; maybe it can explain what really happened to her.

I'm hoping you'll take my daddy's case, so I can focus on this, but I'm thinking you won't. I wish you the best. I hope whatever cases you're working on come out with a positive result. Bring back someone's daddy for me. Tell them you couldn't take my case, but I'm happy Innocence X took theirs.

Respectfully,
Tracy Beaumont

VIGILANTES GET ISH DONE

I ditch the assembly and head fifteen miles east toward the Pike. The isolated drive sends alarm bells ringing in my head. I ignore them.

I pull into a deserted parking lot and leave my car away from the main entrance so I can explore. As I step out, it's eerie, only the sound of birds flying above.

The dry grass stands tall around me, except a path twenty feet away where it's been trampled flat, a clear sign that cars and teens have come here and traipsed all over. The hallowed ground of parties. Past this space are the wetlands that go out to Galveston Bay, where the loading dock stands.

On the other side of the parking lot, about a hundred feet away, there's an abandoned warehouse with a weathered sign: SOUTH SEAFOOD PACKING. The dock and the immediate surrounding grass still have yellow crime-scene tape. No other cars in sight, no lingering officers. Angela was found on that dock, strewn out, helpless.

My stomach swirls, uneasy. Most of my reporting is opinion based from the safety of my computer. I've never been to a murder scene. Never imagined I ever would.

I note how from here you'd only be able to see Angela from the dock if you got past the brush. I know I've got to get closer, but my body is rigid, wanting to wait safely in the car and watch from there. I swallow hard. Jamal needs my help, and stopping isn't an option.

My heart races as I approach. I study all the access points to the dock. Three locations stand out: the parking lot; the walking trails; and the path leading to the South Seafood Packing building.

When I move in a little closer, I have a better view of the old building. On the other side is a small parking lot that's so overgrown you almost can't tell it used to be a lot. I scan to see if there's anyone else around me. It's a ghost town so early in the morning.

If someone attacked Angela, there's not many ways to get in and out of the Pike. This gives me hope other witnesses could come forward to tell the full story. New suspects to interview.

At the edge of the dock, I shiver at the thought that this is where Angela's body was found. I stay well behind the police tape. On the dock I can see stains of what's now dark-colored spots and one puddle. Must be from Angela. The hairs on the back of my neck stand up. I shouldn't be here.

"I'm so sorry," I whisper to Angela, knowing she's beyond hearing me, but needing to say it anyway.

It's a relief to turn away and study the parking lot. It would've been pitch-black. I struggle to find a reason that would draw her out to the dock alone. She must have been meeting someone. I just hope that it wasn't Jamal and that there's an explanation to his letterman jacket being left behind.

I'm struck by the police tape only marking around and near the dock, but nowhere past the grass or up toward the seafood packing building.

A few steps farther, hidden past the grass, is a footpath. There's something . . . *off* about it. I move closer and realize the long grass is splattered with red marks, but no police tape. The murder happened less than a week ago.

The blood is easy to miss unless you step deep into the brush. If the police were certain Jamal killed Angela on the dock, then perhaps they got sloppy and didn't search far enough? I take a few photos with my cell, then skirt around the area to avoid touching anything.

Squatting low, I notice two grooves, leading to more scuff marks by the building. Like someone was dragged. Fought and couldn't get away. I blink quickly to take away the image of Angela. How scared she must have been, trying to fight for her life.

I want to say it's my imagination, but I can't—not with the

dried blood. I should call Sheriff Brighton so he can send a team over here again. I move to make the call, but lack of trust stops me.

I believed so much in Daddy being found innocent during the trial, but hope wasn't enough to go against the story the police wanted the jury to believe.

Sheriff Brighton came to arrest Jamal. And Chris's black eye continues to strike me as odd. The sheriff has more than one reason to want this murder solved quickly.

Either way, Chris knows something, and if the police won't disclose this detail of Angela's investigation, a surprise confrontation with Chris might be a solution. If he was caught off guard, he could blow up and reveal what happened. I can only imagine what he'd do if he knew about Jamal and Angela. This could be what he was arguing with her about on Tuesday morning before first period.

Quincy said Jamal got a text from Angela to meet him. If Jamal came searching for Angela and didn't see her, he could've ventured past the parking lot, then saw her at the dock. Maybe he even saw who hurt Angela.

The crime started by the South Seafood Packing building. Then Angela was dragged and carried to the dock.

Her life ended at the dock.

But Angela was alive at some point and free enough to text Jamal, call for help. Something happened between her texts and calling 911, leaving Jamal's name dangled as a suspect. But did she say his name as a warning? Or as a cry for help?

At ten, I take Jamal's phone from the secret compartment of my small purse and send a text to trigger a response.

> Quincy gave me the phone. What happened between you and Angela at the Pike?

Jamal will be pissed when he reads this, but he'll answer. Beverly should be my next call. When I look up at the seafood packing building, I want to check it out first. I don't trust the cops won't bury evidence just to make this an open-and-shut case.

The warehouse door takes only a twist and hard shove to get open from what looks like a broken lock. When I enter, I expect to see a fully stocked building with equipment and supplies, but it's stripped down, almost cleared out. Dust gathers over an old broken-down forklift and a production line the length of the building.

The phone beeps with a text from Jamal.

All you need to know is I didn't do it.
Tell Quincy he sucks as a friend.
I gotta ditch my phone now.

> Wait! I'll only message you once a day. Promise.
> I'm at the Pike. What happened?

Go home. It's not safe out there.
No more texting. Delete. I'm out!

I wait for Jamal to share more, but when he says, *I'm out!* he usually means it. I delete the texts. As much as I want to take Jamal's warning, I also want him home. Free.

Quincy said Jamal wouldn't run too far from home. Maybe he's near here, but that feels too dangerous.

I gulp down my fear of involving the police and text Beverly, asking if the crime scene at the Pike is cleared. Pretending I haven't already searched it.

That's when I hear voices in the distance.

DON'T FREEZE

Alarm bells sound in my head. My stomach drops. I turn and see the tall grass flicking back and forth. The same motion the grass made when I waded through and found the crime scene path to the building. Someone's coming.

There's more rustling, getting closer. I realize I'm caught totally out in the open. The panic rumbling inside me climbs up my throat while I hold back a scream.

The warehouse is dim, except where the sun shines through the layers of dust on windows. I step back, scanning the space for a place to hide. There's a small opening between the wall and the warehouse conveyer belt.

I push through the narrow gap.

My fingers going numb, I try to ignore the icy grip of fear. It will only paralyze me.

Desperate for safety, I scramble farther into the shadows, even though the space gets tighter and tighter.

I take quick breaths in, trying to make myself small, hoping this hulking contraption will be enough to hide me. I hold back a cough from sucking in old dirt and heat trapped inside the building. The dreadful smell of must suffocates my lungs and tickles the back of my throat.

The door opens, broad daylight streaming in. I lower myself, stretching out to fit under a piece of metal. My fingertips reach for anything to pull on to tuck my body beneath the machinery.

Still, my eyes strain. I'm desperate to catch sight of whoever is here. Peering through a gap, I can barely make out two men walking inside, coming closer.

I'm torn, afraid if I see them, they'll see me.

I spot something.

On the ground, near the gap I've shoved myself through, is a cell phone.

The men turn around and walk toward the door, their mumbled voices talking about "a waste of time" and "what are we looking for?"

They finally leave. I breathe a sigh of relief and wait it out a few more minutes before crawling toward the gap, closer to the phone.

The phone looks like it had been flung on the ground, dropped in a rush. Hearts cover the case.

Angela's phone.

It has to be. My left pocket has my cell in it already. I decide to tuck Angela's phone safely next to Jamal's burner in the secret compartment of my purse.

After ten minutes of silence, I push the door out slowly, then step outside.

"Hey!" a man's voice yells. "Over there!"

I curse and take off running past the packing building, thrashing my arms around so the grass moves out of my way. Heart in my throat, I press on, hoping if I go around the building, I'll be able to find the path. Make my way to the car and escape.

A voice yells, "Stop!"

I keep running until their words click together in my brain.

"Police! Stop! Or I'll shoot."

My chest screams out. Pounding. I don't trust what'll happen if I stop.

My instincts say to flee.

My brain says to stop.

I throw my hands up and turn, but I shut my eyes. I don't want to see it happen.

I don't move. I can't move.

The sickly fear of death snakes up through my body.

They yell again, and I can't help but force my eyes open.

One white officer keeps his weapon on me as he walks slowly toward me. My muscles tense, trying not to move and holding back from flinching. Even if the police leave me unharmed, a search would get rid of my only way of communicating with

Jamal and give them Angela's phone before I can take a look. Another tall and thin officer with silver hair follows behind the first, his face much younger than his hair indicates. His badge reads DAVIS CLYDE. He puts his hand on the other officer's shoulder, and they exchange fierce whispers.

"Wait!" a woman's voice cries out to the officers. "Wait. She's with me. She called me."

Beverly passes them, wearing her on-duty cop uniform. She steps between their guns and me. Wrapping one arm around me, she lets out a painful exhale. "She's with me."

I grab on to her tight, so she doesn't let go. I'm too afraid to speak. To move.

"That's the suspect's sister." The officer with the gun on me points with his free hand. "What are you doing at the scene of a crime?"

"Put the gun away," Officer Clyde says to the other officer.

"Tell them what you're doing here, Tracy," Beverly says with wide eyes.

"I came by the dock. I had to see for myself because my brother wouldn't do what you think he did."

"She called to ask if this is still a crime scene." Beverly hands over her phone to show the texts. "I didn't want her walking around here by herself. I came to check on her. See."

"Take a look, Clyde," the other officer says.

Officer Clyde reviews Beverly's phone, then asks for mine.

I hesitate as I reach in my left pocket. I bite the inside of my cheek, worry building that they'll search me and find the other phones. I hand my phone over. Four texts from Beverly scroll up.

Cleared. Why?

You're not there, are you?

Answer me.

I'm coming. Stay put.

"Looks legit," Officer Clyde says. "This is still a crime scene, though, as we search for more evidence. You shouldn't be here."

I watch the other officer with the gun, knowing some of their evidence is in my purse. My stomach swallows itself. Turning and turning.

"Thought we were done collecting evidence," Beverly says.

"There's an unaccounted piece of evidence," Officer Clyde says.

"I'll walk her out," Beverly says.

"Think that's a good idea?" the other officer says. "We should question her. Aren't you in school? You got something you wanna share with us . . . ?"

"N-no. Um, no, sir," I stutter.

"We need you to point out everywhere you've been, so we can add to the report. You've compromised the scene," Beverly says.

I look her dead in the eye and tell her the truth about where I hid. Tell her I was scared it was the killer, not the cops, which is true enough. But I don't tell her about the phone. I want to see it for myself before I turn it over to Beverly. And only Beverly. Then I go over the exact path I walked.

"I noticed blood on the grass, leading to the building." I point out the blood that was out in the open, not marked off with police tape. "I followed the trail to the building."

Officer Clyde pulls out his report, flipping the paper back and forth. Then calls out to Beverly, "This wasn't in the report. We need to call this in. Did you touch any of it?"

I shake my head no. Heartbeat racing that maybe this could help Jamal. Then they'd be forced to look closer at the evidence.

Even though I want to stick around and see what happens, I'm shaken up. I'm glad I'm able to say I got out of here.

Alive.

It's like a tight cork has wound itself inside me since they came after Jamal. I know it won't be long before that cork winds tight again, but at least there's relief for a moment.

When I'm safely in my car, I reach for Angela's phone. I brush it off and turn the power button on.

BABY GOT BACK BURNERS

The power shuts off almost immediately. Dead battery. But not before I see I need a passcode. Dirt and grime fill every crevice. I blow into Angela's dead phone, each breath a lifesaving wish it's not destroyed. I shove the phone back in my pocket, the weight of all its possibilities burning through my clothing, onto my skin.

Now that I'm out of danger, Beverly should be the one I hand this off to, but I don't want to lose the opportunity to look first. Especially if it could cast doubt on Jamal's innocence.

I pull up to my house, see Mama's pacing out on the stoop. She must know what happened if she left work and has been waiting on me.

"Answer your phone, girl."

"I was at school."

"School's still in session." Mama's lips quirk to the side. "But here you are. They called to say you were absent . . . and I spoke to Beverly."

Damn. I bite my lip.

"She said you almost got arrested out by the Pike." A flash of the officer's gun on me takes over my thoughts. My heart speeds up. Mama doesn't look like she knows about that. Beverly must've kept that part from her. Shame also runs through me that after all my Know Your Rights workshops, the sight of the gun threw everything I knew out the window.

"Why can't you stay out of trouble? I don't need you getting into any, not now. Go find yourself a hobby or something."

"I'm on the school newspaper."

"One that pays *and* keeps you out of trouble."

"I'll look." I mean it. We can't keep up with the bills only with Mama's wages.

Mama gives me a hug when I reach her. "You scared me."

"I'm sorry, Mama. I just had to look. See it for myself."

Mama squeezes my hand, then shakes her head. "Dr. Scott from the community center called. She was asking if you doing a workshop tomorrow—there were a couple of calls. I said you'd probably cancel."

I pause. I should. I've got so much going on, but I've never missed doing a monthly workshop in over a year. Even if nobody shows up. Daddy said to do something. I can do this.

"I'll call her back and let her know it's still on." I rush in the house before she asks me more about the Pike.

Upstairs I search through Jamal's room for his iPhone charger for Angela's phone. Then pull out the burner, see if Jamal sent another message since I deleted his last. Nothing.

I go online for how to crack the most common phone passwords. Clicking on a page about password generators, I review the list of password structures. Graduation, anniversaries, pets, kids, and birthdays are the most common.

I check Angela's social media for anything like those I can play off. Her birthday stands out first, July 14. Like the date in Jamal's notebook. I enter several number iterations, then use 0714.

Angela's home screen pops up, and my eyes widen. I study it for a moment, make sure this isn't a dream, before adjusting the settings to airplane mode with location services off.

First, I check Angela's call log. The last two dialed are 911 and Jamal's number; after those are several missed calls from Jamal. The most recent answered call, however, is from Chris. One minute and twenty seconds, another, two minutes and five seconds. All around ten in the evening Tuesday. My stomach sinks because this is the kind of evidence the police need. I hope that her phone bill can provide it for them, too. If they think to look.

Then I go through her text messages, finding a thread between her and Jamal. They texted multiple times a day. A surge in my stomach pulls; I feel betrayed I didn't know this was happening between Jamal and Angela.

JAMAL 4/26:

I thought about what Tracy asked. Talking about
my dad's case on air isn't the right place.

ANGELA 4/26:

But you said Tracy was right? This could
get national attention.

JAMAL 4/26:

It'll just make my moms mad. Chris'll shut you out.
He's already angry.
If he thinks you helped get me on the show.
He'll never tell you more about the Pike.
Let's wait it out.

ANGELA 4/26:

Chris won't be much help anyway.
He's clammed up after talking to Scott.
It's a dead end. This might be your shot.

I skip through more messages.

ANGELA 4/30:

He came to see me! Just showed up at my work.

JAMAL 4/30:

What!
What did he want?

ANGELA 4/30:

IDK. Chris must have told him I was asking about him.

JAMAL 4/30:

Are you okay?
I don't want you seeing Chris anymore.

ANGELA 4/30:

Another week.
I promise. I just need to look through more photos.
Keep the memory card safe for me.

JAMAL 4/30:

All right. I'll keep it in the production room
so you can get to it.

ANGELA 5/1:

Chris is pissed. That's why he showed up at the studio.
I promise it's over.
Where are you?

JAMAL 5/1:

Walking. Don't wanna go home. Interview
went to hell.
My sister goes too hard. This wasn't her deal.

ANGELA 5/1:

Meet me at Herron?

JAMAL 5/1:

OK

ANGELA 5/4:

Chris is pissed at me. Scott told him I've been
going around his back.
Using him for information.
He also knows I took it. I covered, though.

JAMAL 5/4

Return it. I'm tired of getting caught up in drama.
Let it go. You don't need to do this. It's a school paper.
Either end it with him for real or don't deal with me.

ANGELA 5/4:

I'll end it. No more. I promise.
Gotta go, your sister's here.

The messages lead up to the day Angela was murdered. Jamal wanted her to drop something, and that same day Angela asked me to help, to keep it from Jamal. Angela needed information from Chris, and when Chris showed up at NBS World News, neither Jamal nor Angela looked happy. I thought Jamal ran because of the cops, but maybe that was only part of the reason.

I search through the rest of her phone, stopping at her photos, quickly scrolling through. It hurts to see Angela so happy and carefree. The selfies, pics with Mandy, and shots of her family. I pause when I see videos of Angela and Jamal.

I press play and hear Jamal's laugh. It crushes me. My heart jumps hearing Jamal's voice. The video lasts ten seconds.

"This is stupid, Ang."

Off-screen Angela says, "What? No. You have to practice, Jamal."

"I don't want to. Come here, kiss me."

Angela laughs, and the video goes on with them kissing. She captures the moment with her phone. Angela's voice rocks me. My throat goes tight, eyes water. I play it again. Jamal will want to see this.

I take a moment. Wipe my eyes before viewing the next video. Jamal practicing for *The Susan Touric Show*. After some easy questions, he looks away from the camera and seems to lock eyes with Angela.

"What if I just say it? Put all the cards on the table."

"Susan would hate that. She loves thinking she asked the question that broke the door open."

"Are you sure she's going to ask about my dad? What if she doesn't? What's our plan then? Tracy wants me to say something, but my moms would kill me if I bring it up."

"She's going to ask. At least she's going to give you an opportunity to open the door. I know she didn't want to agree to the interview terms; that was all NBS One. Oh, shoot, I was recording that whole . . ."

Jamal was planning to listen to me and say more on Touric's show, but he decided not to. I scroll through her phone quickly, as if secrets will slip from my grasp and I'll lose the chance to save Jamal. Then it rocks me why Jamal is gone.

Jamal knows who killed Angela.

He could tell the police, but not if he knows they won't believe him. What if he claims Chris killed Angela? Chris is surrounded by people who'd protect him. I imagine handing over the phone and it being locked up with all the other evidence in the precinct that was ignored in Daddy's case. Giving it to them would be like giving away all we've prayed for since Jamal ran. I hold on to a shriveled piece of hope that it's better to keep the phone than to give it up.

This evidence might prove Jamal was worried for Angela, not out to hurt her. Without Jamal by my side, and with Angela gone, I know the only evidence left is that memory card.

I tuck Angela's phone in the hidden compartment of my purse. Pull out the burner and ask Jamal about the memory card, hoping his answer reveals one of three things.

1. He has it.
2. He gave it to Quincy.
3. He left it at Herron Media.

SNITCHES GET STITCHES

The last place I want to be is school. The media, the students, even the teachers make it hard. But these are things I swallow. No choice to shy away if I ever stand the chance of discovering Angela's exposé. I arrive at school, thankful there's only one camera in sight. The rest gone since the memorial at school on Monday.

I mentally check off my list of people I need to talk to and set my goals of what I'm trying to accomplish today. Angela and Chris were always locked up together. That's why it was shocking when I saw her with Jamal. A secret like that she had to have told Mandy; she was Angela's best friend. Maybe also Natalie, the new editor of the paper. I despise her now. Still, she might know something. The chances she'll help me are slim, but I gotta try. For Jamal.

Then there's Jamal's friends. Quincy at least fessed up to

seeing Jamal. But Cuddy and Demarcus on the track team have been silent. Claim they know nothing. That can't be true. They had to at least know about Jamal and Angela.

I make my entrance through the west gate, my new escape into school. I'm also hoping to catch Cuddy and Demarcus coming in from early track practice. I've got my Know Your Rights workshop flyers in hand as a way to start a conversation.

I smile when I see Quincy waiting on the other side of the gate.

"How'd you know I'd be coming through this door?" I ask Quincy.

"How do you know I'm waiting for you?" His eyes twinkle when he gives a side grin.

"Tell me you're not?"

"Hey, I gotta make sure you get into school safely. I'm a gentleman."

"Ha!" I playfully punch his arm. "I was planning on talking to Cuddy and Demarcus, but I'm glad you're here. Do you know anything about an exposé Angela was working on, maybe with Jamal, leading up to the Susan Touric interview?"

"Susan Touric's show?" Quincy's voice goes flat. "That's what you want to talk about?"

I trust Quincy won't betray Jamal, so I tell him everything I found on Angela's phone.

"He . . . he was looking into some stuff. I don't wanna say." Quincy looks over his shoulder, his hands shoved in his light hoodie.

"What about Chris? Angela was texting Jamal about getting

information from him leading up to Jamal's interview. The day she died was the same day she planned to end it with Chris. I saw him at the station with a black eye. Did Jamal get into it with him because he knew what happened to Angela?"

"Stay away from Chris. He'll get Daddy Sheriff on you and won't think twice about making your life hell. School's already hard enough."

"What do you think they were working on?"

"If I say something, you're going to go looking, and that means trouble for you."

"Why?"

"Because Angela was curious. Now there ain't no Angela." He looks away and blows out a breath, then catches my gaze. "I don't want you getting in over your head. Talk to Jamal."

"He's not saying much on text. You gotta tell me what you know."

"I don't know nothing. Anyway, I'm not gonna speculate. Then if it turns out to be something and you get into it, it'd be on my conscience. You're gonna have to be mad at me. If I say anything, your head gon' start spinning, then the world gon' spin, then there ain't no stopping it. If Jamal ain't answering, go look for him. He can't be far."

"I'm not stopping looking for Jamal. I'm going to get the truth."

Quincy kicks at the ground. "You're not gonna let this go, are you?"

"No." I feel him wearing down.

"I really don't know much."

"She wrote a note about going to 'the underground.' Also about having Jamal keep a memory card at Herron Media for her. You know about this?"

"You ask him?"

"Waiting until ten, but if I don't hear from him, I'm checking there."

"How? You think you gonna waltz in there? Don't even know where to look."

"You do?"

"Nah. I don't work there no more. Can't get in without getting turned away because of Jamal."

"Did you try?" I study Quincy.

He looks away. "Jamal asked for it, so I been working on that."

"What . . . wh-what else did he say?" I stammer.

"That's it." He slings his backpack over his shoulder.

"I don't believe you."

"That's truth. Jamal's paranoid. He's not talking over text. Just locations for me to drop off food. Clothes. And he asked if I could get into Herron. Look for a memory card."

My eyebrows scrunch, trying to hold in how pissed I am.

"Don't look at me like that. I gave you the phone. Ask Jamal."

The bell rings and Quincy starts walking to the breezeway, but I stay.

"What are you doing?"

"You can go on without me," I say. "I'm waiting to talk to Cuddy and Demarcus."

"Guess I'm staying, then."

"Thought you were rushing off to first period. Get your education on." I flutter my eyelashes at him.

"If you're gonna start interrogating the senior class, I gotta at least supervise."

"Interrogating? I'm just asking questions."

"I've never known you to do anything delicately."

"Oh, thanks."

"I just mean you get shit done. Besides, Cuddy and Demarcus won't tell you jack unless I seem cool with it."

"So, they know something?" I watch Cuddy and Demarcus as they end practice and make their way toward Quincy.

"Here you go. I don't know what they know. And you know what they say, snitches get—"

"Stitches. Yeah. I know the rules. Do you, though? Aka, older sister who's a cop."

"Don't play me. I can't choose my family."

Quincy tries to egg me on more but I'm back out, looking at the track. The team is finishing up, and I notice Scott is missing. He's the one who told Chris about Jamal and Angela messing around. I need to work up a plan to talk to Scott. Maybe check his response, or even learn how Chris reacted to Scott's news. I try to spot Dean, because he might be able to speak to them in a way I can't.

Dean is packing up his things. I didn't even think about him being here until now. As close as we are, he never talks about track with me since I quit. He didn't get why I knelt during the anthem because I knew the coach wouldn't let me get away with it. He didn't get I don't care if I had the clout to influence change. I wanted people talking about it, then maybe it would start a conversation. That didn't work for Dean and me, so we just let it go. That meant letting go of talking about track, too. I hadn't thought about how that's an unspoken part of our friendship.

Dean waves at me, and I wave back. Normally I'd run to Dean, say what's up, but Cuddy and Demarcus are now joining us, and they won't talk in front of Dean. Quincy's saddled up next to me, so Dean disappears down the breezeway.

"Yo." Quincy goes in for fist bumps and side hugs with Cuddy, then Demarcus.

I stand back, waiting for the rest of the team to go into the lockers and get ready for school.

"Cuddy. Demarcus." I give them a nod, handing out my Know Your Rights workshop flyer I'm running later tonight. This should warm them up and put their guard down.

"Yo. Heard from Jamal?" Cuddy runs a pick through his high-top fade and grooms the suspect beard he's trying to grow. I'm immediately deflated at his question. I didn't want his first response to be a question about whether I'd heard from Jamal. I want him avoiding talk about Jamal, so then I'd know that they've been in touch.

"You still doing these?" Demarcus looks at the flyer. "Are they any good? Seems like they're not much help when it's shoot now, ask questions later."

"It's mostly not like that, but you still gotta stay fresh on this stuff."

"I'm always ready." Cuddy towers over all of us.

I look away. I froze at the sight of the officer's gun aimed at me at the Pike. I was able to keep my hands up high, out and in view. But I was terrified. Even armed with the knowledge about my rights, all that went out the window. I couldn't replace the fear with my life on the line.

"What do you know about Jamal and Angela?" I ask.

"This why you out here so early?" Demarcus shakes his head.

"I caught them together, so it's not like you're telling me something I don't know. I'm trying to clear my brother's name. If the word is out about Angela and Jamal, that means Chris knows. You know I saw him at the police station the day after she was murdered, and he had a black eye."

"I trust Tracy," Quincy says. "Maybe not anything else but trying to free a Black man. Yeah, you can trust her."

"Is that a compliment or . . . ?" I try to say it with a straight face, but I feel my cheeks going red.

"Probably both," Quincy says. "But for real, if you know something, you gotta say."

"What about you? If anybody knows anything, it'd be with you," Cuddy says.

Quincy shakes his head like he knows nothing, and I don't

give a clue, either. The less people who know we've been in touch with Jamal, the better.

"Chris's black eye might not have had anything to do with Angela," Cuddy says. "Scott and Chris got into a fight at lunch. I saw them down by the Pearl Coffee and Tea shop off East."

"The same day Angela died?"

"I think so," Cuddy says.

"Was Scott at practice the next morning?"

"Nah." Demarcus sips his Gatorade. "He off the track team."

"Why?" I'm shocked.

"Some shit he did. Coach kicked him off a few weeks ago. He'd been wanting to for a while because Scott was skipping practice, complaining about not being in the four hundred when Todd was out," Cuddy says. "No loss. He was always trying to train without us."

The ten-minute-warning bell rings.

"We still gotta shower." Demarcus nudges Cuddy.

"All right," I say. "If you think of something, let me know."

They nod and leave me and Quincy trailing behind.

"They probably don't know nothing," Quincy says. "You know how Jamal was. After your dad, it's hard to get close. If he had something he wanted to share, I'm guessing it'd be with me."

I nod. It's true, but I was hoping it wouldn't be.

Walking into school with Quincy, I can't help but smile. It feels like we've reset our friendship to where we left off years ago.

Dean and Tasha wait by my locker.

"Hey," I say.

"You're back," Tasha says. "Heard you ditched yesterday."

I see Dean look at me, then Quincy.

"Mom tell you?" I ask Tasha.

"Yeah. You know she's gonna call me first, but maybe I should tell her to call Quincy next time." Her response is soft but flat.

"Nah." Quincy puts a finger up. "I have no claim to what Tracy be doing."

"I gotta go to class," I say. "You ready, Dean?"

Dean and I head to math class.

"What was that all about?" Dean asks. "You trying to get back on the track team?"

"Looking for answers for Jamal. They don't seem to know anything. You hear anything at practice?"

"No one's talking about it. They know better. Cuddy makes sure of that." Cuddy is about the size of M'Baku from *Black Panther*. No one people easily mess with.

We stand in front of math class, not going in quite yet, even though the bell's about to ring any second.

"What about Scott? You know why he was kicked off the team?" Scott off the team took me by surprise. Now Scott and Chris are hard to get ahold of.

"Not really. He was always complaining."

"What about Chris, have you seen him?" Scott and Chris are

best friends, and Chris arguing with Angela might have more to do with her murder.

"Chris? He's the last person you should talk to."

"You can help me, or I'll do it without you."

The bell rings and we rush to our seats. Dean shakes his head, but he doesn't say no.

After class, I head to the newsroom to take another look for any clues about what Angela was working on. When I turn the knob, it's locked. I'm taken aback. Mr. Kaine has an open-door policy. We're all on our own schedules trying to meet deadlines.

My backpack buzzes. A text from Jamal. Finally, he's responding to my question about the memory card.

Can you get access to HM production room?

My thumbs hover over the phone keyboard. I'm not sure how I'll do it, but I'll find a way.

Yes! Is that where the SD card is?

Hidden compartment. Near controller desk.

K. What's on it?

IDK. If you can safely get to it, it could have answers.

I go back and forth with Jamal until he stops answering. Satisfied I've got a new lead, I peek inside the classroom's window and see Natalie at the editor desk. She looks up when I tap the window. She doesn't move. I tap again, and she swoops her blond-streaked hair from one side to the other before finally making it to the door.

"What do you want?"

"What do I want? You don't own the classroom."

"Well, since it got trashed during Angela's memorial, we've been on high alert."

"Trashed?" I jerk my head.

"Don't act all brand-new. I know you had something to do with it. Mr. Kaine saw you in here before the memorial."

"I had nothing to do with that. Why would I trash the newsroom?"

"I don't know. Maybe because you didn't get the editor position. You're mad we honored Angela instead of posting your article. Your brother is on the run, suspected of killing Angela. Should I go on?"

"I didn't trash the class." My face feels hot. I tense my jaw to hold in my anger. "If I'm suspected of doing it, how come no one's called me in?"

"Because Mandy said she locked up behind you after Mr. Kaine left, but we all know you could've come back. You weren't at the memorial."

I don't answer her. I wasn't at the memorial, but what I'm

most confused about was why Mandy would cover for me. She left before me, not after me. I didn't trash it. Who did? And why?

"I had nothing to do with that. Mandy already told you." I step away from Natalie. More puzzled by the fact someone trashed the room. I look to Angela's corner and her desk is spotless, totally cleared out. Natalie's box on top of the desk. She's not only the editor, she's already claimed her desk.

I turn back to Natalie. "Did you know Angela was working on an article with me? To help me show I have what it takes to be editor."

Natalie's lip twitches. Her eyes are steel. I can't read her. Can't tell what she's thinking, but the way she's looking at me now is like she knew Angela wasn't a sure vote for her.

EACH ONE TEACH ONE

I never know what to expect when I run a Know Your Rights workshop. They were bigger back when Raheem Smith was shot, and after Calvin Pascal killed himself in Rikers after waiting three years for a trial, unable to pay bail on a twenty-dollar robbery charge. The horrors of his time as a teen among adult inmates wouldn't let him go, so he made it stop.

The past few months there's been one to two people trickling into the workshops, mostly repeats. Today, I breathe out when more people file in than usual. Most of the campaign spikes come out of news stories away from here, but Jamal is local. He made the news. That's big in Galveston County, even bigger in Crowning Heights.

I smile when I see Cuddy, Demarcus, and Todd from Jamal's

track team. Eight people total. All Black men, except for the man enjoying his free meal provided by the center.

I pass out my pamphlets, with a carefully folded Know Your Rights campaign crib sheet like the one I took to the police station. That's the one most people are drawn to, so they each grab a couple.

Quincy arrives, taking a seat next to his younger brother, Malcolm. He gives me a nod. Quincy's been through this session at least six or seven times. He always stays in the back with his headphones on, not fully covering his ears, leg stretched out, and usually outta here before I can say something to him. Today, though, his headphones are off while he reviews the pamphlet with Malcolm. Malcolm's now thirteen, no longer a boy in the eyes of police or white America.

"Welcome, everyone," I say. "Let's go around the room and share why you're here today."

"Thought I'd come by and refresh my stuff," Demarcus says.

"Yeah." Todd flicks his finger in the air.

I go around the room to a few more people. Malcolm stands up when it's his turn.

"My sister is a cop."

Heads turn to him.

"Her and my brother said I should be learning my rights."

"That's wassup," Demarcus says.

Quincy pulls his shoulder-length locs back, taking his time sitting up. I wait to see if he's going to speak before I start my presentation. He watches me, and with Malcolm here I know he won't play quiet in the back.

"And what are you here for?" I call him out.

"For you."

Snickers in the front take over. My face feels hot. I hold back any reaction so they don't think they can mess with me the entire presentation.

"Didn't want you presenting to yourself," Quincy says when the chuckles settle.

"Appreciate that." I look around the room for anyone else, then begin.

"All right, let's start with common scenarios."

I go through the typical variety: being pulled over, walking on the street, coming to the house for questioning. Then I go over an actual stop scenario.

"Safety is always first," I say. "You're not in a position of power, and it feels bad. You could be angry, scared, defensive. But that officer doesn't care how you feel. You're a suspect, until you're not. And in that moment, you're a threat. You have to control your language and your body movements." I did that first step when the gun was on me at the Pike. Keeping myself still and following directions. I'm lucky it didn't turn south when I ran out of that building.

"Now show me." I put my hands up, spreading my fingers and staying still. "Everyone up."

A few chuckles take place, and only a few people stand.

"I said up." The rest of the group slowly gets up. "You got a gun on you, a Taser, a dog. Don't move. Don't talk back. Breathe in and out slowly to calm your nerves."

"I don't think I can stay calm if a cop's yelling at me," Malcolm says.

"It's okay to be afraid," I say. "Practice helps, but it never fully takes away the fear. Controlling your response can reduce the fear in an officer who's reading you as a suspect, hiding something. Remember, they're thinking in split seconds—all the bias goes up."

"Why do I gotta calm down a professional? Shouldn't he be breathing in and shit?" Demarcus says.

"*They* do, but I'm teaching *you* how to survive. Don't try and reason. It ain't fair, but a gun on you isn't the time to debate. They'll just twist in their head your confusion for anger."

"Yeah, they see your black ass and think you a King Kong or something, D." Todd locks his hands behind his head like he's been through a few stops himself.

"Number one priority is your safety. Not the time to pop off." I put my hands down, and the group takes a seat. "You use your resistance in other ways. Follow instructions. Be calm. State you know your rights if what they're doing's in violation, but always know who's got the upper hand."

"So, heads getting smashed in the ground ain't the time, then." An older guy in the front finally speaks.

"Definitely not the time. Now, everyone download the ACLU Blue app. You or someone else gets stopped by police, you can start filming. You can upload immediately. If they confiscate your phone, they can't delete the video. Or press this button and it goes right to Twitter." I pass out a handout on rights to film police in Texas.

"If you're filming, and they tell you to put the phone down, state you have a right via Texas law, even state you're filming live."

"Yeah, 'cause if they confiscate your phone, you know it's not going public," Todd says. "Sandra Bland's videos didn't get out for years."

"It took ten years for video to go public to prove that BART cop lied about Oscar Grant," Demarcus says.

"Filming is powerful. The app makes it fast, so you don't have to think about filming, then getting deleted. What other scenarios do you have?" I ask the group.

"What about in your car?" Todd says. "Music bumping, you're stopped, and your wallet's in your pocket or something?"

"As you pull over, turn off your music. Don't reach. Ever. Keep your wallet in your drink console. ID and insurance inside. Hands out in front, ten and two on the steering wheel. If a gun's drawn, only move your hands to put them on top of the dashboard. Say 'Yes, sir. No, sir. Officer.' The deference brings down their alarm. So you can move on to having a conversation. Always ask the officer for permission if you're reaching for something. If they look jumpy, don't move until they're calm."

"That sounds like a sucka move. We know a lot of this," Demarcus says.

"Good. Now, do you know how to do it when you're late for something and you're being targeted? Can you control your anger? If so, that's good. Because then you can memorize their name and badge number. Confirm their number and never consent to a search. State their name and badge number, and request an attorney if they plan to arrest you."

I put them in groups and ask them what they believe police are allowed to do. Then review.

"They can ask for name, address, date of birth. That's it. If they believe you have a weapon, they can give you a pat down. Trust this will likely happen. If you resist, the force they use will likely be harder. State you don't consent to a search, but allow the pat down and confirm you do not have a concealed weapon. Don't argue."

Then I dive into what causes escalations and offer some de-escalation tactics, mostly using language that demonstrates that they know the law if they're interacting with police.

"What about if you are arrested?" I say. "Any of you know what to do?"

"Right to shut the fuck up," Demarcus says.

"Yes." I shake my head. "You have the right to remain silent.

You also can ask what you're being arrested for. If you are taken in, who would your first call be?"

"My lawyer," Cuddy says.

"Yes. You have the right to an attorney; ask for one. But you probably don't have lawyers on retainer. Who can you call to work on that for you?"

Demarcus raises his hand. "My sister. Ain't no way I'm calling my parents."

"Yeah," Cuddy says. "I'd have to call my mama, 'cause my pops would probably let me sit for a couple of days before I could tell him what happened."

"Demarcus," I say. "What's your sister's number?"

Demarcus picks up his phone and scrolls.

"Put it down," I say. "You're in a holding cell. No phone. You need at least two numbers memorized. Who's got one?"

Heads shake. Like almost all of my presentations.

"I got one," Quincy says.

My eyes widen as Quincy recites my cell number.

"You have one number memorized, and you pick mine?"

"Ain't calling my mama. Beverly would already know. If I called Jamal, he'd call you. Who better than you anyway? You know lawyers, judges, bail bonds, plus how to set up a GoFundMe account to get my ass outta jail."

"Yo, Quincy," Demarcus says. "Repeat that number right quick."

"Yeah, let me put that in my phone, cuz, so I can memorize," Cuddy says.

"Don't you dare, Quincy." I flick my fingers at him. Quincy grins, knowing he caused this stir. Malcolm asks him a question, then he writes down what's probably my number and Beverly's.

"Pick somebody you know well, somebody who'll answer an unknown number."

"Damn," Cuddy says. "Only my mama does that."

I go through a few more rounds of questions and scenarios. As we close, I see Quincy's getting ready to leave. I pair up the audience and leave the groups with a scenario about an officer at your home. Quincy's about to leave.

"Hold up," I say.

Quincy weaves his way to me, probably thinking I'm getting on him about his memorizing my number stunt. He waves Malcolm on to wait outside.

"You're leaving?" I ask.

"You want me to stay?" Quincy steps a little closer and gives me a cocky smile.

"You are too much. I'm just saying, you make a big scene in my workshop, then bounce? That for show or what?"

"Nah. I gotta get home, you know, especially if I'm going to help you break in to Herron Media." Quincy drops this last line all clever like.

"How did you—"

"Jamal texted. Thought you might be needing backup."

"You're gonna help, huh? You have a genius way in?"

"Swiped keys on my way here." Quincy smiles, then dangles the keys in front of my face.

"What? Really?"

"We been in touch. Grabbed a phone at the convenience store during lunch."

I look away. A little frustrated Jamal doesn't trust I can do it alone.

"Hey, I can also go by myself if you gonna pout about it."

"Nine p.m., after dark. In the back."

"Bet." Quincy whistles at Malcolm and they head toward his Impala, throwing two fingers up before he drives off.

When I get back to the session, they're all done with the role-plays and ready to bounce. In the back, a clean-shaven Black guy in his mid-twenties enters.

"Welcome." I wave him in. "We're about done, but I can give you handouts and a calendar for the upcoming work-shops."

"I'd appreciate that." He steps closer. "Tracy Beaumont, correct?"

I nod. He doesn't look like the typical person who joins my sessions. More like a reporter with his white-collared shirt under a dark blue suit jacket.

I gather the last of my handouts and wait until everyone leaves before approaching him. Curiosity building.

"I'm going to cut right to it." He leans forward. His face looks serious, and he nods as he speaks. "I'm taking your dad's case."

"What do you mean, you're taking my dad's case?" I touch my temple, shaking my head. "Who are you?" I repeat his words, but they're not pulling together to make sense. Did he just say what I think he said?

"Let's start over." He clears his throat. "I'm Steve Jones from Innocence X." Steve sticks his hand out. "I'll be representing your father."

WELL, I'LL BE DAMNED

"You're Steve Jones?" I squint my eyes at him.

"Yes."

"From Innocence X?"

"Yes."

"Bullshit."

"I—" Steve pauses. "My dad is Stephen Jones, founder of Innocence X. I'm his son."

"Oh." It finally clicks. I couldn't put his young face together with the man I've been writing letters to for the past seven years.

"Innocence X is taking his case?" My mouth hangs open. I have to repeat what he said, over and over again. This is impossible. Years of writing, believing, sometimes it felt like I was writing a journal to myself instead of letters to Innocence X.

I'm heaving in and out, crying in joy. Steve pats my shoulder, and I throw my arms around him in a hug. He fumbles around like he don't know what to do, either. When he realizes I finally get it, he hugs me back.

"Does my mama know?"

"After all your letters, I thought you deserved to know first— well, after your dad, of course."

I pause to catch my breath.

"You've met with my dad?"

"A few exploratory phone calls. Met with him in person this morning. He agreed you should hear directly from me. Then I'll contact your mother."

"Can I call her?"

"Yes." Steve laughs. "Let's do that."

When Mama answers, I put her on speaker and blurt everything out, ending with "He's taking Daddy's case."

Mama wails on the other side of the phone.

"What's happening, Mama?" Corinne's excitement bounces through the phone.

I wish I was there to see my little sister. I know she always feels left out because she wasn't born when things turned bad. Her present is tied to a past that she was never a part of.

"Daddy's got a good lawyer, baby," Mama says.

"Daddy's coming home? Jamal too?" Corinne's voice cries out. The pain rocks me because this doesn't mean much for Jamal's situation.

"What about Jamal?" I ask Steve, hoping Corinne's questions can be answered with a yes.

"I've been following what's going on with Jamal. We might be able to lend some research, although he'll need to have his own attorney. We focus on conviction repeal cases, not ongoing—"

"But Jamal." My voice goes weak.

"Get him to come home. It doesn't help your father's case if he has a missing son as a suspect in another crime."

"How long before my husband is free?" Mama doesn't even touch getting Jamal home. We want him back, but not if it means they'll take him away from us.

"This is a long process, ma'am. I won't lie to you, one in forty of our cases ends up in exoneration. It's a big commitment to take on a case, so we maximize as many as we can in the area. I'll be positioned here for a year, focusing on a handful of cases." Steve pulls the phone closer to him. "James is my first priority. I have a small budget, and I'll need to fund-raise to get everything set up for an investigation and find an office space to work out of."

"I have a few ideas for office space." I hide my own doubt. I can persuade Mr. Evans to rent out the loft space above the antiques store, but Mrs. Evans . . . I'm not sure.

Every ounce of hope that Daddy would be freed was riding on Innocence X. With Jamal gone, I dug deep to keep that belief. Inside, I feared I wouldn't have the stamina. I wouldn't have enough to give Daddy and Jamal. Now I no longer have that fear. No longer have that burden of doing it alone. I stand straighter. My ancestors' strength pouring into me, fully armored so I can fight to prove their innocence.

OUTLAWZ

I leave the Evanses' store happy to have gotten Mr. Evans to rent the loft space above the antiques store as a temporary office for Steve. I dip out as Mr. Evans shows Steve around the space, a convenient alibi for Mama that I can use as I sneak out to meet up with Quincy at Herron Media.

I finally feel like we're catching a break. I text Jamal before I meet Quincy.

Innocence X came through.
They can help you too.
Going to HM with Quincy.
Come home.

I weave my way through the streets; evenings are fairly quiet, as storefronts close early. When I reach the store before Herron Media, I zip a right to walk down the alley.

I turn the corner, and a low whistle rings. I almost take off running when I see someone by the back door. Then I realize it's Quincy, in all black. He lifts up his hood, whistling "The Farmer in the Dell" like Omar from *The Wire.*

"Seriously," I whisper.

"I didn't want to shout your name."

"You scared me. And look at you. It's hot as hell out here still."

"I'm not doing jail time because I got caught."

I huff. "Do you have a way into this place or what?"

"This is your show. How were you planning on getting in if I couldn't swipe keys?"

I shrug. "I hadn't thought that through yet."

"No plan whatsoever, huh?"

"Nope."

"Come on." Quincy waves me over.

We walk farther, around the back of Herron Media. We're now shielded between two fences and the next building that's farthest away from the employee entrance. It looks like the loading area for deliveries.

I sweep my eyes to the top of the building, looking for a camera. Seeing none, I tap Quincy to let him know I think we're good.

Quincy takes out a ring of keys, messes with a few until he finds the one that fits the service door.

"Have you done this before?" I whisper.

Quincy doesn't answer, then takes my hand, and I follow him

into the building. I take in quiet, measured breaths, so I don't miss a sound in case we're not alone. I take slow steps as he guides me near the wall. He points to the only location of a camera that could catch a sliver of us if we're not careful. I lean my back against the wall, our fingers touching as we extend them out, scooting until we turn the corner.

Although we're out of view from the camera, we don't speak. Just fumble our way through hallways, passing closed offices. Quincy said we gotta watch out for one or two people that stay late.

The only thing we see in the hallways are the blink of small red and green lights above when we pass smoke detectors. We reach the front of the building where the glass windows are near the reception desk, then turn the corner to slowly climb up the stairs.

Upstairs is quiet. I take the lead now that I know where we're going. Quincy hangs back, looking out to see if anyone's in the hallway.

I pull down on the door handle to the main media room that Jamal used—the last place I saw Angela and Jamal together. It's unlocked, so I wave Quincy over.

"Where do we start?" Quincy asks, shutting the door behind him.

"There." I point to the cabinets near the audio recording controllers. We each take a side of the cabinets and go through them slowly.

Fumbling through books, files, supplies. Nothing looks like a personal place to keep something private. We spend more time going through each one until there's nothing left. I walk to the middle of the room, turning, looking for a place to store the memory card. Whoever trashed the school newsroom could be looking for it, too.

"Did he say more than 'near the controller desk'?" Quincy asks.

"Nope," I say. "He kept it short. 'Hidden compartment, near controller desk' is all he said. Maybe it's gone?"

I sit on the flat, open space that's to the side of the controller desk. I kick my leg up to rest it on the other side of the desk, and the corner tumbles, causing the phone and schedule board to fall. A loud crash sounds.

"Damn. You always this subtle." Quincy shakes his head, but he's still grinning. I let out a nervous laugh, holding my hand over my mouth. Then his face freezes. He puts his finger to his lips.

I stop.

Then I hear it. The sound of someone coming down the hall. Under the door the hallway light flickers on.

"Someone's here," I whisper.

Quincy whispers, "No shit."

My mind racing as the person goes door to door. The click of the door. Footsteps. Then the closing of each one. Getting closer and closer. Click. Footsteps. Close. Click. Footsteps. Close.

Quincy and I lock eyes when we know our door is next.

There's nowhere to hide, nowhere to go. Even if we shut off the lights, the second the door opens, the light from the hallway will showcase us in plain sight.

I whisper to Quincy, "We're screwed," and push away the fallen items slowly with my foot so they're not in view.

"Trust me." Quincy takes my hand, pulls me close.

The door opens.

FUNNY THING ABOUT FIRSTS

Quincy wraps his arms around me, then kisses me softly.

"Oh! Excuse me," a guy says. "I didn't know anyone was here."

"Dang. Sorry, B. I lost track of time." Quincy turns to the man in the doorway, blocking me as he answers.

I hide my face, acting embarrassed, unsure who's at the door. I might not know them, but they certainly would know me. My heart's still beating fast with fear and with the shock of Quincy kissing me. His lips rushed to mine so fast, I didn't know if I should push him off, pull him in, or slap him from trying to get in a kiss before we go to jail. Still, I touch my lips, the memory of his soft lips lingering there.

The door shuts. I'm still in shock that Quincy's plan worked.

"Warning next time."

"I'm sorry. No time." He swings around and gives me a tentative look. "I couldn't think of anything else."

"Was that your secret backup plan?" I try to play it off and catch my breath.

"I just thought about Jamal the last time we were here. How you caught him. So my brain just went there as a cover." He looks regretful. "But that was a last resort."

I pull my hair back and let it settle around my burning-hot face.

"Sorry. I should've . . . They opened the door. I acted quickly."

"It's fine." I put my hand up, so he knows there's no need to talk about it.

Quincy gives an embarrassed chuckle. I'm surprised by his bashfulness. I didn't think he was capable of being shy about anything.

"Thanks, Quincy." I look away, now not wanting him to catch that I'm still thinking about his kiss.

I pick up the part of the desk that broke. When I put the frame back on, I feel under the desk. My finger catches on a broken edge that's not fitting easily.

There's another small drawer.

I take the corner off, running my fingers along the desk for anything out of the ordinary. I push in the simple lock with the key that swings by the wall.

Inside, I find Jamal's small notebook, a photo of my family at a visit with my dad on Christmas . . . and a micro SD memory card for a phone.

"Think this is it?" I flash it in front of Quincy. "We use these at school in the newsroom."

I take a paper clip and pop out the SD card I have and insert this one into my phone, then wait for it to load in the location folder. Hundreds of files and photos load up.

I scroll through, searching for something that speaks to what Angela and Jamal might have been looking into.

"Think he'll come back to check on us?"

"Nah. Brian is cool. I caught him smoking weed on the loading dock and never ratted him out. He's probably just worried he went out for a smoke and didn't do a full sweep before locking up."

I search through hundreds of photos while Quincy paces back and forth, standing guard by the production door. I study snapshots of games, pep rallies, and school-year highlights. Typical newspaper images. Then I see it. Photos off campus.

The old tattered sign of the South Seafood Packing building in the background. These were taken at the Pike, weeks before Angela was murdered. A group of about fifteen white guys gathered around a firepit, drinking beer. Two of the dates are in April. I check my calendar, both taken on Tuesdays. The photos are mostly hazy, like it was taken from afar. I zoom in closer. A flash of adrenaline hits me. Chris and Scott, along with a couple of guys from school. They don't seem to notice they're being watched.

"Find something?" Quincy leans over my shoulder.

"Bunch of guys from school at the Pike, near the building where I found Angela's phone."

Quincy takes my phone and zooms in. "Yip. Nothing weird about a bunch of white guys hanging around a firepit near the Pike."

I look again. Nod because there's something to it.

A tingle runs up my spine. I'm not sure what I've found, but it feels important.

I let Quincy lead me as we go down the steps.

"Front doors this time?" I ask.

"We should be good now that we're leaving with nothing obviously taken." Quincy leaves the keys on the reception desk, before we walk out the main entrance.

"What are you gonna do now?" Quincy asks.

"Ask Dean to keep a lookout for Chris or Scott. Then head home. My mama will be expecting me. I've been out way too long and gotta get the car back."

"What about getting this to Bev?"

"Yeah. I should." I flip my phone in my hand, back and forth. I know I need to get the SD card and Angela's phone to Beverly, but then she'd know I didn't listen to her.

"You should, for real. Doesn't mean you can't look into it, but this could help Jamal."

I nod.

Quincy walks me back to the Evanses' store, where our cars are parked at the end of their parking lot.

"Next time I'll ask," Quincy says when I open the car door. He jogs off to his car without waiting for my response.

"Next time I'll be ready," I whisper.

TRUTH SERUM

Dean's got eyes on Chris. I'm planning to ambush Chris at the worst place possible—Angela's grave. In texts back and forth with Jamal, it's clear he wants me to have nothing to do with Chris. I have to know why.

Before we go, Dean helps me carry boxes of my daddy's evidence to the loft above the Evanses' antiques store. The collection will no longer be shoved inside closets and under beds, but with Innocence X.

The loft space is cleared out except for stacked-up boxes, a table with a laptop, a heavy-duty printer, and a copier. On the walls, several whiteboards with dates, names, and deadlines. What captures my attention is Steve's master board laid out with Daddy's case. Motives and suspects are what I'm mostly caught by: *Exculpatory Angles* written on the side. That's the holy grail of death penalty appeal cases. Error in the defense or prosecution often has the most success in identifying innocent clients.

As Steve sorts through boxes, he lets out a low whistle. "I can't wait to get more familiar with your dad's case."

I check out an accordion file about two inches thick with black ink: *James Beaumont*. A bubbling excitement builds—I'll finally be able to discuss everything I've wanted to tell Innocence X over the years.

"I'll need to review the entire case transcript," Steve says. "Do you have that?"

"Our first attorney requested it, but he didn't leave us with everything. Now, if we want them again, we need to file and pay for it."

"I'll take care of that. Hopefully they'll be cooperative and not delay us."

"They can do that?" I ask.

"Do you have an hour, Tracy? I can ask a couple of questions to orient myself?" Steve switches topics.

I look to Dean, worried we might miss our window with Chris, but also torn because Daddy needs my help.

Steve takes my silence as agreement. "Good." He pulls out a notebook and a small recorder. "During the Touric interview, you mentioned there are new suspects that Galveston County Police haven't looked into."

"About that." A pang of guilt hits me. How exactly do I tell Steve the truth?

Steve studies my face. "No suspects, then. That was for the television?"

"I wanted to get Innocence X's attention." I look down, ashamed.

"I knew it!" Steve snaps his fingers. "I used it anyway to make my argument to make this case a priority."

I blush. He knew I was lying.

"Who do you think killed the Davidsons? Is there a remote possibility Jackson Ridges was involved? I'll have to clear that aspect first, question the family so I know where to focus."

I rub my forehead. I don't want to be part of dragging the Ridges family to benefit Daddy. Mrs. Ridges has been torn apart, and Quincy's life has been much harder than ours. I can't question them. It would be a betrayal. I turn my back to hide my queasy feeling.

I look out the window, searching for a distraction. A glint catches my eye, light reflecting off glass. A guy parked in a white SUV across the street watches us through binoculars. He's in direct line of sight of the loft's window. Spying on us.

"Someone's watching us," I say.

Dean moves next to me as Steve drops his file and waves us away from the window.

"I saw him yesterday, too, when I was heading to your workshop." Steve closes the blinds. "He could be looking for Jamal—an undercover cop."

We head toward the door as Steve takes the exit to the outside stairwell and down to the street. The guy drops his binoculars and peels out, almost sideswiping another car.

I whip my phone out and snap some shots. The SUV veers toward the highway exit.

What exactly are we up against? A sinking feeling tugs in my stomach.

"I snapped some photos, might have caught the plates," I say when Steve returns.

"I'll get someone on these plates." Steve calls Innocence X headquarters. "If it's not a cop, it could be one of our organization's adversaries. In order to get a retrial, we often start by seeing if there was an error made by the prosecution or the defense attorney. Sometimes our investigation finds something beyond an error, something criminal: lies; coercion; a judge with a certain reputation. Locals usually don't get too worried this early. Some people think we're martyrs willing to burn down the whole justice system because one person might be innocent. But an outsider—"

"Sabotage?" I ask.

"Perhaps an organization dead set on increasing the private prison system. Building more prisons requires more prisoners, and Texas was the first state to adopt private prisons. Texas continues to have the highest incarceration rate in the United States in those private for-profit prisons. One prisoner can mean twenty thousand dollars a year. Bodies mean dollars. Over three *billion* dollars a year. Think. It's big business. Innocence X threatens their profits."

"How will we know which one he is?" I ask.

"They'll make themselves known. Proving someone's innocent stirs up trouble."

"Like how?" Dean steps closer to me.

"A crime was committed. Somebody did it. And if it wasn't your dad . . . Then there are the prosecutors who don't want their cases being turned over, the judges, and the police. No one wants to believe they sentenced an innocent man to death."

I shake my head. Unable to believe that anyone would try to stop me from saving Daddy, from exposing the truth. But the same might be true for Jamal. Jamal is silent about what happened. He's only said he didn't do it, and that I need to stay away from the Pike. Jamal was there; he must know who harmed Angela and left her for dead from a head injury, from what the newspapers are saying. This might be why Jamal is on the run.

I know what Steve's getting at. This won't be a fairy-tale ending. At least not until we pass through the eye of the storm.

I reach for my purse and grab Angela's phone, but I keep the micro SD card to myself. Whoever is watching us might be the same person who killed Angela. I hand the phone over to Steve for advice. His eyebrows raise, puzzled.

"A few days after Angela was murdered, I went out by the Pike. I found Angela's phone. I didn't turn it in because I ran into some officers and they threatened to charge me with trespassing. They had me by gunpoint. I froze. I didn't want them to think I was messing with evidence, so I kept it."

Dean stays silent, but the tips of his ears are red. He's mad I kept this from him. I've kept a lot from him lately.

"You could have been killed. And you keeping it *is* messing with evidence." Steve shakes his head.

I show Steve the texts and videos. As Dean looks over Steve's shoulder, a confused look is on his face. I know I should give up the micro SD card, but then I'd have to admit I broke in to Herron Media.

I wait patiently for Steve to give me direction about how to get Angela's phone in the hands of the police. Maybe take it back to the South Seafood Packing building and give Beverly a tip. Something that keeps me out of it.

Steve gets up, then passes over today's newspaper.

I look at today's headline: MANHUNT.

I skim the story for updates, but there's nothing new. Until I see it. They say they've located her cell phone. A lie! I gasp and quickly finish the article.

Maybe they've stopped looking for Angela's killer and settled on Jamal? There will be no justice for how she was left injured, attacked, and thrown away. Now it's not just about freeing Jamal, but giving Angela justice.

AT A CROSSROADS

Dean gives me the silent treatment as we leave Steve's new office. He was the first person to show up to the police station when everything went down with Jamal, but I've kept him out of the loop. I know it's not fair, but he'd want to stop me from looking into things. And now I know I can't tell him I've been communicating with Jamal.

"I'm sorry I haven't shared everything," I finally say.

"That was dangerous to go out to the Pike alone. You should've called me." Dean's eyebrows knit together. We feel distant and I didn't realize how much I've missed him.

"It was the day of Angela's memorial—you know I couldn't stay. I felt like I needed to do something, so I went to the Pike. Only found her phone on accident."

"You go with Quincy?" Jealousy flashes in his eyes. They've

never really been cool. Only Jamal tied them together, but even then, it was estranged.

"Why would you think that?" I flick my eyes forward. Hope he didn't catch me leaving Quincy's car after Herron Media last night. My chest goes tight, thinking about the kiss that Quincy and I shared. It wasn't a real one, just a cover to keep us from getting busted. But it put a shock in me, forced me to think about Quincy and me in that way.

"What if Chris doesn't show?" Dean changes the subject, and I'm thankful.

"He'll have to show up at school sometime. And if he doesn't, I'll go to his work."

At the station Chris was visibly injured, shaking under the arm of some guy. Each time the image of his face runs through my mind, I can't help but be more convinced that Chris killed Angela. I run through the approach I need to take with him, and the questions to ask. Thinking in procedures helps silence my fear of confronting him.

I look over at Dean, who gives me a half smile like he's over it. He thinks it covers his thoughts, but it doesn't. Not to me. I see the disappointment—and sadness?—lurking beneath.

"What's wrong?" I ask.

"This thing with Angela. It's got my mom all riled up."

His mom always knows how to get under his skin. Mrs. Evans thinks Dean's on the wrong path. She's ultra-conservative, praising Christian values while voting in ways that seem to contradict that. I try not to let him see it bothers me.

"She doesn't want me spending time with you anymore. It started with the office loft, then she just went off . . . Tracy, it was . . ." Dean's eyes look glazed. "She said so many things about us . . . Why it never mattered if your dad was arrested . . . or if Angela was still alive and Jamal home. Our lives are too different."

I'm frozen. Dean's using softer language, thinking he's protecting me, but I've long decoded this meaning. She doesn't want us to be close because I'm Black and he's white. That's what he's been hiding from me, and this wasn't their first conversation about this.

"What happens now? Is this it? I talk to Chris, and then we can't be friends any longer?"

"You're my best friend," Dean says. "She can't stop that."

"You're mine, too," I say, and I mean it. Dean is closer to me even than Tasha.

I don't care what his mom says. I'm glad he doesn't follow everything she believes. We've always pushed the boundaries that were set before we had a chance.

"What if I'm as bad as her?" Dean chokes up. "That everything she's raised me around is so ingrained in me I won't even know, and then I do something to mess us up?"

"Why would you think that?" I touch Dean's arm. He slowly turns to face me, his arms resting on the wheel.

"When Jamal's story came out . . . my first thought wasn't he's innocent. It was wondering, how could he do that? At the table, my mom was going off on how rampant Black crime is, it was only time before something like this would happen again . . . I didn't respond. I was still trying to understand, sort through Angela being dead. I went to the police station because I was worried what Jamal being guilty would do to you. Not . . . not because I thought Jamal was innocent." Dean looks away.

My throat aches. How could he? It feels like he punched me in the gut. Betrayal.

"Then when you got out of the car with your mom, it shook me. I saw how broken you both were, thought about my friendship with Jamal, and felt ashamed. It's been eating me ever since. How easily I could turn against someone I know so well, and what would I do if it was a stranger's story on TV. I have these thoughts sometimes that I know are wrong. What if I'm just as bad as my mom?"

He wants answers I can't give. I can't make him feel better. Before hearing this, I wanted to take all Dean's pain away, and now . . . There's so much I don't know about Dean.

He breaks down crying in front of me, waiting for me to pick him up, but I can't. I want him to know how much it hurts. How angry I am that at one point he thought Jamal was guilty.

The hurt he feels now is something I live through every day. Never knowing what lurks, what kind of ugly, racist bullshit will rear its head and hurt me. How a thing like that can easily shift my day badly. I won't fix it for him. Not in the way he wants it to be fixed—easy, without vulnerability. It's *never* been easy for me.

"I'm sorry I doubted Jamal." Dean pulls my hands closer to him. I leave them limp. "I promise I haven't done that since the police station. I just needed you to know I've got some work I need to do, but I'm here for you. Things will be different this time. It's not going to be like your dad. Not if I can help it."

I don't respond. I've seen this before. How the veiled language in news stories and police reports contain coded phrases like *suspicious behavior, acted like a monster,* and the all-too-common *the officer feared for his life* that can change how people you thought were your friends act around you. And now I know Dean isn't immune. Somehow, I thought he was different.

Dean watched the same news updates I saw and easily believed their portrayal of Jamal, his friend, the one he's known for years. The one he ran alongside during track. Dean went to the same party and posed for the same photo that made Jamal look like a criminal. He should have known better.

When I watch the news, I can tell without even looking at the TV if the suspect is white or Black. A "young man who lost his way" or "was afflicted with mental illness" but "had a promising future" = white. A "thug" with "trouble in school" = Black.

Dean changed his mind only after seeing me. Because he knew my family. Everyone else watching will be like sheep. Unwilling to doubt the nonstop coverage of the hunt for Jamal.

Susan Touric failed Jamal by rushing to convict him in the court of public opinion without a full investigation.

I want to be angry that Jamal ran, but I can't blame him. What else are you supposed to do when the world treats you like a monster?

NO DISRESPECT

Dean and I sit parked in his truck down Buckhead Road, near Angela's gravesite. Rumor has it Chris was too distraught to go to Angela's ceremony, but each night he visits her plot here. The graves change from ones a hundred years old to modern ones, with fresh flowers and flags staked near a few shiny marble headstones.

A heavy weight of guilt pulls at me because we're not here to pay respects to Angela. Ten minutes of silence go by between Dean and me, until Chris arrives. I step out, taking a deep breath, and prepare myself for a confrontation.

Dean paces in front of his truck. Even though things are tense between us, Dean was dead set on coming with me. I don't want to scare Chris off from talking about Angela, so Dean knows he has to stay far enough away that Chris can let his guard down. Say something stupid.

Chris doesn't hear me coming up behind him. I walk cautiously, posting near the spreading oak by her grave, until I notice he's so upset he won't hear me. He hovers over her grave that's still adorned with flowers, teddy bears, notes, and candles. Her marble headstone reads BELOVED DAUGHTER AND FRIEND.

I hate myself for not knowing how to feel about Angela's death. Any other situation, I'd be paralyzed with shock or grief, even if I didn't know her much. No one deserves being murdered, but her death is tied to my brother's freedom. Each time I grieve for her, I feel like I'm choosing sides.

I look back at Dean, bite my lip, as I prepare to confront Chris. I clear my throat. We meet eyes. He stands up, pulling on his orange Texas A&M hat. I feel the color drain from my face when the vein in his neck pulses.

"What do you want?"

I take a step or two back. Then catch my breath.

Chris pulls his hat down to cover more of his face, but I can still see his eye has settled to splotches of pink and some green since the police station.

"Angela was on the paper with me. I care about what happened to her."

"You don't deserve to be here. Not after what your brother did."

"My brother cared about Angela, too."

I swallow hard. Attempt to keep my cool, but I'm uneasy. I look back at Dean, confirm his presence, and then speak: "I know my brother had nothing to do with her death. You tell me." I take a chance and say it with confidence. Like I know exactly what happened.

"He murdered her. It was him." He steps to me fast, and I fall back but stay on two feet.

My eyes go wide, voice stuck in my throat. I want to scream but can't get it out. From the corner of my eye, I see Dean run toward us. Chris backs up.

"How dare you come here and . . . harass me while I'm grieving." He spits his words at me, face flushed.

I study his reaction. He's so jittery, it's possible he killed Angela. I swipe the air toward Dean to show I'm okay, but he ignores me. He waits by the tree near us, arms crossed over his chest.

"You think you're gonna scare me with Dean being here? You can get the whole track team out here, with Jamal. I'm not going to hide what I saw. You know who my father is, right? You don't think I told him everything? If something happened to me, he'd be out here looking for who did it. Looking at your family."

Inside the back of my neck is tingling; what's he talking about?

"What happened to Angela?"

"What happened?" His voice rises, angry. "Your fucking brother couldn't keep his hands to himself. Thought he could get everything he wanted, even if it meant her life."

"You're out of your mind."

"She loved *me*. Jamal wasn't shit to her. He confused her, made her think she could get out of Galveston Bay. But he wasn't meant for her, and he couldn't handle it."

"Jamal wasn't ruining her life, and it's not his fault you two didn't work out. It's high school. Sounds like you're the one who was angry enough to get revenge." I know it's a risk, but I poke at him to get a response.

Chris shakes his head. "I was ready to forgive her for getting caught up with Jamal, take her back by convincing her what the whole town already knows: Jamal is just like his dad."

"Jamal didn't kill Angela." I'm trembling. "She was out by the Pike because of you and your friends." I know I'm reaching, but I need to see his response.

"What do you know about the Pike?" Chris's eyes widen, and his voice is shaky. Something about the Pike has him scared.

"*You* tell *me* about the Pike. I know all about what happens there," I lie. The memory card had a lot of photos that I'm still sorting out, so I put the only pieces I know together. Angela went to the Pike and was continuing to date Chris because he could help with whatever she was researching.

"Angela is dead because of Jamal." Chris is crying, choking on tears while he's talking.

I can't get over his face exploding in pain, but is it pain from losing her or guilt because it's his fault?

Dean closes the distance between us, grips my shoulder, and holds me close to him.

"Jamal is the reason she's dead," Chris says. "If he would've stayed away from her, none of this would've ever happened."

Chris is hazy talking. Like he's reliving the horror of seeing her body. But he said Jamal was the reason she's dead, not that Jamal actually killed her. There's a difference.

"Did you find Angela alive or dead?" I ask.

"What does it matter?" Chris cries out, shaking his head. "It's his fault."

"Did Jamal get there before or after you?"

Chris grabs his things and walks away, mumbling to himself, "He killed her. He killed her."

"Chris is getting away," I say to Dean. He wraps his arms around me, holding me back, shushing me to keep my cool. "He's getting away."

"Let him go," Dean says.

"Chris!" I shout.

He turns to me and cocks his head like he's remembering we're still talking.

"Did you see Jamal with Angela before or after you found her body?"

"It doesn't matter." He keeps walking.

I calm my voice, so he knows I'm not attacking him. "Before or after?" I just want the truth.

"After," he whispers, then jogs to his truck.

A sudden lightness washes over my body. Jamal was with Angela after she was killed. Chris just admitted it.

RECEIPTS

Jamal's been silent on text. Steve, Quincy, and Dean all think I should turn in Angela's cell to Beverly. They're right, I should. At least I conveniently uploaded the images from the SD card to the cloud, so I won't have to admit I've conducted two break-ins.

I pull up outside the police station.

Beverly comes over and leans on the side of my car. "What's with the cryptic call?"

My ears get hot and I take a long breath out before speaking.

"I found Angela's cell inside the South Seafood Packing building . . . before I was caught."

"You're mistaken." Beverly snaps her head up, studies me. "We have Angela's cell phone."

I squint hard, confused. "No, *this* is her phone. She used it at school. I can tell it's hers because of the hearts on the cover." I flash Angela's phone and turn it on. "All her calls, texts, and photos are on here. I wasn't sure who to trust, but I can't hold on to it any longer if it has something that can help find Angela's murderer."

I hold out the phone. I expect her to ask questions, but she's got a tight grimace on her face.

"What are you going to do with it?" I ask.

"I stuck my neck out for you." Beverly sweeps her hands out, then puts them on her head. "You took this from a crime scene where two officers were ready to arrest you. You could've been killed out there. Then they would've grabbed this phone and found cause, say you were helping Jamal hide evidence."

"I was scared when they went after me." I grip my hand on the edge of the car window. "Then when I read in the paper her phone was found, I didn't know who to trust. Not when Chris is referenced so many times in texts between Angela and Jamal. Sheriff Brighton was the one knocking on our door looking for Jamal."

I look up at Beverly with hopeful eyes.

She takes her time, then speaks. "Don't bring this phone up to anyone else. Don't mean I'm not going to turn it in. I need to think about how not to get you in trouble over this."

"They lied about having her phone."

"Exactly. Thank you for bringing this to me. Tracy, don't ever do anything like this again."

"I won't."

"Promise me."

I touch Beverly's hand. "I won't." I pause, debating about sharing that I also confronted Chris. Then I look at the station; he's already made a statement on record. My information could conflict.

"I talked to Chris. He blames Jamal for her death, but he admitted to me that Jamal arrived after Chris found her body. It didn't sound like he actually thinks Jamal did it. Just that it was his fault that caused it to happen, for whatever reasons."

Beverly nods. "The window for Angela's murder is tight between the calls and when Chris found her. That's why this phone might help. We also need to hear from Jamal."

"But Chris was out there with her body. Couldn't Jamal say he caught Chris in the act—killing her?"

"If Jamal hadn't run, and if he'd called the police right then and there, he'd be better off. But he ran. Now he looks guilty."

I take stock of the police station. Everything probably happened so fast, and it's too late for Jamal to backtrack and share his statement. No one's going to believe him.

"What do you know about the Pike?" I ask. "Angela took photos on a couple of Tuesday nights. Can't be a coincidence . . . Angela . . . was murdered on a Tuesday?"

"The Pike is generally empty, known for parties, and that's it. Don't know about Tuesdays. I don't usually have that route. I can ask around."

"Good," I say. "Let me know."

"Tracy." Beverly puts both hands on the edge of my window. "I'll find out more. You're going to have to trust me, though. Police investigations are—"

"Police business, I know." I search her eyes. "Beverly, if you find out something you don't like, be careful who you trust."

Beverly takes a step back, glancing all around before taking the phone, tucking it into her pocket, and entering the police station.

I want to trust her, too, but I don't know if I do enough to put my brother's life at risk.

I also don't think I have a choice.

PLUS-ONE

Some would call this party crashing, but technically I'm Dean's plus-one. The senior graduation party is the most exclusive party of the year, held at the biggest house. Which means usually most of the white kids go, and everyone else hitches rides with their white friends so the cops aren't called by neighbors— neighbors who are perfectly fine with ragers, but not a car full of Black and brown kids. It would've been at Angela's this year, but now it's at Mandy Peters's.

"You sure this is a good idea?" Dean asks.

"What?" I step outside, readjust my dark green off-the-shoulder minidress. "It's just a party."

"Neither of us is graduating."

"You went last year." I fumble through my bag to apply more lipstick. Then stretch out my natural hair that's now all blown out.

"I crashed with the track team last year," Dean says.

"Track team's crashing again, so no big deal."

Dean stops and runs his keys around his finger.

"Listen," I say. "No one at school wants to be caught talking to me. Drunk classmates are about the closest chance I have of interaction."

"What about angry, drunk classmates?"

"That's why I have you." I hit his shoulder, then chuckle when he looks pissed. "I kid."

"Funny. For the record, this is a horrible idea."

Dean states the obvious. It is absolutely a horrible idea, but I also don't have many options.

We pass cars and trucks jammed in spots in front of Mandy's house, a mini mansion compared to homes farther inland at Crowning Heights.

As we approach it, Dean turns, giving me a last chance to bail back to the truck. I swallow hard, but I came with a game plan.

"Let's split up. You see what you can find out about Tuesdays at the Pike. If I get a bad vibe, I'll wait at your truck until you're done."

Dean nods, then enters the party first.

Thirty seconds later, I beeline through the house, keeping my head down. Music blasting, the smells of beer, cigarettes, and weed taking over. It's not that late, but it looks like people have been going at it for hours. There's no way I could ever get away with throwing a party if we had a house like this. Mama would have everything covered in tablecloths and clear plastic. Carpet runners to protect the floor.

I settle a bit when I see everyone is into themselves, laughing and talking. Not worried about me.

I make my way to Mandy's massive kitchen. My mouth drops when I look out the window. Tasha and Quincy are out on the back deck.

Betrayal sets in. I asked both of them separately if they were going. Quincy practically begged me not to go, so I had to play off like he was right.

I go to meet them outside. Greeted by the sound of Tasha laughing at Quincy telling her something.

"Surprise seeing you here," I say to Tasha, then glare at Quincy.

"Changed my mind," Tasha says.

"And you weren't gonna say something?" I lean against the post.

"I knew I'd see you. Seems like you've been the one too busy for me lately." Tasha's tone is icy; there's not even a hint she's joking around. "I'm not sitting around to wait for you to call me, then come running at your begging."

"You shouldn't be here," Quincy says to me. "I tried to tell you."

"Why? Am I ruining a fun night for y'all?"

Quincy furrows his brow and lowers his voice. "No, because your brother is a suspect in the murder of the girl they've memorialized with photos up there."

Quincy points inside at a white poster board with Angela's

photo in the middle, signatures and notes written on it by people at the party.

"Anyone could feel like dragging you outta here, and you wouldn't find anyone to help. Everyone drunk. This is dangerous. This how mobs get started," Quincy says.

I don't speak. Hurt flits in my eyes, because I still feel betrayed.

"I'm going inside." Tasha begins to walk away with a drink in her hand.

"I'm trying to help my brother," I say. "You not the only one who's got shit falling on them."

"All right, both of you, stop," Quincy says. "Come here, Tracy."

Quincy leads me to the edge of the deck, leaving behind Tasha, who's sipping on a beer even though she hates to drink.

"Track team's here. Coach was pissed the team's been fighting. Pro- and anti-Jamal camps. I thought I'd come to help ask around. I'm not here to party. But seriously, *you*, here? Come on."

"I'm not alone."

"Dean?"

"Yeah."

"Figures," Quincy says. "Just let him ask around."

"He is."

Quincy leans in closer. "What did Bev say?"

"Kept things close to her chest," I say. "Said she'd look into it. Jamal's not answering my texts anymore. I'm worried time is running out for him and it won't matter what was going down at the Pike."

"So, you came here to talk to Chris again?" Quincy was livid when he found out I confronted Chris at Angela's grave. He thought I was reckless, even though I brought Dean.

"No." I avoid his eyes because that would be ideal. "I came to talk to Mandy. I thought maybe she knew what Angela was working on. She was her best friend. She lied to Natalie about seeing me leave the newsroom so they'd stop suspecting I trashed it. She could be an ally to me."

"And you thought going to a party with the entire school that's been treating you like trash was a good idea?"

"The sooner I talk to her, the sooner I can go."

Quincy huffs. Then leans his back against the deck rail.

"Over there." Quincy points to Mandy, who's out in her backyard, rocking on an old swing set, while the rest of the world is getting high and drunk.

I walk down the steps toward Mandy. Quincy pulls at the hem of my shirt for me to stop, but I don't. He hangs back by the gazebo and watches me.

I take Mandy by surprise when she looks up. She stomps her feet down to stop from swinging and opens her mouth to speak. Before she can ask me what I'm doing here, I interrupt.

"I won't be here long. I know this is hard on you with Angela gone, but I'm here because I also want to know the truth about what happened to her."

Mandy doesn't answer right away. I notice her eyes are puffy and red. I can sense the ache of pain shuffling through her body. I know the feeling, when you've been through so much you can't even talk because it hurts so much.

"Did you know Angela and Jamal were seeing each other?" I take a chance and let out their secret.

"Of course." Mandy musters an eye roll.

"Did you know she wanted me to work on some exposé?"

Mandy nods slowly. Looking around, checking to see if anyone else is within hearing distance. I look to where Quincy was waiting and notice he's gone now. He's moved up the stairs to the top deck where Tasha waits.

"You think my brother killed her?"

"I'm not talking about it." Mandy grips the swing handles and takes a seat. She's not yelling at me to leave, so I take a seat next to her.

"I know that Jamal was worried about her," I say. "Before she went to the Pike."

"I can't talk about it."

Mandy flicks her eyes. There's fear there.

"If you know who killed Angela, you have to say something."

"I don't know who killed Angela."

"But you don't think it's my brother." I hold my breath, hoping she agrees.

"Jamal wouldn't hurt Angela. I don't think he's the type to

let anything ruffle his feathers. If she was arguing, it was always with Chris."

My chest explodes in relief. If Angela's own best friend doesn't believe it, then maybe Jamal stands a chance.

"What was she working on?" I croak out. "I can help."

"How can you help? You're talking to me, which means you know nothing more than I do."

"Angela had a micro SD card with photos from Tuesday nights at the Pike. Angela was out there on Tuesday—"

"You found them?" Mandy whispers, leaning toward me. I stay silent. I need Mandy to let something slip. "I couldn't find them anywhere."

"Was that why you were cleaning out her desk, putting things in a backpack?"

"If they knew you had them, you could be in danger, Tracy." Mandy grabs my arm. "You have to stop looking around. Angela is dead because of those photos from the Pike."

"I don't get it. Why because of the photos?"

I don't share that Beverly has them now.

"Not because of the photos—what she uncovered."

"Who trashed the classroom?"

"I don't know. Just that you didn't. It's not your style. But someone wanted to make it look like you did it. I just wasn't going to let them get away with that."

I give her a nod of thanks. "Who do you think killed Angela?"

"I don't know." Mandy looks away, toward her house.

Something catches her attention, and I hear shouts from inside. It jolts us both.

"What's going on?" I jump off the swing.

"I wish they'd all just leave." Mandy shakes her head. "My parents wanted me to have this more than I did. They think it will distract me."

The noise gets louder. Yelling, cursing. We run across her yard and into the house, following the sounds of the fight. The crowd is gathered in the living room. As I get closer, I see Cuddy and Demarcus shoving guys out of the way. The crowd chants, "Fight. Fight. Fight."

I touch my face when I see Quincy pinned in a corner with Scott.

I step closer to the chaos.

CRASH AND BURN

Quincy and Scott are shoving each other, throwing punches when they can reach. With each movement, Quincy is off balance, but so is Scott, since he's clearly drunk. Dean cuts past me, and some of Scott's friends think he's there to help Scott, but he's not. He pushes Scott off to give Quincy space.

Scott sees me, and the anger in his eyes makes me take a step back. He's thin, but drunk he's scrappy and doesn't seem to mind the punches from Quincy. Like he's numb to the pain he'll feel tomorrow.

"Get the fuck out." He charges at me. "You don't belong here."

I try to dip away, but the crowd is pressing in on me, shoving me back toward Scott. He rips at my arm, and I feel my socket pull. Then he's yelling at me. My heart races, and I try to back up, but the crowd is locked up tight. Keeping my friends from being able to help me.

"We can't get Jamal, so how about you pay?" Scott says low and deadly as he grips my arm.

My chin trembles, trying to form words, but all I can let out is a weird, throaty sound. I look back, hoping to spot an escape. A place to catch my breath and think. Far away from here.

Quincy frees up from the crowd and jumps at Scott. Cuddy and Demarcus join him. The mob finally opens up to avoid the blows. Chris makes his way through the crowd, my first time seeing him. Dean shoulders his way in front, blocking Chris from joining in.

"Cool it, man," Dean says.

"Get the fuck out," Chris says. "You people, get the fuck out. I'm calling the police."

More track team members help Demarcus, me, and Quincy get out. People start trying to calm down the room, but my being here caused a ripple of tension across groups on different sides. I look to Mandy, who avoids eye contact. Only Black folks start exiting the party. A group of white guys circle, to make sure we don't turn back.

Scott tugs on Chris's arm, but he pulls back. They say a few words that don't look friendly. Like they've been beefing, too.

On my way out, I whisper to Dean to stay. He's torn, but he knows what's up. People will be talking, and it could lead to more information.

On the steps, Tasha's by my side, coming from nowhere. She must've been waiting outside.

"I was looking for you. Hoped you'd already left. That was stupid, Tracy."

"I know." But Tasha's not fully mad, because she's holding my hand, shaking as we rush to get away from the party.

"You okay?" Quincy reaches for me. Tasha drops my hand.

Quincy touches my face, then goes over my wrist that'll surely bruise.

"I'm gonna kill him."

I shake my head. "He's not worth it."

"I can take you home," Quincy says.

I'm about to tell him I can ride with Tasha, until I realize he offered because Tasha's leaving without me.

"Tasha!" I yell after her. She turns back, giving me a hard look, then opens her car door.

"Tasha!" I run to catch up, my feet pounding, and climb into her car.

"Why you riding with me?"

"Tasha. It's been us, together, always." She's hurt about Quincy, obviously. I can't let that push our friendship aside. It's clear Quincy's back in my life, but she's taking it the wrong way.

"It sure don't seem like it," Tasha says. "Since when have you been feeling Quincy?"

"We have history, Tasha." She's never really known our history; no one has. Not what we've been through. All the things that are unspoken. But I also need Tasha. Tasha needs me.

"You know you're the reason that fight started. He could've been hurt."

"Quincy's been helping me with my brother. There's so much going on you don't know, but it's not like I'm trying to keep it from you. We been through a lot, too. And you're mad, so yeah. I'm going with your stubborn ass."

Tasha isn't happy I joined her, but she also doesn't kick me out.

We drive past Quincy's Impala, where he's leaning back on his car, nursing his leg and giving us a nod, but I look away. Won't let Tasha see how badly I wanted to ride with Quincy.

WE GOT A SITUATION

On Sunday after church, I head to see Dean at work. Dean rings up a customer, then joins me in the corner where I have my favorite view to the street. Steve is out doing interviews, so I don't mind waiting for him at Evans Antiques. I've got my laptop pulled up, searching online for anything around the dates the photos at the Pike were taken and catching up with what I missed after we were all kicked out of Mandy's party—at least all the Black kids.

"Party didn't last much longer," Dean says. "Everybody knows I'm cool with you, so no one said much to me."

"What about Mandy?"

"She kept to herself. Seemed relieved when everyone started leaving. Scott and Chris stuck around, helping her clean up, but she was jumpy with them."

"Mandy doesn't think Jamal had anything to do with killing Angela. She thinks the micro SD card got her in trouble, and all the questions she was asking."

"You find anything on there?"

"No." I share a copy of the photos out at the Pike. "Does this spur anything?"

Dean shrugs. "Just a bunch of guys out drinking. The only thing weird is they're from different cliques. Don't usually see them all together."

Dean gets up to help the next person in line. What Dean doesn't say is that they do have something in common—they're all white. Just like how the party last night was pretty much segregated. He can't see it, but the absence of color is striking to me. It also gives me a thought. I search online, up and around a few days before the photo was taken.

Eventually, I see one small reference to a Black Lives Matter peace rally against a hate group planning on marching an hour away. It ended up being a mob of around forty guys. A girl who was part of the peaceful march was shot by a stray bullet that hit the crowd.

I covered the march in "Tracy's Corner." It started a debate in history class when white kids asked why it's not racist to say Black Lives Matter but a problem to say White Lives Matter or Blue Lives Matter. What they don't get is that those lives have always mattered. Ours are treated like we're less than equal. Like we don't deserve the same respect. A school shooter can come out alive but a Black kid in handcuffs on the ground can be shot, unchecked. An AK-47 in a white hand has more rights than a Black kid with Skittles.

I search through social media tags, scrolling until an image jolts me. A guy with a Texas A&M hat with the number 27 on the side. Chris. His mouth opened wide, yelling at the anti-racist protesters, Blue Lives Matter flag in his hand. Right next to him, much clearer now, is Scott with his varsity jacket on, TRACK & FIELD on his shoulder.

I get up to show Dean.

Through the window of Evans Antiques, I see a guy get out of his SUV. He's dressed in a crisp blue shirt, gray slacks, and shoes too shiny for Texas. I strain to see his face, but his hat and sunglasses are a good cover from this distance. He strikes me as familiar, maybe from around town. He doesn't head into the Evanses' store. Instead, he makes his way down the alley.

"I think that's the guy who had binoculars watching Steve," I call out to Dean.

"You sure?" Dean comes over and puts a hand on my shoulder, looking over me to see the guy, but he's too late.

"What else is down the alley?" I ask.

"Garbage. It's a dead end." Dean pauses, then looks at me. "And the stairs to Steve's office."

I'm certain it's no coincidence that he's here as soon as Steve's gone.

I pull out my cell and call Steve. "Did you lock the office?"

"Why, you need to get in?" Steve asks.

"No. The guy in the white SUV went down the alley behind Mr. Evans's store. All that's there—"

"Call the cops and stay away," Steve says. "I had his plates run. He's not someone we want near our case files."

I hang up the phone and dial 911 while repeating to Dean what Steve said. His brows furrow and his jaw clenches, and then he swiftly moves past me as I talk to the 911 operator.

"Dad!" Dean yells, then hops over to the counter, enters a passcode on the gun safe, and pulls out a shotgun. He grabs a handful of shells and grips them, two by two, locking the gun back in place.

"What are you doing?" I block Dean from moving, my hands trembling.

"Stay here." Dean points his finger at me in such a demanding way I almost slink back.

"Dean. No." I'm hyperventilating, wanting Dean to stop and wait for the cops.

He doesn't stop; he jogs out the front door carrying the shotgun. I quickly give the store address to the operator and chase after Dean. When I step outside, an alarm goes off upstairs. I breathe out a sigh of relief that this'll scare him off. But it doesn't stop him.

"Dean, it's not worth it," I yell after him, and run out to the alley.

Dean is halfway up the outside staircase to the office on

the second floor, gripping the banister as he looks down at me. I'm shaking in place. He takes one step up, looks at me again, and stops. Mr. Evans runs out the door, followed by Mrs. Evans.

She's not going to like this.

"What is going on?" Mr. Evans quickly makes his way to Dean.

"Someone's breaking into the office upstairs." I avoid eye contact so I don't have to be the one to explain more to Mrs. Evans.

"Get downstairs, Dean," Mr. Evans's voice booms.

Mr. Evans is a few inches shorter than Dean, but he makes up for it with his commanding presence. Dean's foot hovers over the next step up, pausing. Then he backs down and meets us in the alley. He keeps watch on the door, expecting the guy to come down any second.

Mr. Evans grabs the shotgun from Dean and posts with it at the bottom of the stairs. This is the only exit and entrance to the loft. We watch from afar. Nothing is moving Mr. Evans out of his place, his boots firmly on the ground.

Mrs. Evans has her I-told-you-so face on, with eyebrows raised. This will be trouble for Dean. I mouth, *Sorry,* to him.

A police car arrives, then another. They park between the alley and the front of the store, and then meet Mr. Evans at the stairs. He must have turned off the blaring alarm, because it's finally silent. After ten minutes, officers go in and out. The guy is nowhere to be found. Either he hopped the fence and never made it upstairs, or he scaled down one of the windows from the back room of the office.

Dean leads his mom and me upstairs, where we meet Mr. Evans and three officers. One of them is Officer Clyde, the silver-haired officer from the Pike.

At first glance the room looks the same, except a window's open. The closed file boxes in the back have been tampered with. I know for a fact they were sealed, since I taped them shut myself.

The officers walk around. I study them. Watch how they open up the boxes, sifting through and pulling files out. I make a noise with my throat to catch their attention. Mrs. Evans is also examining the loft. Her mouth is tight, disapproval on her lips. When she heads back downstairs, I can't help but feel relief that we won't have to tiptoe around her anymore.

"What you say your name was?" Mr. Evans steps up.

"Clyde," the silver-haired officer responds. "Not sure what we're looking for. You saw an intruder?"

I hope he doesn't recognize me, but my hopes are dashed when I feel his recognition laser in on me.

"Yes, sir," I say. "This is the second time we've caught him out here. The first time with binoculars looking up into the office when I was helping the tenant move in. We've got a license plate from before."

I grab a photocopy of the SUV's license plate and hand it to Officer Clyde. The other officers continue rifling through the boxes. Another officer stands in front of the massive board that

Steve's been working on. They take photos of the boxes, pulling out files and reading through Steve's notes. Then they take a photo of Steve's board. They don't seem too concerned about a robbery.

"Well, I don't think there are any valuables here," Mr. Evans says, beginning to usher the officers out. "But I'll be sure to check in with my tenant. I'll be in contact if he identifies anything missing."

"Didn't know you had a tenant," Officer Clyde says.

"Yip. Things been slow, so thought I'd try and make a little more money."

"You filed the appropriate paperwork to rent a space? You know how the city is about pop-up establishments. You never can be too careful who you bring into town."

"I've got the paperwork. Nothing to worry about here, Officer Clyde," Mr. Evans says.

The cops finally exit, and Mr. Evans shuts the door behind them.

"What do you think?" Mr. Evans asks us.

"That was weird, right?" I say. "The break-in? The cops?"

"Small town. Folks don't like new people coming in and being nosy," Mr. Evans says.

There's being nosy, and there's conspiring against the investigation. Someone was looking for something. The question is, what?

Two hours later, Dean and I jolt at the sound of the key jingling in the door. Steve carries his briefcase in with a weary look of exhaustion.

"What took so long?" I ask.

"Interviewee was an hour late. Some emergency."

"Coincidence a break-in occurred in the daytime?" I ask.

"Not sure I believe in those anymore," Steve says. "It's time we take precautions."

"I agree," Dean says.

I think about how quickly Dean pulled out the shotgun. I don't like the way this is going.

"All right, what happened?" Steve asks.

We walk Steve through everything. From the moment the guy got out of his SUV, all the way through how the cops seemed more interested in searching Steve's office than looking for a burglar. When we're done, we point out all the boxes the cops focused on. Steve checks each one.

"Did they take anything?"

"I didn't see," I say. "They were more poking around."

"Yeah. I didn't see them take anything, either," Dean says.

Steve looks over at the security alarm that apparently only makes noise and doesn't actually stop intruders.

"I've got an order in for a new system," Dean says. "This time I'll install it myself."

"Thanks," Steve says. "How long before you say he was out of sight?"

"He went down the alley right before we called you," I say. "Two minutes or so before Dean had a shotgun and was down there."

"Three minutes, tops," Dean adds.

"It's possible he could break in that fast and grab something, but highly unlikely," Steve says. "I have a hard time getting in the door, let alone orienting myself around the files."

"What do you think he was after?"

Steve scans the boxes and the case files and then the lists on the board of all the case names he's considering taking on. "I'll have to look through everything to know for sure what might be missing. Innocence X has a reputation for revealing botched cases, dirty cops, politicians, and bad cover-ups."

"I gave the plate number to the officer. Who do you think he is?" I ask.

"I was hoping we'd have a couple of weeks before things got complicated." Steve rubs his head, then pulls at his chin. "The cops don't need to run the plates. I was able to get the name of the organization that owns the car, but they wouldn't provide the driver's name. Said I'd need a subpoena. The cops should be able to get that. The organization is called Liberty Heritage for a New America. They're a special-interest think tank funded by ultraconservatives. This one has ties to white supremacists who use conservatism to cover their agenda. We've run into them before, but I thought they were stopping harassment and stepping up their fight through lobbying state representatives. This is aggressive, which means we must be on to something they don't want me looking into."

A shiver runs down my spine. This is the last thing we need.

"What's the status of my daddy's case?" I ask.

"The case is officially pending review for direct appeal," Steve says. "They could review it thoroughly or treat it like the others. The hope is I can get more evidence for a new trial."

"My dad has less than two hundred fifty-two days left until his execution date."

"We can't spend time thinking about the obstacles. You'll lose your mind trying to make sense of it. We file. We research. We push. We make noise. We put pressure—"

"We pray," Mama says at the door.

"Yes, we pray," Steve says. "Come in, Mrs. Beaumont."

Mama leads us in prayer. "Father God, let your holy power fill us with strength and protection." She continues, but I lose focus, things rushing through my mind on what we should do next. Whatever it is, we must be on the right track or we wouldn't be getting blocked like this.

I open my eyes when Mama says, "Amen."

IF IT WALKS LIKE
A DUCK . . .

Before I head off to school on Monday, I stand close to Mama. She folds the newspaper, a late attempt to keep the head-lines away. I've already seen them. Jamal on the cover, and Daddy on page 7. *Galveston Times* with a personal countdown: Fourteen days Jamal's been on the run; 251 days until Daddy's execution date. My chest aches.

Her worry lines compound with each day Jamal's been gone. I take a seat at the kitchen table.

"I was thinking—"

"That statement never ends well." Mama winks.

"We don't really know Steve. Like he's doing all this stuff for Daddy . . . and Mr. Evans gave him a great deal on the office space."

"Save it. Where's this going?"

"We should have them all over for dinner tonight."

Over a meal, guards can come down. Steve can get insight into things Mama hasn't told us yet, and Mrs. Evans might warm up more to the idea of Steve staying at the loft after the break-in. I also want to thank Steve; his words last night meant the world. And I don't want him regretting taking our case.

"I'm sure this has nothing to do with Mr. Evans calling last night to say Mrs. Evans wants Steve to move out."

Mama has no chill to hear me out. Having Steve move out would be a setback. He's making progress—the break-in proved that.

"Mrs. Evans might change her mind if she got to know Steve. Anyway, isn't this something you normally would do? It seems . . . kinda negligent."

Mama has always used food to bring people together. Our hardest days in courts were accompanied by other memories. Guests joining us for family dinners. Until it got too much. Until it was clear Daddy wasn't coming home.

"Steve does need a break," Mama says. "He shouldn't be spending those late nights in that office by himself. When the day is done, tell him he's coming here for dinner. I'll leave you the grocery list."

"What about the Evanses?"

"I'll talk to them when I get into work." Mama cranks her neck my way.

I smirk at Mama, who only needed a push. Then send

another text to Jamal. He's been silent since Quincy told him about me crashing the party.

I step out of the car to get to Elm's Grocery store. When I run across the street, I almost don't see Mr. Herron, Angela's dad, standing in front of me. Out of habit, I attempt a wave, but stop midway because he's visibly shaken seeing me. As much as I want to comfort him, my presence won't give him peace.

I want to say I'm sorry. Scream out Jamal's innocence. That I wish Angela was still here. None of that happens. I'm frozen.

"How can you act like everything's fine?" Mr. Herron's jaw is tense.

"I—I—I'm sorry. We have someone who can help find out what happened to Angela." I point down the street to the loft above Evans Antiques. I want to make it true, even though I know my focus has been on Jamal, and freeing Daddy.

He throws his hand out. "Bring my daughter back, if you want to help. Can you bring her back?"

My breath catches. Stunned. He knows that's impossible.

"You can't." His eyes go wet. "Stay away. I hope they find Jamal and he rots in prison like he left my baby girl outside to do."

I want to be outraged at his behavior, but I can't. It's shame. Pure shame running through my body, even though Jamal didn't do nothing.

I escape to Elm's Grocery, my cheeks red as I pass customers who witnessed the interaction outside. I hurry through the store, picking from Mama's grocery list. I go to check out, and the grocer doesn't speak. Doesn't look up at me. They all know who I am. All itching for me to leave.

When he's done, he rings me up. "That'll be forty dollars and twenty-seven cents."

He's rushing me so fast he almost forgets to take my cash. I wave two twenties in front of me. He halfway apologizes but doesn't meet my eyes while I fish around for the change.

"That's okay. Forty is good."

I ignore him. I'm not gonna have him say I shorted him. As I turn to exit, I bump into another customer.

"Sorry," I say.

Without looking up, I scoot around to pass the guy.

He steps between me and the exit.

I glance up to give him a glare. My face drops when he stares at me with cold eyes. I almost let it slip out that I know him—the guy from Liberty Heritage for a New America. I now realize he was the same guy with Chris at the police station. He looks like a slightly younger version of Sheriff Brighton. My throat constricts when I know for sure he recognizes me, too. That's why he stopped me.

"Excuse me," I force out, shaking as I move left, then right, to get past him.

He blocks me again. Then finally he lets me pass, his hateful expression unchanged.

Relief sets in when he goes the other way. My steps are tentative. I'm so light-headed from the blood rushing through my body.

I cross the street and then call Officer Clyde, tell him about being harassed by the same guy from the break-in. I hear him write down a few things, and then he hangs up. Immediately, I text Beverly. I can't take the chance Officer Clyde will let this pass because Sheriff Brighton might have a closer connection to it all.

I wait to see if the guy will leave, but he walks down the street toward another office building. Without hesitation, I sneak behind the white SUV to get a better look. Inside, sitting on the back seat, are boxes from the copy store. An image of the original copy is taped on top of the box, but it's too hard to see unless I go on the street side. I strain to search the other half of the car, trying not to look suspicious. When I can't take the curiosity anymore, I go around. My heart beats fast for fear of getting caught, or worse . . . facing him again.

In broad daylight, on the street side, I peek in the white SUV's window. Taped to the top of the box is a sign, a drawing of a white, straight couple holding a baby. The words at the top: *Don't let white guilt control you. Join together and honor our heritage.*

My heart is racing. I read again, searching for the name of the organization. Nothing states Liberty Heritage for America, though. The posters are clearly recruitment flyers. The flyer doesn't state a meeting location, but my guess is Tuesdays at the Pike is one of them. This could be Angela's exposé.

I move closer to the driver's side, but out of the corner of my eye I spot the man leaving the office, so I cross traffic. He doesn't see me but turns toward his parked car. We'll be forced to walk by each other. I duck into a store and hold my breath until he walks past.

I close my eyes to picture him in the police station. Then our interaction in the grocery. The hate in his eyes was the same. My breathing gets labored. I suck in air to calm myself, but my panic grows.

I don't forget a face. Spent my whole life observing everything around me. It was him. I didn't catch it before because he was so far away, his sunglasses and hat covering his eyes.

I race to Jamal's car, dumping my groceries in the back, then lock the doors. I scroll through my phone, searching the Liberty Heritage for a New America staff directory. I find a Richard Brighton. Google his name. His image is as clear as day. Brother to Sheriff Brighton.

I check my other phone, not having heard from Jamal recently. At a stoplight, I blow up his phone with desperate texts. With the hot, dusty air outside rushing in through the open windows, I feel like I'm riding in our evacuation bus all over again. I shut the windows because I don't want those memories to chase me home.

GUESS WHO'S COMING TO DINNER?

Promptly at six, the doorbell rings. I loosen my two-twist strands before opening the door. Mama insisted I wear a summer dress. Corinne, too, although we couldn't stop her from wearing her favorite cowboy boots. I force a smile at the door so any evidence that I was terrified earlier disappears. But inside I'm spinning, each move I made today still bouncing in me like a pinball looking for a safe place to land.

Three smiling faces greet me: Steve, Dean, and Mr. Evans. Followed by a sullen Mrs. Evans. Dean towers over them all, wearing my favorite blue-checkered shirt, the one I got him for his birthday. Mr. Evans lets them enter first, his arm around Mrs. Evans. More pushing her in than ushering.

"Welcome," Mama calls out from the stairs, dressed nicely, like she hasn't been on her feet, cooking. She greets everyone with smiles but gives Mrs. Evans an extra-long hug.

"All right, all right. I told you I was coming, Lillian." Mrs. Evans laughs. "I'm not going anywhere, so you can stop hugging me."

Mama has that way about her. She claims her cooking is her visible weapon—praying's the invisible one.

I immediately glance over at Dean, who gives me a half-cocked fake smile that lets me know it was an ordeal getting here.

"Who is this young lady?" Dean says over my shoulder. Corinne's playing shy at the bottom of the stairs.

"It's me, silly." Corinne gives a bashful laugh.

"You clean up well, little sis." Dean picks her up for a hug.

At the table, Mama leads us in grace. All heads bowed and thankful at a break from everything causing pain. Mama's cooked a traditional New Orleans meal. In the middle of the table is a mound of boiled crawfish, with corn and potatoes. She overdid the crawfish because it's the last of the season. Then red beans and rice, corn muffins, and okra. Plates pass around, a miracle the way it washes away fear from earlier.

Steve's laughing, talking, shoving food into his mouth and sucking down crawfish. As dinner goes on, though, you can tell he's fading away.

"I should've had you over sooner. Not like me at all." Mama smiles, but it's a heavy one. Weighted. Painful. Steve's sitting in Jamal's seat after all.

"Understandable. I went right to work on the case. Barely

had time for anything else. Thank you, Mr. and Mrs. Evans, for the use of the office space," Steve says. "I can do some real work there."

"What exactly are you doing?" Mrs. Evans dabs her napkin at her mouth before placing it on the table.

"Judy—" Mr. Evans places his hand over hers.

"I'd like to know. Because all I see is trouble. We've never had break-ins before."

"That's not Steve's fault," Mr. Evans says. "We talked about this."

"I don't mean any trouble." Steve waves his hands. "I'm doing my job."

"I didn't have y'all over here to argue with each other." Mama puts her hand on the table. "Let's not start a war before we even have dessert."

"I don't mean to disrespect your home," Mrs. Evans says. "But since he's here, I want to know more about this business that's going on upstairs, from Mr. Jones himself. There's a difference between someone who might mean well with their social justice interests and actually having proper legal training."

"I can assure you, my Harvard law education and my work for my father's legal clinic, Innocence X, have given me the adequate skills to take on this case." Steve sits up and covers his chuckle at her knowing so little about his background.

"I, uh—" Mrs. Evans hesitates.

"I don't intend on causing trouble, but some people don't

want me to be successful. We're a nonprofit with highly trained lawyers; we work for people without the funds to successfully support their cases. I believe every person has the right to a fair trial, regardless of income."

"That's all fine." Mrs. Evans's face turns a shade of red. "I'm not saying I disagree, but sometimes organizations like yours stir up problems. Like all those anti-cop workshops Tracy does. People get riled up, making nothing into something, and I don't need to have my family mixed up in that."

I open my mouth to correct her. She's never directly said anything about my workshops. They're not anti-cop—they're pro-rights. Mama's giving me the eye, so I force a bite of food to swallow my words. I look over at Corinne, who seems to have lost her appetite. I give her a wink. She doesn't react.

"If Dean were accused of something he didn't do and was sentenced, you'd want justice, a fair defense, even if you couldn't afford it," Steve says.

"I just wonder, why now? What can possibly be proven after all these years?"

I choke on my food, guzzle some water down. Mama looks like she's five seconds away from cursing out Mrs. Evans talking like this in her house, over food she made.

"The Beaumonts believe it's worth it." Steve points around the table at us. "The first family appeal letter I read was from a stack my father took home every night. That's when I stopped hating him for working so much and realized he was a hero.

Tracy's letters have come in like clockwork every week for seven years. While I'm here, this case is *the* only case to me. I'm not worried about a town's wish to get back to normal."

I hold back a sob, thinking about my daddy's life on the line and someone actually reading my letters.

"Well, I, for one, am glad you're here," Mr. Evans says, then looks at his wife. "I've always given you room for your opinions, but we're in someone's home right now. Lillian's worked for us for years counting books, helping expand our sales online when the business was damn near ready to fold. We know her kids, and there's nothing wrong with an investigation to help bring justice for James if they can prove he was innocent."

"Don't make me the bad one here." Mrs. Evans raises her voice. "I want to protect my family. I don't want to get mixed up in this like I'm choosing sides."

"Choosing sides," I say. "There's one side. The side of justice."

"I'm not saying anything about your dad's . . . situation. But with that poor girl dead, people are asking questions. Now, if it looks like we're helping, we might lose business."

Mama's face goes tight. Mrs. Evans is talking about Jamal now, and it don't sit right.

"I didn't mean to hurt your feelings, Lillian. I don't mean anything by it. I'm saying what it looks like to other people might have an impact on my business. My home."

"I don't want to get anyone upset." Steve shakes his head.

"But if causing disruption in town is asking questions and finding evidence that might free an innocent man, then call me guilty."

"I'm gonna start on dessert now." Mama sits up. "Corinne, you wanna help?"

"I'll get the bananas." Corinne races to the kitchen, finally a smile on her face. Mama goes to follow Corinne, but Mr. Evans places his hand on hers.

"No. No. Sit down," Mr. Evans says. "I think it's due time Judy sits and listens. If she'd change the news channel every once in a while, she'd see real issues are going on with police and Black folks. And you know it's no different than it's ever been around here."

"Don't get started on this Blacks and police." Mrs. Evans shakes her head. "None of this has anything to do with race."

I've always suspected her feelings but didn't know for sure. Dean's hidden them as much as he could from me until recently. But the more I hear from her, the more I'm boiling inside. I grip my hands under the table to control myself and avoid looking at Dean, who is desperately trying to capture my attention.

"That's enough." Mr. Evans taps at the table with his fist. "Steve, the office space is there as long as you need it. I'd be more than glad to let it be used for something good. Now, I don't want to hear another word because I want Lillian's famous bananas Foster, and I'm not leaving without a bite."

Mrs. Evans stays silent.

Mama spends a few minutes in the kitchen, then enters the dining room with a flaming pan as Corinne runs to turn down the lights. That's Corinne's favorite part about eating bananas Foster.

There's complete silence as each bite is finished. My mind is on everything Mrs. Evans said. Anger seeping in as I watch her, I decide I'd rather do the dishes than sit at the table any longer.

Dean follows me to help clear up.

"No, sit down," Mama says. "You're a guest."

"You know I'll be hearing the hawing over there if I don't join her," Dean jokes, then grabs a handful of plates.

"I'd be fine," I say. "But since you're offering, you're washing and I'm drying."

Before we get to the kitchen, a booming noise explodes outside.

A roaring thump follows, and a hard pop and crash.

I recoil, my hands covering my head as shattered glass shoots across the room. I'm stunned until I hit the ground, Dean hovering over me like a shield. The chaos is deafening. My world just exploded.

AMERIKKKA

Our front window is destroyed.

Unsteady, I get to my feet to check on everyone. Hold Corinne close. Still unsure what happened. Mama is covering her mouth, her eyes teary and wide.

I feel the temperature warm up, a crackling sound. I whip around to look out the busted windows.

Dean runs through the kitchen's back door to go around the house while Steve goes through the front door. I'm stuck, staring. Confused why it's so bright outside. Until I realize there's a blazing cross, over ten feet tall, that's staked into our dry grass. The flames are catching the ground on fire. Bright and flashing.

I cry out at the tall cross burning in our front yard. The fire is blazing; I look away. Shut my eyes, but the image of the cross stays even in darkness.

"Good Lord." Mrs. Evans stands there, with shards of glass around her, fixated on the yard. My eyes lock on the brick on the ground, paper wrapped on with what must be rubber bands.

"Judy, you all right?" Mama wraps her arms around Mrs. Evans, since more of the glass hit her. Mrs. Evans's face is as white as a ghost's. She doesn't speak, shaking, but shuffles along as Mama guides her, directing her closer to the kitchen while calling the police.

"Take Corinne upstairs, Tracy." Mama waves her arm at me, and it breaks my gaze away from the glass-covered floor.

I head upstairs, ushering Corinne and leaving her door open. Grateful that her room is on the backside of the house. Corinne doesn't speak; she goes silent, gripping one of her dolls. My adrenaline still up from the window blasting, but also at what this is doing to Corinne. She's become numb to our nights evolving into terrifying disturbances. I worry about what this will do to her long-term.

"It's gonna be all right." I push her hair back.

Corinne nods. I look away, so she doesn't know I'm afraid. I turn on her sleep noisemaker to drown the outside. Then leave.

On the porch, Mrs. Evans has a blanket wrapped around her, crying out that everyone needs to be careful. She's shaking like they came for her, not us.

"You hurt? Any glass get you?" Mama tugs at my chin, checking my face. "How's Corinne?"

"Shocked. This is too much for her, Mama."

Mama nods. "Stay out here with them while I call the fire department. I'll go check on her."

Mr. Evans, Dean, and I stand behind the fiery cross, watching Steve hose it down. Our shadows elongating in the dark, hot night of Texas as the flames extinguish.

"See anyone?" I ask.

"They were gone by the time I got around," Dean says.

"Where were the police?" I point down the street where they were parked for two weeks until now. "Is this what you meant when you said it was going to get ugly?"

Dean touches my back, shaking his head.

"I'm from Mississippi," Steve says. "I've seen this before, but I didn't expect it here. There's definitely something bigger going on."

My throat closes. I haven't heard from Jamal in two days.

"What do we do?" I take a step closer to Steve.

"It means we've got more work to do. This something that happens around here often, Mr. Evans?"

Mr. Evans doesn't answer right away. He watches the cross, then glances over at Mrs. Evans. I wonder if he's thinking the same thing as me. If Mrs. Evans considers this a part of stirring up trouble, or if it makes her realize that trouble was already here and we're just trying to survive.

"Klan was here." Mr. Evans hesitates. Like he wants me and Dean to leave so he can talk to Steve.

I'm not going anywhere.

"All this land from here to the Pike was seized twenty years ago by the FBI in a big bust. White supremacists had bought property and businesses so they could launder money in and out without the government knowing. Some lost property, money, and some went to jail."

"Wait," I say. "Daddy and Mr. Davidson were planning to build homes on land that had been owned by the Klan? Does my mama know?"

Mr. Evans doesn't answer. I'm shocked. Why is this the first I'm hearing about it? All this time we've been looking at Daddy's case all wrong. There could be more around Mr. Davidson choosing to do business with a Black man.

"Who could be involved?" Dean asks his dad.

"I don't know." Mr. Evans looks off in the distance. I think he's avoiding eye contact, but then I hear the whirring sound of a fire truck and police cars.

With the sirens in the background, I rush to the house for the brick that broke the glass.

Dean follows. "Should you be touching that?"

"If we don't read it, there's no promise it'll be shared with us," I say.

I carefully pull off the rubber band with a napkin, brushing away any lingering glass, and read the note. Swallow hard as I take it in. The note flutters in my hand, and I almost drop it before Steve urges me to read it.

I bite the inside of my cheek, steady my shaky hands, then read it out loud.

NO MORE WHITE LIVES LOST AT THE HANDS OF
A BEAUMONT. NEXT TIME IT'LL BE A BODY WE
BURN.
                              —THE BROTHERHOOD

UNTHINKABLE

The world feels upside down, like I've been dropped—then left broken. Nevertheless, I need to flip that switch in my brain so I can believe these police officers are here to help.

I wish I could trust them automatically, but I can't. History has a way of latching on to you. Like touching a hot stove—you only need to do it once before you know better.

When the police arrive, Mama waits by the door. Shaking. I meet her, wrapping my arms around her waist. I know she's doing the same as me—putting her armor back on. I gaze up at her, then quickly look away. It hurts to see her forcing herself to be strong. Especially when Mrs. Evans was allowed to fall apart. Allowed to be human.

When I'm ready, I force myself to study Mama, because I

need to learn that strength so I can pass it down, like a family recipe. An heirloom. A curse.

The officers walk toward us, black smoke and kindles of fire crackling behind them. Officer Clyde takes off his hat. I haven't heard from him since my call earlier. He's joined by two more officers and the firefighter crew. Beverly stands off to the side, her eyes huge. She pulls herself together and joins us. Relief pours through me.

"Ma'am," Officer Clyde says with a sullen demeanor before he shakes Mama's hand and introduces himself again.

"Officer Clyde." Mama pauses. "Beverly."

Bev's face doesn't show an immediate expression, but there's a dazed look in her eye when she turns to the cross.

"We'll take the cross down as soon as we can, Mrs. Beaumont," Beverly says.

"Thank you, Bev," Mama says. "How's your mama doing?"

"She's doing good, ma'am. I'll tell her you asked about her."

"Please do. Get the word out to the church and folks in Crowning Heights," Mama says firmly. It's code for "the Black community better meet about this." I already have a plan formed on getting the word out tonight.

I can understand those who stayed away from us because of the criminal cases we were dealing with, but a cross burning is serious business. One that holds stories of blood and death. We should all be worried.

"Tell me, boy, does trouble always follow you?" Officer Clyde says to Steve. "You're new to town, correct?"

"Stephen Jones," Steve checks him. "I haven't been called a boy since I was ten years old." He says *boy* with a little smile, but the veins in his throat are pulled tight. He's pissed. Calling a Black man a *boy* has its own racist history and connotation. Steve ain't having it. "And no, I'm not from around here."

I study Officer Clyde. If he's comfortable saying "boy" to Steve, then he won't be helpful tonight or with Richard Brighton.

"Stephen," Officer Clyde corrects himself. "Sorry about that. I thought that Stephen Jones was an old lawyer in the South."

"My father."

Mrs. Evans stands alongside us, but it's like she's not here. Like fear struck her the moment she dropped to the dining room floor. She's shook in a different way from us.

Perhaps because she's never had to walk in fear. Every day my senses are on alert, expecting something to happen. Sure, I'm shaken. Scared. Never imagined something like this could happen so close to home. But deep down this feeling is familiar. It runs through my veins, the blood from every generation before me passing down this fear, coded into my DNA.

Mrs. Evans tugs at her shirt like she's about to have a heart attack. I know she needs help right now, but I don't have sympathy for her. All of this is happening to my family. Not hers.

I nudge Dean, steer his attention to his mom. He goes to her and whispers in her ear. She looks out at the shattered glass like he's not there. But he's able to get her to sit down.

"What are we going to do about this?" Mr. Evans asks. "We can't have people living in fear. This town is better than that." He rubs his beard and shoots a meaningful glance at Mrs. Evans when he notices she's seated on the porch.

I wonder what this will do to Steve's office space.

"You're right," Mama says. "We should keep this quiet till we know more."

"We're not keeping quiet," I say. "We need a community meeting. To keep people safe."

I think Mama is about to protest, but she doesn't.

"We'll keep watch," Officer Clyde says.

I point toward the police car. "You've been here up until tonight. What's that all about?"

"Tracy," Mama says.

"That's quite all right," Officer Clyde says. "Whoever did this must've been watching for an opportunity."

"Why pull back in the first place?" Steve asks.

"It's been two weeks. We don't have the manpower to keep a detail here forever. Best bet if Jamal comes home, and you fine people encourage that b—" He pauses. "You encourage that *young man* of yours to turn himself in."

"My brother wouldn't hurt anyone," I say.

"That's what court cases are for," Officer Clyde says. "Running don't point to innocence, if you ask me."

"Nobody—" I say.

"Let's focus on their safety," Steve says. "This is a serious threat to the Beaumont family."

Officer Clyde studies Beverly, who's inspecting the smoldering wooden cross. The note is now placed in a clear plastic evidence bag. Beverly takes a few photos. The irony of a cross being used for such a disgusting act sickens me.

"You haven't updated me about my break-in. This could be the same guy," Steve says. "We should be worried someone might be coming after the Beaumonts."

"He didn't do this," Officer Clyde says.

"How can you be certain?" I ask. "He could be dangerous."

"Because he's in our custody right now for questioning. Sheriff Brighton called him as soon as he got word that's who we were looking for."

Steve and I study each other. This must be news to Steve also.

"Is there a reason we weren't called?" I ask.

"I planned to update you in the morning. Then when I received word about this"—Officer Clyde points at the cross—"I made sure to aid Officer Ridges."

"If it wasn't him," Steve says, "we should be worried more people are involved."

"This won't happen again." Officer Clyde puts his hat on as he gets closer to inspect the damage with Beverly.

"How can you promise that?" Mr. Evans asks.

"We don't have Klan out here, probably some kids playing a joke—"

"This isn't a joke," I say. "You should check for prints. Look into this."

"I plan to." Beverly gives me a quick glance. "I've turned in Angela's phone I found out by the Pike."

I nod at the cover story she must have made up for me.

"There might be other suspects at least for a cross burning like this," Beverly says.

The same suspects floated to me, knowing that Richard Brighton was under arrest but his minions were free to take action like this.

"I'll take some nights watching the house." Beverly walks toward us.

"Not sure if we have the budget for that." Officer Clyde follows Beverly back to us.

"Seems to me you certainly had the budget to have someone watch the house for Jamal," Steve says.

Officer Clyde takes his hat off again and puts it to his side.

"I'll see if I can get overtime approved by the sheriff for tonight in case someone thinks about coming back. But you might want to stay away until things calm down."

"Thank you, Officer Clyde," Mama says.

Officer Clyde helps the firefighters put up the particle board we use during hurricanes over our broken window.

I take photos of the cross so I don't feel helpless, then move closer to the windows, but I can't get the image of the burning cross out of my mind. If it wasn't Richard Brighton, then who?

TAKING CHANCES

The house is nearly silent by midnight. The only other sounds are the soft click of Steve on his computer before he shuts it down and goes upstairs to Jamal's room. Mama's letting him sleep here for the night. It took some planning after the police left, but Pastor Jenkins from church agreed to help lead a meeting tomorrow evening at the community center where I hold my workshops.

Dean and I pace by the large kitchen window, hiding behind its pitch-blackness. Instead of the smell of Mama's kitchen, I'm overtaken by a damp, smoky smell that's seeped through the broken window. A stain that will be more than charred black grass outside.

I check my cell, watch the online confirmations for tomorrow's community meeting grow with each refresh. Hoping for a text from Jamal, but nothing. I send a few messages to Tasha, who's freaking out. Then text Quincy last, because I know he'll hear about it from Beverly.

I grab a glass of water at the sink, letting the water overrun before I notice how long I've been standing here.

My phone beeps and Dean glances over. Instinctually, I turn it over in case it's Jamal. Just another text from Tasha.

Come stay at my house. Bring Corinne and your mama.

Maybe tomorrow. Steve Jones is staying in Jamal's room. Bev is watching out.

This is scary. Stay safe.

I will. Love you.

Same.

☺

I tuck my phone in my pocket. Dean eases his arms cautiously around my shoulders, resting his head on top of mine. The clock ticking in the background reminds me that Dean will have to leave soon. I'm at least grateful that the uneasy feeling that was churning inside me, the one that screamed in fear but was overpowered by the need to be brave, has finally calmed down, like a smooth ocean wave after high tide. Rocky and shaky, but softening up with each faltering wave.

Air catches on my neck from Dean's even-patterned breathing as I sort through how to solve this all.

"When I saw Richard Brighton, I looked into his car while he was in another building. He had flyers recruiting white folks. Like he's rallying a hate group. Then this cross burning. Hear anything more from school?"

"No. You know people don't talk to me. Do you think Chris did this?"

"Who else? Before, when we didn't know who Richard was, it was between him and Chris, but now that we know it's his uncle, there's no other obvious suspects."

Dean takes another heavy breath, resting his chin on my shoulder now. "We won't find out tonight. Don't let it control you."

Tears escape. They travel down my cheek, and it's getting too difficult to breathe normally.

Dean holds me. He touches my face, tracing his thumbs down to my neck and then back along my cheek. I watch him, knowing I won't have to speak. I don't want him to pull away. He has a glint in his eye, watching me. Tears are now pouring out. His thumbs can't keep up, so he stops. The next tear trails down my face, and Dean kisses it away, then another.

I press into him as if I'm melting in his arms. He leans in to kiss me, and I don't stop him.

His lips are gentle, soft. He kisses me again, and this time I respond. Careful to not go too far, not to risk one of us pulling away. Making up for all the moments we'd never had the courage, never had the chance, never sure if our feelings for each other would be returned.

Upstairs there's a creaking noise, followed by a door opening, and we jump apart.

"It's midnight. Your mom's probably making sure I get back like I promised . . ."

"I know." I hold back an embarrassed smile. "I'll walk you to the door."

Dean takes my hand, making his way to our front door. Everything tells me Dean and I should only be friends. That's what I've convinced myself over the years, but what if I've been wrong?

Dean opens the door, and at first I think he's leaving, but then he pushes toward me and I'm pinned between the door and him. This time Dean doesn't move to kiss me first. I tug on his shirt, and that must be all that he needs before he kisses me again. This time he's not as gentle. And I'm not as fragile. This time he holds nothing back, rushing to me in desperate kisses. My body shaking, grateful for the door holding me up.

"You don't know how long I've wanted to kiss you like this," Dean says in hot, stuttering breaths.

I kiss him deeper, knowing we should stop, but it's not what I want. I want to feel better, without my brain in overdrive, thinking too hard about every situation, every reason I've told myself we can't be a thing. We can't happen. But each kiss tells me different.

When I'm confident he won't disappear, I hold his face. His breathing heavy. Our lips slowing down and my mind catching up to my body that's on fire. Aching not to stop and knowing I want to feel this good forever.

ONE DAY AT A TIME

I'm guessing I'm not the only one who doesn't sleep. The house feels unsettled, creaking with each shift—toilet flushing, fridge opening, lights flicking on and off.

Finally, when I smell breakfast, I go downstairs. Corinne sips juice while Mama reads the paper. I scrunch up my nose, confused at Steve cooking.

"Morning, Mama." I kiss her cheek, run my fingers over Corinne's black coils.

"Steve's making breakfast." Corinne grins.

"I see that," I say. "Don't burn my bacon."

Steve shakes his head.

I laugh because it's the kind of thing I'd say to Jamal. It breaks the heaviness weighing in my chest.

No one outside our family has ever been caught cooking in

our kitchen. I give Mama a puzzled look until I see the view out the window—a blackened char where the cross was set ablaze. The boarded-up window. Mama needs a break.

"Tracy, better hurry up," Mama says. "We leaving soon. You coming with us? I can drop you off."

"I'll take Jamal's car to school." With everything going on, I need to be able to get around.

"You sure it's safe to be alone? Steve's riding with us, so we can all leave together."

"It's daylight; Beverly's still here. I want to get the word out about the community meeting. I'll meet you there after school."

"I wanna go to the meeting," Corinne says.

Mama's face goes tight, like it's not the time for this conversation. Downtown hasn't been friendly, and if I was getting looks through town, being pushed around at school, Corinne must've been, too. Corinne's been through a lot; the community meeting might scare her. Guilt sizzles through me because I didn't think how things have been affecting Corinne.

"We'll have a separate playroom for the kids. It'll be fun," Mama says.

"I guess it'll be all right." Corinne's face droops.

"The meeting will be long. Lots of people talking," I say. "I'll fill you in, though. All the big highlights."

"Yeah? That'd be nice." Corinne gives a half smile, then takes a bite of food.

I know she's trying to process all this. Just like when I was her age, eavesdropping on all the hushed conversations Mama had about Daddy. Corinne might be young, but she notices how when she enters a room it sucks our conversation dry about what's happening. Jamal used to be the one to smooth things over.

Corinne was born after Daddy was sentenced, so she didn't know what life was like with Daddy. But she did know with Jamal. He filled in in Daddy's absence. A big brother to protect her. He made sure she could look up to him. At her school events, all her friends loved seeing Jamal. He'd race them at her playground. He never treated her dropoffs like a chore, not like me. Jamal was the string tying us all together. Making sure the hole wouldn't be so empty that if Daddy came back it'd still be impossible for him to fill. Now I see that hole turn gaping. I hate that Corinne will have to carry that shadow behind her, those invisible chains that say who her daddy was. Who her brother was. I don't want that to swallow her up, replacing her with somebody new. I just hope it's someone with armor, not someone who can break. Not someone like Tasha or myself. But someone better.

I get up and grab paper to write a note to Corinne that I'll slip in her lunch box, just like Jamal would if he was here and this went down.

Have a good day, Bighead. I Love you.

I go back to the table to finish up breakfast. Mama sends Corinne upstairs to brush her teeth before they leave. Steve finally sits down.

"Have either of you heard from Jamal, since last night?" Steve asks.

There's tension in the air. No one wanting to put the words out loud that we've been in touch with him at all. The trust that our house is sacred, gone. Mama's eyes are wide, hopeful, but she lowers them when I don't respond. Steve doesn't know us well, but even he's picked up that our family is tight. Jamal might be on the run, but he wouldn't forget about us. He'd be worried if word got to him. I hope this means he'll reach out.

I check my phone. Nothing.

"You think they'll catch whoever did this last night?" I ask.

Steve takes a bite of food, then looks up. "Hopefully, when they question Richard Brighton, they'll find out who he's affiliated with. Could be more suspects to look into."

"He's family to them. You think much will come out of his arrest?"

"He was taken into custody for questioning. If he's released after a break-in, we'll know exactly what side the police are on." Steve takes a sip of coffee.

"Why do you think they did this last night?" I ask.

Steve pauses, then looks at Mama. "Was James harassed when news came out he was going into business with Mark Davidson?"

"A bit," Mama says. "It wasn't easy fitting in a few months after we moved here and it became clear we were staying."

"What kind of things were happening before the Davidsons were killed?"

I sit up straight. I don't remember much about before, just everything that fell out after.

"Phone calls. Then hang-ups. Cold shoulders out in town. But nothing we weren't used to," Mama says.

"Was he worried about going into business with Mark Davidson?"

"James never worried about nothing." Mama laughs. "He said the land was there to be built on, but people were too scared to buy it up. If he didn't do it, someone else would eventually. When he explained it like that, what could I say?"

"James should have told me about this," Steve says.

"Told you what?" Mama says. "If the murders had anything to do with the Klan, then they would have killed James, not Mark and his wife."

All those visits, talking about the case, Daddy never mentioned any of this. I wonder what else he might be hiding. Steve stares at the boarded-up window, looking like he's having the same thought.

Mama takes another bite and doesn't say more. Then she grabs her plate to clean up.

"Come on now, Corinne, I got to get to work," Mama yells up the stairs.

"Are you going to ask my daddy about this?" I ask Steve.

"I am." His mouth is a thin line.

"Good," I say.

"He might have kept things to himself to protect you all. You ever seen any harassment?"

"Just about the case," I say. "People driving by, name-calling. But all things that were related to the trial."

"There might not have been a need to bother you all once your dad was convicted."

"But now . . ."

"Now your dad is represented by an organization known to help those wrongfully convicted. And there could be something bigger going on with your dad's case."

"Connected to my brother?"

"I don't know about that. But you all weren't visible, or a threat. Until—"

"The interview Jamal did. Then Angela being killed and you coming to town to work on my daddy's case."

Steve doesn't respond. It only makes me worry more about Jamal. Steve clears his dishes, then meets Mama and Corinne by the door.

I stand up, pull out my phone, and log on to the community meeting invite. Refreshing the page for an update on attendance to the meeting, I hope that folks show. It's one thing for people to say they're planning on showing up, a whole other thing when the day comes. A piece of me wants to pray for Jamal to be there, hanging in the back of the room. But he can't. With each day he's farther and farther away—never more so than last night, when our sense of safety was stripped away by the sound of shattering glass, the flash of bright orange, and the flames waving among the shadows of a cross.

EAGLE HAS LANDED

I step out of the shower and get ready for school. As I do, I note a sound downstairs. I'm supposed to be alone, but the bones of the house scream: *intruder.*

At first, I wave it off to the house adjusting to the heat, but the creak repeats. I peek outside. Beverly's patrol car is long gone.

The back door slams. I jump up, race outside. There's movement by some bushes before the trail reaches the trees. My eyes skitter around cautiously so I don't run blindly through the woods. I know my way around, but also how easy it is for someone to lie low in the shadows to catch me by surprise. Someone from the Brotherhood. Never mind that, hope that it's Jamal propels me toward what might be an ambush.

On the run, the dry grass scratches at my ankles. I reach the trees; shadows and dark patches block my ability to see far. I enter, and ten steps in, I'm instantly engulfed, struggling to keep up with a person zigzagging through the woods.

A flash of a white shirt catches my attention. My throat tightens with fear, but I don't slow down, moving so fast my feet barely touch the rough and cracked debris on the ground. My arms pump hard like Jamal taught me.

The crack of a branch breaking in the distance steers my movement. I follow the sound, pushing my fears aside. Allow nostalgia to fill me instead. We pounded across this grass so much as kids it stopped growing and created this trail. I'm at home out here.

Memories of hot summer days flood me. Times we knew our parents were out working and we could spend the day here. We'd break away through the trees, dipping and diving, running to an overgrown section. Make our way through the woods and eventually crash at an old shack with busted-out windows. It was high up on the trail and became our lookout spot to everything below.

I should've thought of it sooner.

Jamal.

Of course. The way this person is snaking through the woods, they're running with precision.

Quincy said Jamal wouldn't go far, but he never knew about this old place. It's Jamal's and my secret.

At the thought of finding Jamal, I run faster until I reach a break in the trees. The shack still stands. Neglected, with paint chipped away from years of rain, sun, and storms. The windows shaded by old, tattered pillowcases and bedsheets.

My breath goes heavy. Feet hollering, hot and burning, but not in as much pain as my aching heart for Jamal.

I look behind me, confirm I didn't bring trouble for Jamal. All clear, I touch the shack. My fingers crumble the paint, wood splinters digging into my skin.

When I'm certain that I'm completely alone, I go around the back and peek through a side window.

The door handle is kicked in, so I enter.

I'm overwhelmed with stale, dusty air, years of the shack dying inside with no one there. I want to scream out Jamal's name in victory, like we would as kids playing hide-and-go-seek with Corinne. I wish she were with me now.

My fingers touch along the yellowed, lined walls as I walk across the half-rotten floors that were damaged by a leak from the roof. I pass a kerosene lamp hanging on a rusty hook. The dust swept away, recently used. I notice a small table with newspapers, the dates as recent as a week ago. I steady my breath, heart beating fast, then go to the second door that's ajar. You can tell the foundation's cracked and the door can't stay put. A Texas wind rushing under doors and through windows would be strong enough to open it. But I hope that was Jamal and not some storm.

With the light touch of a hand, I push the door and see the broad shoulders of someone sitting on the floor in a makeshift bed. His back is turned against me. Hands over his head, rubbing it, with his black-and-red headphones he's taped the cord to stay in place.

Typical Jamal, in his own head—when the whole world is looking for him.

"Jamal." I muster a whisper. The ache builds in the back of my throat.

I found him.

Since he's been gone, it's like he's been a ghost. Swept up away from us, almost worse than Daddy being gone. Because at least we could see Daddy weekly.

Jamal tips one headphone off his ear and stays real still before he gets up to look out the window.

"Jamal."

Jamal jumps and whirls, then studies me, and it's like he sees a ghost, too. He flips his headphones all the way off, the cord dangling around his neck. I wait for his response. Anger. Happiness.

He leans in a bit like he's had the music on so loud he doesn't know if he's missed something I said.

"Anyone follow you?" He looks past me, worried I'm not alone. I grip my fingers on the door handle, tense.

"No," I say. "I don't think so. You were so far ahead. I checked. No one else was in sight."

"Well?" Jamal opens his arms wide, then lets a big old smile out. He looks like Daddy.

I run to his arms, and they wrap around me. The rush from finding him settles inside me. Survival. Always in survival mode, keeping on the move, so the impact of real life doesn't leave me paralyzed. All so a moment like this can crash into me. It practically knocks me over.

"You been here this whole time?"

"Only this week, since the house detail stopped, and I knew they'd stop checking the woods. I couldn't stay at Quincy's, so I kept out in the fields by the highway, got supplies at the convenience store that's busy off the 55. I got the paper there to see what the cops were saying and see what I needed to do to prove my innocence. When my photo kept hitting the front page, I knew I needed to lay low."

I study him, his eyes sunken in. He's been gone fifteen days now, but it feels like so much longer.

"How'd you find me? I was in the woods before you even left the gate."

Jamal's shoulders relax as he lets go of me and goes to the window, moving the makeshift curtain slightly open to peek out again.

"I wanted to catch a closer sight of who ran from the house. You scared the hell out of me."

He gives me a look but must know better than to give me a hard time. He left us.

"You ran in the woods like you were born out there. All I could think about was us racing up here. I knew it had to be you."

Jamal closes the curtains and takes a seat on an old blanket I recognize from our attic. I move a book out of the way and sit beside him.

"I heard the fire truck last night, then saw the flames. I almost came home until I saw the patrol car."

"It was Beverly," I say. "She was watching out for us last night. Why'd you come this morning?"

"Thought you were long gone to school, left with Mama. I had to see for myself what happened. Charge my phone so I could reach you." He lifts up his burner.

"I've been blowing up your phone," I say.

"Battery drained. After your texts about the photos and the march, I started searching for motives. How it connects to Angela going to the Pike."

"Thought you were hurt or ignoring me. You could've come home. I wouldn't've ratted."

"I couldn't risk it. And Mama's been staying up lately. I can see her light on every night."

I nod. I've heard her pacing.

"How's Ma? Corinne? I saw a lot of people outside, but not Corinne."

"I took Corinne to her room so she wouldn't have to see it." I go over with Jamal what happened last night.

"Pops will be upset when he hears about this. You seen him lately? He ain't mad, is he?"

Jamal's eyes well. Leaving Mama, us, was a big deal for Jamal, and he would've never wanted to disappoint Daddy.

"Mama's going to visit him before a community meeting I'm holding at the center." I touch Jamal's hand. "He's not mad, Jamal. None of us are. We're scared."

Jamal looks away, wiping under his eyes.

"We got a lawyer. Innocence X, they answered my letters."

"You serious?" Jamal grabs on to my arms. His face is pure joy. "I thought you were playing so I'd answer your texts and turn myself in."

I feel that excitement inside me like I did in the beginning, before the cross burning.

"They're filing paperwork for appeals. There's so much to tell you." I bite my lip, not sure where to begin.

"How close are they?" Jamal nervously rubs his fist.

"Closer than we've ever been."

"That's good, T. That's real good. Daddy can be out, take care of Mama now." He puts his arm around my shoulders. He's drifting off away from us. Like he can let go now. It makes me angry.

"They could help you, too," I whisper, because I don't know how Steve can help without knowing the truth yet.

"Nah. They can't help me. Not right now anyway. Pops's time's running out."

A virtual image of a clock above both of us. The one that's been looming since the day Daddy was sentenced. Jamal isn't thinking about himself, just Daddy.

I don't know what else to say, so I ask what I've been waiting to hear. "What happened with Angela?"

Jamal runs his hands over his face. "We'd been seeing each other since after homecoming. Wasn't serious . . . until it was. She was going to break up with Chris, but then she suspected something strange when his uncle started spending more time with him. She'd gone a few times to the Pike to see what Chris was doing there."

"Richard Brighton. He's been watching Daddy's lawyer. Ran into him just yesterday, found flyers in his car about a white hate group he's recruiting."

"Damn. You doing too much." Jamal runs his hands over his scruffy half beard that's grown in.

"We have to find out who killed Angela."

"Still. I don't like it."

"This goes with my theory, though. Explains why she was there that night," I say. "The SD card is in Beverly's hands now."

Jamal gives me a hard look.

"I downloaded everything onto my phone first." I put my hands up in defense to explain I didn't just give everything away.

I tell him more about my suspicions around Chris and Scott not wanting people to know they were at the rally where the girl was shot in the crowd.

"Chris didn't like that Angela supported your stories in 'Tracy's Corner,'" Jamal says. "He thought your articles were anti-police. When I got my Susan Touric interview, he wanted Angela to stop it because he thought I'd play the sympathy card about Dad and blame the police for a botched investigation."

"That the real reason you both were upset after the show?" The pieces I'd been trying to put together are starting to line up.

Jamal doesn't meet my eyes. My throat constricts. My lie about having suspects was tangled up with Jamal and Angela's strategy to find the truth about what might be an underground hate group. I don't know if I can forgive myself. Jamal turns away until his emotions settle and he can speak again. He clenches his fist in front of his mouth.

"Angela was supposed to meet me after work. She never showed. She was like that. I thought she was mad you walked in on us together, so I didn't worry at first. I waited at Quincy's."

My heart races. Finally I'm hearing more about what happened that night.

"Angela called me to meet her out by the Pike. When I got there, Chris was down by the dock. That's when I saw Angela on the ground."

Jamal's voice is shaky. I can see how much that night messed him up to see Angela, and maybe nothing he could do about it.

"Chris yelled at me like I did something. He was freaking out. I was trying to get past him to Angela and he was freaking out, so I decked him. We started fighting." Jamal chokes on his words. "I got past Chris. That's when I saw it—blood seeping from the back of her head. Chris kept saying it was *my* fault. Angela's eyes were open, but she was gone. I yelled at Chris to get help. He ran to his truck. I laid my jacket over her. Then I realized he was driving away. I could hear a car coming off the highway."

Jamal faces me, his eyes clouding and guilt washing over him.

"Why did you run instead of wait for the police?"

"She was already . . . gone. I was out of my mind, not thinking about my jacket. Just knowing I didn't want to leave her like that, but also knowing I had to get outta there. They weren't going to believe me . . . Chris left. And he'd been saying it was my fault. I realized he probably killed her, and him leaving meant I'd be the main suspect once he got to his dad." Tears fill his eyes. "Sometimes I feel like we're cursed."

"It's not your fault," I say, even though I know the feeling. We've never caught a break. All those years praying, going to church, looking over our shoulders when we didn't do anything wrong.

"Nah, you don't hear me. See all these books." Jamal points around to the scattered books I hadn't noticed are from the collections we've rotated in and out to Daddy. W. E. B. Du Bois, James Baldwin, Thurgood Marshall, Michelle Alexander, Ta-Nehisi Coates. Then a week's worth of newspapers.

"They all say the same thing over and over again—it doesn't matter when they were written. The laws might change, the systems might look different. All these books say what the problem is. Working ten times harder to get half. Seems to me, all the blood that's been spilled ain't our debt. But we paying it over and over again. And the world acts like there's something wrong with us. They hate us so damn much."

Jamal's voice is cracking, desperate words that have been suffocating him.

"Four hundred years, and we still ain't American to them, T. All that blood. *We* built America. Black labor built the greatest nation in the world for free. They ripped us from our family then, and they do it again with new laws disguised as change. I'll be in prison doing that labor for free."

"But we have a superweapon: Innocence X. A real chance. Not like before."

"If I turn myself in, I'm getting the death penalty. Unless what, I plead? Unless I say I did it, I killed Angela? Then I get what, life without parole?"

"It won't be like Daddy."

"It will be!" Jamal's hand grazes over the newspapers and they whoosh, floating to the floor. "Them cops weren't ever going to think I didn't kill . . . Angela." Jamal gets choked up. "Not when the sheriff's son says different. Not when I ran. Not with Angela gone."

"But you had to know . . . leaving your jacket . . . they'd come after you."

"I was in shock, seeing Angela." Jamal chokes up again. "When I got home, I cleaned myself and was planning to call in like I was worried about Angela, that she'd gone to the Pike. Then they'd find her. If they asked about the jacket, I was gonna say I left it in her car. It was a stupid idea, but it was a plan. But all that fell apart when the police showed up before I could get my story out. And the first to arrive was the sheriff. I knew Chris must've pinned it on me, and I wouldn't stand a chance."

A hot flush creeps up my face. I touch my neck like I can stop it. My questions being answered, terrifying to think Jamal went through all of that. No wonder he ran.

"We need to get you to meet with Steve Jones from Innocence X. He'll know what to do."

"I can't risk it. If the police find me, I'm done. And if they even think you might know, you're in danger."

Jamal doesn't budge; he's not going to stop hiding when we don't have any evidence yet to prove his innocence.

"I'll call Steve—he'll know what to do. Then we go from there."

"Then what, I walk home? If they find out you know where I am, they'll be all over looking for me."

"What, then?"

"Can you get hold of Mandy? She's the only one I can think of that Angela would've told about what she was doing."

I swallow hard. Angela was going to let me in on her exposé but never got to it. Mandy knew a little, but I don't think she knows as much as Jamal's hoping for.

"I'll talk to Mandy again. I got a little bit from her before. She was scared, but she doesn't think you did it, Jamal."

Jamal's eyes soften.

"We got a community meeting this evening about the cross burning. Then I'll track down Mandy. If she speaks out, saying you wouldn't hurt Angela, maybe we can get Beverly to safely bring you in for questioning. They can't do anything in front of a whole station. The entire police force can't be crooked."

"Oh, they can't?" Jamal huffs out.

"They can't." I look away because I honestly don't know who to trust. I just know Jamal can't keep hiding out here. He's gonna get caught.

Jamal's eyes settle like he's thinking hard. Then he tightens the laces in his shoes, knotting them up like he always did before a big race. He must know as much as I do, that he's got few options other than running the rest of his life if he doesn't try to find out the truth. Jamal can't run forever.

You can't outrun the inevitable.

LET THE SAINTS SAY AMEN

The community center is bustling. Every seat taken, looking like Easter Sunday at church. I take a glance around the room. In the middle sit Tasha and her younger sister, Monica. Tasha smiles. I quickly text her, since it's hard to reach her seat.

Thank you for coming

☺

Pastor Jenkins stands in front, next to Lucinda Scott, the community director. Seeing Pastor Jenkins takes me back to times Mama tried to describe what court would be like.

Ten-year-old me didn't know what to expect until she explained that court was gonna be like church. I felt better because I knew church. Sunday was all-day dedication. Monday, you drop off dishes from Sunday service. Tuesday, Bible study. Wednesday, choir. Thursday, the good choir. Friday, Savior's night. Saturday, cleanup.

And court was supposed to be like a sinner's testimony: truth on a throne.

The way God's message reaches the pastor and spreads like wildfire until it touches someone's soul at the altar for prayer circles or getting saved. Then you'd have as long as your truth-telling was gonna be.

I kept waiting for the judge to catch the Holy Ghost. Get all swept up like the hurricane that took everything away from us. Then we could pretend we never stepped foot on that evacuation bus to Texas, and Daddy wouldn't have met Mark and Cathy Davidson.

But court didn't resemble church. No one riddled with guilt came bursting into the courtroom asking for forgiveness. And after, we didn't have a church home anymore. Not the same, anyway. After the sentencing, we were pushed to the margins. Whispered about. It took a long time to grab that place again for Mama. I never fully did. Not again. Not the same. Instead, I ran to the community center for my workshops a few years later. Never as full, but at least filled with purpose.

Lucinda waves us to reserved seats in the front. I follow Steve and Mama, passing Quincy, who gently reaches for my arm, stopping me.

"You okay?"

"I think so." I give him a half hug.

"Let me know if you need anything." Quincy squeezes my hand.

"Jamal can't keep hiding in that shack," I whisper to Quincy. He's the only one I trusted to share I've seen Jamal. "It's not safe. We gotta find a way to clear him, get his side of the story out."

"I came by. Last night. I was thinking I would stay there, you know, in Jamal's room. Watch out for y'all."

"Why didn't you come in?" I think about last night, my kissing Dean.

"I felt weird about it. Didn't want to just pop up, you know. I stuck around with Bev." Quincy looks away. Dean didn't say anything about seeing Quincy when he left. Maybe he was gone by then.

Quincy leans in. "How Jamal look?"

"Tired. Hungry. Needs a shave, but good. I dropped him off more supplies, but he can't stay there long. It's a miracle he hasn't been caught yet."

"Did he tell you anything?"

"Everything points to Chris and the meetings at the Pike. I haven't heard from Mandy. Maybe we confront Chris again, or his uncle?"

"That's dangerous, T. You gotta step back."

"Someone's already after my family."

"Right now, they're giving you warnings. If they think you know what Angela knew, you might be next."

My phone beeps.

It's Dean.

Can we talk later? I'm back row.

I look out to Dean, who gives me a small wave. I nod, face getting hot. Embarrassed about last night now that I see him.

Ok.

I glance at Quincy, who has a twinkle of mischief in his eye. I put my phone down, wiping any expression off my face. It doesn't work. Quincy's all up in my business.

"He's in love with you. Did you know that?"

"Who?"

"Who? It's obvious." Quincy shifts his head toward Dean.

"You watching me?" I look away to play it off.

"You showcasing your business everywhere." Quincy shoves his hands in his pocket.

"We're friends," I say.

"Uh-huh, right."

"We are." I punch his arm playfully.

"Poor guy doesn't even know what he got himself into, does he?"

"Okay, stop. I know you ain't talking. Your dating calendar stays packed."

"You know I be out there."

"Oh." I make quotation marks with my fingers. " 'You be out there.' Yeah, I've noticed."

"I didn't mean it like that." Quincy bites at his lip, and I swear he's embarrassed.

"Nothing serious. Too many expectations. Always forgetting birthdays, Valentine's, the things good boyfriends are supposed to do. Bet Dean never forgot your birthday."

"You damn right," I say. "But that's because I don't let him."

"You're such a pain in the ass." Quincy laughs.

I chuckle. Then Mama catches my eye—she's waving me to my seat.

"Come with me if I hear from Mandy?"

"Bet." Quincy walks to the side of the room, closer to Beverly.

More people continue to filter in, so extra seats are pulled out from the storage closet. Officer Clyde and Beverly stand next to each other, surveying the room. They position themselves on opposite sides when the doors close, and Dr. Scott goes on the stage. I take my seat with Mama.

"Welcome," Dr. Scott says. "There's room, keep coming. Raise your hand if you have a seat next to you. Before we begin, let's hear from Pastor Jenkins from the First Ebenezer Baptist Church."

"Thank you, Dr. Scott. We here today because our brothers and sisters need us, Lord." Pastor Jenkins prays over my family.

My eyes flutter, tempted between listening to opening prayer and keeping watch.

Pastor Jenkins finishes, and Beverly takes the mic at the front of the room. She's greeted warmly because she was raised in Ebenezer Church.

Beverly shares the state of things, what happened last night and that although it probably won't happen again, we should be keeping an eye out. Lots of heads nod while she talks, until she mentions that the Galveston County police force is asking residents to be careful as they conduct their investigation. She opens up the floor.

An older Black man with a Kangol cap stands up. "We can't live like this."

A man speaks from the other side of the room. "First it's a cross, then what?"

"Yes!" More shouts from the crowd.

"Why aren't there arrests already?"

"We've begun an investigation." Officer Clyde steps in, standing next to Beverly. The crowd grows uneasy. Energy shifting.

"An investigation?" the man who spoke first repeats. "Then what are you going to do when you don't find anyone? They said they'd burn a body."

"We believe it's an empty threat," Officer Clyde says.

The crowd erupts. Angry. It's chaotic. Parents hug their children close, some pacing in the back. I'm glad I'm not the only one upset by his words. Too often I've felt like we've just been fighting this battle ourselves.

"Is this a threat to all of us or someone looking for the boy?" An older woman in the middle of the room raises her arm while she speaks.

That stings. I knew there'd be some blame on our family, but I wasn't ready for this today. This just adds more reasons Jamal should stay in hiding.

Beverly taps Officer Clyde on the shoulder, relieving him at the mic.

"I know you all are scared," Beverly says. "I was, too. That's why I'm here today. Me and Officer Clyde. We don't want anyone scared, but we need your help to be vigilant. Contact the police if you see something suspicious."

"Call the police?" Murmurs rise, hesitant voices repeating the same sentiment.

"Call. Me," Beverly says. "Cross burning has no place here. It's possible someone's angry over the death of Angela Herron, placing the blame on the Beaumonts. Regardless, we can't take chances it won't happen again."

"Or something worse," Quincy calls out.

"Or something worse," Beverly says.

Officer Clyde looks like he wants to address the room, but Beverly has it more in control than he could, so he must know it's better to stay in the background.

Beverly fields more questions. Community members sharing their stories, speculations. Some angry. Some see it as an isolated incident. Translation: It's Daddy's fault. Jamal's fault.

It burns inside to hear a crowd filled with confusion and putting the blame on my family.

Beverly points to me; it's time to address the crowd. I have my comments folded in my hand, but I don't open them when I get to the microphone. I speak from the heart.

"I know you're all scared. I'm real scared, too. My mama—" I point to Mama. She's gripping her purse tight. "My mama's scared. Even though she don't let y'all know. But someone's out there who might know more about what's going on with my brother, Jamal, and my daddy, James Beaumont. Some of you even testified as an alibi for him, so you know my daddy wasn't where they say he was."

There's a hush in the room. Each person hanging on to my words. My breath is labored, emotional, but I'm trying to hold it in because Daddy's bigger than life to me. Bigger than anything in our house, our family. He takes up so much space, and he's not even here. The way they watch, I know it's because they feel bad for me. For Mama. But the room is filled with those who also don't know how to feel about my daddy.

There are moments when my thoughts are a betrayal to him. Uncertainty wrapping itself around me, poisoning my mind. But out here, visible to the world, there are no doubts about my daddy's innocence.

"Last night that cross burning wasn't just a message to my family. A statement was being made to *our* community. People outing themselves to let us all know what place *we* supposed to take. There's a hate group growing in our community. Recruiting people. We can't let our town, our home, be threatened by violence. By hatred. My father went to prison, not because of guilt, but because it was easy to think an *outsider* like a Black man killed the Davidsons. Now that generational curse is passing down to my brother. The son . . . of a 'killer' must be a killer."

My voice catches. I take a breath to calm myself.

"But we can stop it. We can be vigilant and look out for each other. And now my father has a second chance. Some of you know about Innocence X and what they do. Well, a representative is here tonight because he's working on my daddy's appeal. Many of you were here when my daddy went through his trial. Some of you even shared or tried to share information with the police, but they didn't follow up. This is your chance to right that wrong. Retrace that time seven years ago. Every memory is important. He's a good man. An innocent man. And he has less than two hundred and fifty days to live. If you know something, anything, please help us free my daddy. Free James."

The audience rises, fists up, and chants, *"Free James. Free James. Free James."*

I'm taken aback by the crowd being moved. Hope fills me up, and I'm glad I took the moment that was supposed to be about last night to focus on Daddy. When the crowd quiets, I introduce Steve and give out his number. Frantically, people take down his information. Then I end by sharing the dates for my next Know Your Rights workshops.

Pastor Jenkins closes out, using this as an opportunity to highlight the church, so I dip out into the hallway to catch my breath.

I spot Dean. I know him too well. He's never been good about pretending things weren't the way they were. I can see he's burning to talk about what happened, in a lot more detail. He follows me into the hallway, catches me by surprise, and kisses me on the cheek.

I step back. "Not here."

He bites that side lip, and his dimple appears and disappears.

"You think this will help with catching whoever was sending that message to us last night?" I say.

"I hope so. If people can stop making it about themselves. It was driving me crazy that everyone was making it about them," Dean says. "All the complaints about the police. Why can't they focus on you and your family? Y'all are the ones that were hurt."

I pause. I also wanted everyone to focus on how to help my family. But I get it. Trusting someone who's been harassing all our lives to now stop harassment from escalating isn't easy. This isn't one moment in time, but a longer one that bleeds in and out of all our lives. Our history of Blackness in America. Dean doesn't get that. I watch him, wondering if he ever will.

Dean takes my hand, leading me away from the doors and around the corner, like we're a couple. I take my hand back. Not here. Not now. I have too many questions, like will his mom make things harder for us? And really, I want to get back to the community meeting, hear what people have to say. I wish he didn't come so I could focus on this and not him.

"You okay?" Dean asks.

I'm about to answer him, but then I realize he's talking about what happened before our kiss—the attack. A sick billowing feeling rushes through my stomach.

I nod unconvincingly. "You?"

There's more to what I'm asking him. It's one word that wants to drill down to the scare last night, our kiss, my uncertainty.

Dean doesn't answer. My eyes well; it hurts too much. I want to run from facing a decision.

"Will you ride with me so we can talk . . . about last night?" Dean's eyes carry so much pain, hurt from me pushing him away. It stings to watch.

"I'll meet you after." I tug his shirt when he looks away. "I promise."

Dean nods.

Last night, Dean was everything I'd been waiting for, but then at the community meeting he was the farthest thing from my thoughts. All I could think about was rushing back to the community meeting. The flutter from seeing Quincy. I swallow hard because I don't have an answer about Dean or Quincy—who I can't seem to shake.

WILL WE EVER BE
THE SAME?

Dean hangs by his steps, so I perch myself on top of the rail. I mist up at the carvings DE + TB TAKE THE WORLD and run my finger around our initials. I can always tell what kind of mood his mama is in based on whether we go straight inside the house or hang out on the porch.

I'm worried things will never be the same. There's weird tension now since the community meeting. I don't know how our kiss might affect our friendship, but I also don't want to run away from facing the truth. I take a long breath as Dean keeps his head down.

"Ready to talk?" A lump builds in my throat. The things Quincy was saying about Dean have my head spinning.

"We kiss, then today you push me away. I don't know what you want," Dean says.

"What do you want me to say?"

"So, you regret last night?" Dean runs his hands through his hair. I don't answer fast enough. His eyes get wide.

"I don't know."

"God, Tracy." Dean gives a heavy sigh. "Please don't act like you regret it. Don't say you take it—"

"I don't. I don't take it back. But there's so much going on right now . . . What do you want, Dean?"

"I wanted you last night." Dean's lips quirk, and my heart races.

"I did, too . . ."

"But now?"

I've loved Dean for so long, but that love was something different. When we crossed that line, it didn't feel bad; it felt safe. And last night, I needed safe. Now I know I need something different.

"Do we have to have an answer about us?" I look at Dean. "There's so much going on right now. I don't want you to be weird around me now. I need you. As . . . the friend you've always been."

"I'm not in a rush." Dean swallows hard. "A lot is going on."

"Then let's forget this for now and get back to normal? Because I need normal right now." I'm not sure that's true. But one thing that I do know I need: my friend Dean. I don't want to lose him.

"Sure, I want to forget it all . . . because our kiss was terrible."

"What?" I slap his arm. "Terrible? Who was terrible?"

"It wasn't for you? I practically had nightmares."

"Dean." I dig my elbow into his ribs.

Dean wraps his arms tight around me. "How could anything with us be terrible? You're too easy to mess with, you know that?"

"Well, thank you for clearing that up." I dig my elbow into him again. I know there's a lot more we should say.

"I don't take it back, though. I love you," Dean says. "I always have."

There's a silence that sits between us. I want Dean's words to swallow up the pain that's been suffocating me. His eyes look heavy because I don't make him feel better. It breaks me seeing him like this.

My throat burns from holding in the words *Dean loves me*. I knew it. But I'd been in such denial that Dean would always have a bigger piece of his heart for our friendship. That it was so big, there would be no more room for anything else. All of this runs around in my head while Dean waits for me to say something.

"I . . . I love you, too. It's so hard with everything going on. If we didn't have the attack at the house, would you feel the same? What about your mom?"

"If you'd be with me, I'd choose you, Tracy. I'd always choose you over her, over anyone."

"I'm not asking you to choose." I pause to breathe in again. "I want to know you won't change your mind."

Another silence takes us over. I wish we didn't start talking about it at all, just moved on. Because this is so much harder.

"If we were together, would you tell your mom?"

Dean pauses before saying, "Probably."

"Two important questions: (a) Will she ground you forever? And (b) Will she kick Steve out of the loft?"

"I don't know what she'd do." Dean breathes out. "But I don't know if I could hold it in. I shouldn't have to lie. It's not how I'm built."

I don't respond. The world will always try to push us apart. It already feels like it's happening. Because I don't feel that pull to Dean the way I feel like I should. It's a bond through friendship, maybe nothing more.

Dean's mom calls for him. I follow him inside, and he motions for me to wait in his dad's study. Mr. Evans'll be closing up the shop tonight.

I notice there are open boxes all over the desk.

My curiosity building—Mr. Evans is always tidy—I peek inside.

A gasp catches in my throat.

I tear through the box in disbelief. Stuck, shaking my head and mouthing, *No, no, no,* as I try to convince myself the image isn't real.

I think I might be sick.

SECRETS DON'T STAY HIDDEN FOREVER

With trembling fingers, I pick up a black-and-white photograph. A man hanging by a noose. His feet splayed, and a bloated face much darker than the rest of his body. A burning cross next to him. Like the one that was staked in front of my house. Men in white sheets stand beneath the dead man. They are surrounded by women and children. All white. Those without hoods are beaming like it's the Fourth of July.

Dean enters the den with a wide smile. I don't return it. His smile shrivels.

"What's wrong?" Dean rushes to me.

"I don't know why I looked. I . . . I . . . Did you know about this?" My hand shakes as I hold out the photo.

Dean takes it from me and gasps. I feel sick inside all over again as I watch the horror cross Dean's face. He drops it as though he's been burned, then sifts through the box.

Dean picks the photo up again and looks closer, then points to a girl near what must be the Grand Wizard's feet. Another slightly older girl locking arms with her. He flips the photo over.

In my shock, I didn't even notice a list of names with a date, November 17, 1979.

"I think . . . I think this is my mom."

I shut my eyes. Sickened.

"And if that's my mom as a little girl, that means this is my grandfather." His voice cracks when he points the Klan leader out.

"I can't . . . Tracy. This can't be real. Why was she there?" Dean looks through more of the boxes, and I can see he's putting the pieces together.

"You don't even know if it's—"

"It's her." Dean bends over and grabs another box. This time he pulls out a white cloak. "And this is my grandfather's?"

Dean's mom comes downstairs, calling for him. I cover the cry escaping my lips. Dean runs out of the study to cut her off. I can tell he knows that now is not the time for me to see his mother.

I've never been so close to something like this before. In this town I call home, a man was lynched, and people are living here who were complicit. Involved. Dean's parents knew it. I think back on the way Dean's dad stood by the burning cross on our lawn and glanced over at Mrs. Evans. He'd known all along who had been in the Klan.

The white cloak haunts me with its bloody history. The fear

it shaped, and the lies they told to incite terror toward Black people. My stomach's nauseous; shivers run down my spine.

The door opens.

Dean. Alone. Thank God.

"Put it away." Dean shoves the cloak back into a box with a heavy weight of shame.

"Has this stuff always been here?"

I'm hoping he says no. That he's never seen it before, because then I could try and believe that Dean's dad wasn't involved.

"I remember my mom having boxes of my grandpa's stuff delivered after he passed away. She wanted his things, so my dad helped gather them for her."

Dean keeps a slight distance, like he wants to touch me but can't.

"Does this mean my mom's involved with the Klan? My dad?" Dean puts his hands to his head. "What does that make me, Tracy? Klan legacy?"

I think about Daddy, how the town accused him so effortlessly. My anger grows. I'm not sure I can contain it.

"They couldn't be involved," Dean continues. "I've never heard my dad say one racist thing in my life. Hell, he voted for Obama. Klan wouldn't do that, would they?"

"I don't think he's Klan." I sigh. Mr. Evans has always been good to us. I wouldn't think someone active in the Klan would have dinner over at our house, much less hire my mama.

"But my grandpa was, wasn't he?" Dean pauses. "And my

mom . . . it's no secret, her thoughts. She's said things, things about our worlds being too far apart. But nothing that would lead me to something this . . . heinous. She can't think like they do, can she?"

There's nothing else to explain the robe and the photos of his grandpa. His mom was certainly raised around it.

"Why do you think your dad was pulling these out?" I try to keep my voice flat, even though I can feel a scream building. I have to stay calm.

"What happened at your house could've triggered him. Like he wanted to get rid of it? Or he thinks he can find out who did it by going through the boxes?" Dean's voice sounds hopeful, but it teeters and cracks, because he's not convinced. Neither am I.

"He said he'd get Steve information. He could've already done that. If he has, that's good, right?"

I think about something Mr. Evans said to Officer Clyde. How this shouldn't be happening in our town. That's what he was thinking. That it died out with the previous generation. I'm sure the town doesn't want to raise skeletons of the past. Even though it's been lingering at the Pike—infecting the next generation.

"What about the rest of the boxes?" I point to the pile in the corner.

"I don't know," Dean says.

I begin searching the rest of the boxes. Sorting through

papers, unearthing a few more photos that I pull out and stack together. We comb through the boxes for an hour, silence taking over the room.

I skim through a notebook. At first it looks like nothing in particular, but then I notice initials, names, almost like attendance records.

"I think this is a membership list," I say. "Meeting records of who was there? Like it's a damn community organization or something."

"What?" Dean takes the notebook. "All the writing is the same."

Dean's hands rattle. I place mine over his, so they stay steady. Both of our hands are cold.

"What is it?" I ask.

"I recognize the handwriting."

"Tell me it's not your dad's." A sinking feeling weighs me down. I hope it's not true.

"No," Dean says. "The squiggly-lined cursive and the loops on the *t*'s that aren't supposed to be there—they're like my grandfather's writing on birthday cards. I—Tracy, how could the person I loved be filled with so much hate?"

I don't say what I'm thinking. I don't want to hurt Dean. But if he recognizes the handwriting, and all this came from his grandfather's house after he passed, he was definitely some kind of leader in the Klan. My mind is spinning. There's Klan in my community. People I know could be members. Raised to think these things. They burned a cross at my house. They went after my brother.

My dad.

"We've got to take a closer look at this stuff," I say.

"But what about my parents? My dad will notice." He doesn't say "mom."

"We can take a few things and put everything back like it was. We'll replace it in a few days."

Dean holds on to the box. I can see why he wouldn't want things to be exposed about his family. The photo of the man being hanged. I can't stop thinking about that man's family. Their pain.

I feel lied to. Crowning Heights had its own set of rules—a life could easily be taken if you're the *wrong* color. No wonder they were so quick to blame Daddy.

"We have to use this," I say. "Learn more if it'll help my family."

"You should do it. I don't want to stop you, but I don't think I can face anyone in my family. They were involved in . . ." He points back to the box with the photo, then where the white robe is shoved back in a box. "All of that."

"Don't you want to find out, though? Maybe your grandpa changed." I've been through hell over the years with my father's sentence, and Dean so easily wants to give up. I shake my head.

"Find out my dad knew about my mom's history, or worse, that he might be a member? That everything he taught me about treating everyone equally was a lie? I . . . I can't face that. I know it's wrong to hide from that, but I can't." Our eyes meet. "Even if you'll hate me forever."

"It's not a lie."

Dean looks away, a tear escapes, and he quickly wipes it away. I don't want Dean to see that I think differently about his family. About him. But I can't help feeling betrayed that they kept these boxes. I don't understand the intent of keeping it. Why would Mr. Evans allow his wife to keep memorabilia and records if he didn't agree with these beliefs? Last night my house was threatened. The same hate I see in these boxes put the cross on my lawn, lit a match, and threw a brick through my window.

I pull away from Dean and create some distance, my heart breaking all over again.

SKELETON IN THE CLOSET

I couldn't think of where else to go, so I went to see Quincy. Quincy and I don't say a word as he goes through the box of Klan artifacts. His face is stern, but his hands tremble.

"Unbelievable." Quincy flips through the last few pages of what must be an attendance sheet or membership roster.

"Why do you think they kept all this stuff?" I ask. "Mr. Evans said he'd find out names, but he hasn't followed up since. Do you think this is why?"

"Don't try and figure it out," Quincy says. "People get nostalgic about weird shit like this. Look at the Confederate flag. The South lost, representing slavery. And they still try to play it off like it's just pride for the South. The Klan weren't a threat to them. The Klan were just the people they knew, even walked their kids to school to *keep them safe.*"

"All I see is hate."

"He could've been planning to talk with Dean first."

"I'd bury it."

"Maybe boxing everything up was his version of burying it," Quincy says. "All you need to know is if the Klan knew you had this, it's dangerous."

When I first saw the box, I felt sick with an overwhelming sense of betrayal. Quincy's words got me terrified. Klan aren't to be taken lightly. And for what? Daddy's appeal? Because of Jamal?

"What do we do with it?"

"Let's focus on keeping you away from any trouble."

"Trouble already found me. You think you can stop me from looking for answers now?"

"I'm not qualified to do that." Quincy lifts an eyebrow and laughs.

I chuckle.

"What's this mean for you and Dean?" Quincy pauses. "You good still?"

"I think he was shaken, too," I say. "And I for sure didn't know how to process his family history. This is a lot."

"You came here. If you were feeling him, you would've stayed."

"How could I go on looking at this stuff, with him there?"

"You here because we fit." Quincy sits closer to me. "You can't deny that. As much as I've tried to keep myself away from you, I'm always falling right back here. And you know that magnet that pulls us together is the same one that pushes you away from Dean. Won't ever change until you flip that switch and make that decision. He's had all these years to show you what he's about, while I waited for you. Tried to not be a reminder, haunting you with our dads' memories."

"You've never brought bad memories," I whisper, tears forming in my eyes. I made myself think Quincy was trying to live a separate life from me. I told myself that because it was easy to believe. "I thought you wanted out. Dean and I . . . He was good to me. A friend. I'm sorry I wasn't there for you."

"I had Jamal. We were young, but I don't like feeling like I'm supposed to stay on the sidelines anymore. I'm not stepping back unless you ask me to."

I let a small smile slip, face flushed. Quincy takes my hand. It's like we were ripped from each other, our friendship splitting when our families' lives got torn apart. We had to survive through it. It was already too hard to face our community as children tainted because of our fathers. I think I was too weak to try to face my history with Quincy. But now, with his hands holding mine, I feel us melding back together. Becoming stronger. Becoming something bigger together than apart. It's all so much to take in. I can see it in his eyes. We need time to let our lives fall back in place. There's one thing I know now: I won't let anything pull us apart again.

I know I've overstayed my welcome the way Mrs. Ridges keeps passing Quincy's room. We're hip to hip together. Bonded again, like we were as kids, but this time grown. I'm not ready to leave Quincy, so we search online for anything about the Klan and white nationalists in Texas. They've erased this from *their* history. But the burden is on *our* backs like whips cracking our skin and leaving us to bleed out.

I search for articles about a Black man lynched, using the date on the back of the photo. Nothing pops up. I grow frustrated until I find a story about an FBI raid in Crowning Heights, a short article on the second page of the local newspaper. Illegal guns, racketeering. Then I see Richard Brighton's name as charged but not convicted. Richard was one of the few men who weren't sentenced.

The thought makes me sick, but I need to see that photo again. The one with Judy Evans as a little girl. I look at the online scan, blow it up on my screen, and cover the body of the man who was lynched, focusing instead on Mrs. Evans looking up at her dad, another girl, slightly older, with her hand on Mrs. Evans's shoulder.

I go back to my search engine, this time looking for a murder in the weeks following the date of the photo. A shiver runs down my spine when I notice something about a missing Vietnamese shrimp packer. Curious, I click on it. The article says his family had been looking for him for weeks. The last day he was seen was the same day as the lynching photo.

"It can't be," I whisper.

"What is it?" Quincy comes up behind me and looks over my shoulder.

I compare the article's photo with the lynching picture. The man's white shirt peeks out underneath a work apron. A shrimp-hook design on the corner of the apron, white pants with stains. When I saw the white hoods and people gathered around the body by the cross, I'd assumed the man was Black. Now I see he could be the Vietnamese man, with brown skin darkened by long, hot days outside. The apron isn't on him, but his clothing is almost exactly the same.

"You see this?" I point at the photo and the image online, then shut my eyes tight.

"Is that . . . ? Can't be . . . Is that the same guy?"

The missing man in the article must be the same as in the photo. I search his name, Minh Nguyen. The only thing that comes up is that he went missing, possibly ran away from his family to move to New Orleans or another location near the Gulf for better work conditions. No mention of him being found.

They got away with murder. I count sixteen people who witnessed his death and never said a word.

People who can keep a secret like this are capable of anything.

I go over the details with Quincy. He keeps a calm face, but he's tapping his foot hard.

"You should stop looking into all this. Give this to Steve Jones! Stay out of it." The crease in his brow is getting tighter.

I know he's trying to protect me, but I'm already smack-dab in the middle of it. Somehow, I feel like I'm still chasing my daddy's secrets. Jamal has Daddy's case on his back—like father, like son. I know I should focus on helping Jamal, not get lost in old skeletons that, if woken, could be ghosts I'd regret waking up.

KILL TWO BIRDS
WITH ONE STONE

Wednesday afternoon, Mandy steps out of the Pearl Coffee and Tea shop a few blocks from school. Her hair is in a messy bun again, and a black apron's still tied around her waist. I wait in the parking lot for her.

"I don't have a lot of time. I'm on a break." Mandy's dark circles under her eyes share all too much of her pain.

"We both want the truth," I say. "I know Angela went out to the Pike, but she went alone. Without Jamal. Why?"

She scans the lot, a nervous look bouncing in her eye.

I lean on the driver's side of my car until Mandy gets the courage to speak.

"Chris caught her in a lie, and she was trying to backtrack what Scott was saying about her messing with Jamal."

"But the Pike, alone?"

"The first time Angela went to the Pike, it was back in April. Angela thought Chris was up to something out there because he was saying some real wild stuff and hanging with a new crowd."

"Like racist things?" I say.

Mandy nods. "Chris kept going out to the Pike all secret-like. Hushed conversations and cryptic texts. She decided to go out there, see for herself what was going on."

The photos on the SD were back in April; the timeline matches up.

"Angela realized Chris was part of some new hate group. She didn't know exactly what but called it a bunch of angry white boys."

A shiver runs down my spine thinking about the flyers in Richard Brighton's SUV.

"A few weeks later, Chris demanded Scott give back a gun of his. Chris had let him mess around with it after he found it in his uncle's storage. Scott gave it back, but before Chris could get a chance to return it, it went missing from his truck."

"What happened to it?" I jump in.

"Angela. I told her to mind her business, but when Angela was determined about something, there was no stopping her. Scott suspected it was her, so he told Chris about the rumors going around that Angela was seeing Jamal. And . . . and it sounds like you already know Chris confronted her the same day she died at the Pike." Mandy's voice cracks, her hands shaking.

"I saw them arguing that morning," I say.

"She told him she was worried that he was planning on doing something dangerous. That he'd changed since he'd been hanging with a new crowd by the Pike. She'd seen the gun in his glove compartment and took it. Chris wanted to prove to her they were 'good guys.' That they were just pushing back on 'liberal PC bullshit.' That there was 'nothing wrong with wanting to protect their own.'"

I shift uncomfortably.

"His words. Not mine," Mandy says. "She told him she'd return the gun if what they were doing at the Pike was harmless."

"They killed her instead?" I rub my head trying to make sense.

"I wanted to go to the police, but they *are* the police. Who were they going to believe?"

I'm realizing it's not just us who are skeptical of going against the sheriff's family. Mandy is, too.

"My grabbing her things was a last-ditch effort to look for something to prove it. I had nothing. Especially after the newsroom got trashed. Her small purse she always carried was never found, either." Her lower lip trembles. "Then after the party, Chris, Scott, and Justin stuck around asking if I knew about the gun. I kept denying it, but they threatened me until they believed I knew nothing." Mandy looks away.

"What?" I ask.

"By the way they were acting, they weren't being friendly

with each other. They were arguing, like it was only the gun drawing them together."

"Wait." I put my hands on my head. "The gun is still missing?"

"I searched *everywhere*. Her house. Car. Locker. School. The *Susan Touric Show* studio. It's nowhere."

"Did she say where she'd been hiding it?"

"She was bringing it with her to the Pike. She figured the closer she got to their circle, the more information she could have for her story. Giving back the gun was supposed to prove she was on their side. I think she was going to work with you to get the truth into 'Tracy's Corner.'"

Mandy looks down at her watch. "I'm sorry. I gotta go. If I knew anything more, I'd tell you."

"Mandy." I pause. "Be careful."

Mandy looks over her shoulder, nods, and then returns to the coffee shop. I text Jamal's new burner, the one I provided in the backpack full of supplies I took to him after Mama left this morning.

Then I call Quincy; he picks up on the first ring. I don't wait for him to ask. Jump into everything Mandy told me.

"We've got to find that gun," I say.

"How's a gun supposed to help us?" A car door slams. I know Quincy's already getting in his car. He knows me too well. I'm not gonna sit back and wait for answers.

I think about that box of things that Mr. Evans pulled out after the cross burning at the house. Quincy said people like to keep memorabilia. It's also evidence. And the gun might be evidence of something Richard is hiding.

"What if that gun was used to shoot the girl's car the night of the rally? If the gun is found and ties Richard to it, that's not good for his hate group, and the larger organization he represents, Liberty Heritage."

"Maybe," Quincy says. "Or it's even deeper than that."

I swallow hard. The same thought crosses my mind. Maybe the gun isn't about Jamal but about Daddy.

Richard Brighton's been scoping out Steve's office. He has no reason to care about my daddy's case—unless his gun makes him a suspect.

I AIN'T NEVER SCARED

I don't know how, but I persuade Quincy to join me at the Pike. This time, it's closer to dusk. He parks his car farther away than I did, near some large brush so it's hidden from view. Quincy is shaking his head when we walk across the grass. As much as Quincy doesn't want to be here, he doesn't leave a gap between us.

"Where we looking?" Quincy says.

"The path. The building. Until we cover every inch."

We take slow, methodical steps. I retrace my route where I found the splatters of blood and flattened path in the tall grass. This time it's darker inside the building, with less light coming through the dusty windows.

We stop in front of the warehouse doors. I look to the parking lot that's completely empty, hoping it stays that way.

"Let's walk the perimeter of the building. Maybe Angela got around here first before she got caught up in trouble."

"Bet."

We pace around the building, kicking the tall grass down and stepping over it to make sure we don't miss a gun tossed in the grass.

"Wouldn't the police already comb through this area again after Beverly turned in Angela's phone?" Quincy asks.

"They don't know to look for a gun."

"They weren't *not* looking for a gun."

"I didn't know you scared so easily." I chuckle, and Quincy gives me a side-eye.

"This would be much easier if it was daytime," he says. "It'll be pitch-black out here in a few hours."

"I know," I say. "But I've tried morning—I was held at gunpoint by Galveston's finest."

"I notice how you remind me of that *after* we're already out here."

Once we search around the building, we enter through the wooden doors.

"Over there." I point to the small opening I crawled through the first time. "That's where I found her phone."

"You fit through *that*?" Quincy asks.

The space looks smaller, but I was so desperate at the time. I shoved myself through, had the bruises the next day to prove it. Angela could've been in a worse situation. She made herself fit.

Quincy scans the building. "This would be the only space to be unseen. Spy on someone."

"That's true. She wanted an exposé, doing everything she could to get something on them. Maybe she was planning on taking photos from here. Documenting this meeting? But she dropped her phone."

"Think you can fit through again?"

I walk closer to the narrow gap that's sandwiched between the conveyer belt and the wall.

Before I get down to crawl, Quincy tugs me closer to him. Our foreheads touch. Our lips close for the first time since Herron Media, where our kiss was for cover, not the real thing.

"Be careful," Quincy says.

I give a shy grin and nod.

I use the flashlight on my phone as a light. I crouch down, eyeing the gap, not looking forward to shoving myself through. I scratch my neck as I try to catch my breath. I look to Quincy, then take another breath. Quincy lifts the bottom of the conveyer and moves it a few inches out. It makes a difference. I crawl on my hands and knees, scooting myself slowly along the ground.

Even though Quincy's here, he can't help me if I truly get stuck in the machine. Each breath is a struggle as the space becomes more and more restricted. No clear way out except behind me. Panic rises in me when I realize I probably can't turn around.

I can hear my heart pounding. My skin goes clammy. Small lights dance across my vision.

How can I move forward?

"You okay?" Quincy calls out. "You're quiet."

His voice snaps me back. I have to get control. I take another deep breath. "I will be when this is done."

Sweat drips from my forehead, and I scan the floor with my flashlight. Inch my way closer. Then I see the marks of dust wiped away when someone did the same.

"She came from under here," I yell. "There's a bigger gap farther along. It looks like it opens up . . . I think I can fit."

I scooch in like I'm crab walking. My arms are exhausted from dragging myself through the narrowest, most difficult part. Sweat and dust blending together, my eyes start to burn. But I don't stop. I can feel that it's getting easier the farther I go.

I swing my light around and see wooden panels that are busted, possible openings. Then glide my body over and feel along the wall.

"What do you see?" Quincy asks.

My voice quivers. Chest squeezing tighter, freaking out because I'm so deep below the conveyer I'd be cornered if we're caught. But I keep reaching, going farther. I feel something, then stretch my fingers until I have a good hold to pull it to me.

My eyes well because I'm touching something of Angela's.

"Angela's interview bag," I say. "She'd keep her phone, notepads, and pens in there for quick write-ups on the go."

"Her phone must've fell out," Quincy says.

I rest my head against the wall and feel cold metal instead.

"I think I found something," I say. "Can you get through?"

I rub my eyes, the dust getting to me. I take my shirt and wipe my face. Then I scoot closer, swinging my light back and forth, looking along the wall and in little crannies as Quincy pushes the belt more so I can go deeper and he'll have room to crouch under.

I swing my flashlight, see nothing around except Quincy's eyes meeting mine. He looks away so the light doesn't blind him.

"Over here." I tap the vent.

I hand him my flashlight.

"Shiiiit."

"Is right."

Inside the vent is a gun.

PILLAR OF SALT

Two screws are loose. It'll be easy to bust open. Quincy reaches for the vent.

"Wait." I stop Quincy's hand. "Let me think first."

"This's the whole point we're here, right?"

"Yes, but maybe we shouldn't be the ones who find it." I roll my head from side to side, stretching my neck. The urge to grab the gun still itches, but the pause gets me to think more like a cop, rather than a girl who wants her brother back.

"The thought of leaving it here is hard," I say. "We gotta do it, though."

"This wasn't covered in one of your workshops, was it? Like, I didn't sleep through a section on how to not get caught up."

I release a smile.

"We should call Beverly when we get out of here," I say.

"You sure?"

I sit for a minute. Think of all the scenarios. If I touch the gun, then it'll look like I planted it. This gun could mean nothing, or it could mean bringing back Daddy and Jamal.

"We gotta wipe up our prints, too," I say. "Run over everything we touched on the ground, the conveyer belt, the walls."

Quincy takes his top shirt off, leaving his sleeveless undershirt on. I scoot back on my knees as I wipe my side down. Duck out the space and run over the belt.

By the time we're done, we're both drenched. Coughing at the dust now stuck in our lungs.

"Thanks for being here," I say. "I wouldn't have been able to move that belt. It doesn't feel good leaving evidence, but if it's been okay this long, we might be fine."

"Yeah. We should be—" Quincy stops.

The sound of a truck parking, an engine rumbling. Then turning off. Voices carrying, getting closer toward us. Searching for something outside, just like we were an hour ago.

"We've got company," I whisper.

"Back down here." Quincy points to the narrow gap we crawled out of a minute ago.

Something in me knows I can't trap us back in that small space again. And if these people find us, we'll have led them straight to the gun.

I scan the building. The thumping of my heart in my ears gets faster and faster. Light-headed, I lean on Quincy's arm. Scan the space, studying all the large windows. Then I see an office, and it looks like another exit that I must've missed the first time I was here.

"There," I whisper.

Quincy nods. We head through the office, test the back door. I slowly push on it, expecting it to stay locked, but it opens. Quincy moves to exit. I look back through the building.

"Wait," I say. "We could stay here, see who it is. Last time I went running out there, I ran right into guns being drawn."

Quincy squeezes my hand.

We squat, wait it out. A few minutes later the door opens.

Someone's here.

"Go," Quincy's voice chokes out at me. "I'll stay. Cause a distraction if it looks like we're in trouble."

I shake my head. I won't leave him here.

He begs with his eyes. I don't budge.

Chris and Justin enter the building.

Quincy and I exchange glances.

Quincy creeps closer to the door. I follow behind as he nudges it open a crack. His T-shirt clutched in his hand, so he doesn't touch the knob. My breathing gets shallow as I lift my phone and press record.

I swallow hard, hoping this won't be a full-on crew of people entering.

"It's not here, man." Justin stalks around the room. "This place has been searched up and down by cops."

"I don't care," Chris says. "Angela's phone was found in here. That means *she* was in here, and we've gotta get that gun."

I squeeze Quincy's arm. He nods back.

"Maybe Scott got it back," Justin says. "Just call him."

"I'm not doing jack with him."

"You act like he's the one who killed Angela."

"Maybe he did." Chris's voice is ice-cold.

"That's fucked up, man. He's your friend. Why blame him when you know it was Jamal's black ass? Cops'll find him."

"How do we know he's still running? Maybe Scott got rid of him, too," Chris says. "Scott's the one keeping secrets. He knew I was meeting Angela early."

"Wait, you're not serious, are you? Thought we were supposed to stick together."

"He stole that gun. Used it out at the march and got that girl killed. Angela would still be here if he hadn't done it."

"No. Angela would be here if she wasn't messing around on you."

Chris shoves Justin.

"Sorry. Your new theory doesn't make sense."

"Just keep looking. Whether it was Jamal or Scott, my uncle needs that gun. If it's found by the cops, he could be in big trouble."

"You hear that?" I whisper to Quincy, who's texting on his phone. "What're you doing?"

Quincy shows me the phone. He's texting Beverly.

Found the gun.

In a vent at the Pike building.

Behind the belt table.

Chris and Justin searching for it now.

Get outta there!

"Quincy," I whisper. "We can't get caught in here."

"I know. Come on, let's go." He grabs my arm.

I nod in agreement. We gotta bounce.

We creep to the exit door as they are occupied looking under the forklift. I turn the handle slowly, scoot out. Quincy follows. We close the door behind us. My neck tense from straining in one spot, eyes blinded after moving from the darkness to the outside.

"Run on three." Quincy counts down with his hands. Then whispers, "Run."

Mama said my biggest weakness is I don't have self-control. She joked about me being like Lot's wife from the Bible. That I'd be just like her, turning my back to watch when God said not to. The burning flames of the city too tempting to watch. Then she turned into a pillar of salt. But when Quincy says "run," I run. Fast, like I'm being swept by the wind. Don't stop until we're safely in the car.

There's a moment of panic when he starts the engine—no way Chris and Justin don't hear us—but then we're peeling out and flying ninety miles an hour down the highway, quickly taking an exit when we see a fleet of police cars coming toward us. When they race past us, I gulp.

Then turn to look back.

COMING HOME

After a quick shower, I meet Quincy outside my house. We sit close on my porch; he wears a borrowed shirt of Jamal's. My leg leans into his as we try to sort out what we know so far. Our fingers dangle next to each other's. They touch, and a warm zing goes off inside. A soft smile escapes from Quincy, but we don't speak. Too much at stake right now.

A truck speeds toward my house. It's Steve.

As Steve parks, I bite my lip. I'm light-headed and dizzy. We can bring Jamal home now.

I text Jamal.

> Steve's here.
> We found the gun.
> He's going to help.

Meet us at the house.

Everything's going to be okay.

I pray I'm right.

Fifteen minutes later, the back door creaks. Jamal's hands are shoved in his pockets, his thin white hoodie draped over his head. I wrap my arms around him like I haven't seen him in days.

Home feels normal again. Until he takes his hood off. His face is stormy, as Daddy used to say. All his feelings trapped in his body—wind, rain, heat, thunder—all spinning inside.

Quincy comes down the hallway and jumps on Jamal. They hug. Wide smiles, half hugs before doing their handshake routine.

"Man. It's good to see you," Quincy says.

Jamal gives his first wide smile. "Thought I'd be dead, huh?"

Jamal's joke falls flat with Steve, who chuckles uncomfortably. Jamal sizes Steve up. In many ways, Jamal and I are the same. He's better at hiding it with a big grin, while at the same time he's judging your weakness.

"This is Steve." I fumble around, letting go of Jamal when the creases around his eyes settle. "From Innocence X."

"Pleasure, man," Steve says as he gets up to greet him. "You don't know what it means to finally meet you in person."

I don't move until Jamal takes a seat in our family room. The boarded-up window still not replaced. His shoulders slump back and dig into the couch. I'm filled with hope, lightness inside, watching Steve and Jamal meet for the first time. The knots riding up my throat relax, and I can breathe normally.

Steve looks at me, asking for my permission to begin. I nod, taking a seat next to Quincy, who keeps his hand softly around my side. Jamal's face looks suspect about this situation here, too.

I share with Jamal and Steve everything Quincy and I learned. That when we left the Pike, the police were searching for the gun. I just hope Chris and Justin were caught out there, too. Just like I was.

"Gun or not, I got you, Jamal," Steve says.

"I got you, too, man." Quincy gives Jamal a dap. "Forever."

"I'm gonna ask you a few questions," Steve says.

"I can't go public," Jamal says. "This might just be a case to you, but it's my life. If I go in, I can't trust I'm coming here of this alive. I don't know what that gun means yet."

"I've been in touch with my dad. He's flying here tonight. We're taking your case on, along with your dad's."

My heart swells. Steve hadn't shared that with me yet. Quincy squeezes my hand.

"Thank you." Jamal presses his palms to his heart. "That's good for my dad."

"It's good for you, too," I say.

Jamal shakes his head. "We don't know what's gonna happen when the cops find that gun. I can't risk my life. My freedom. They could plant evidence, even if I've never seen that gun in my life."

"I will do everything I can to protect your family," Steve says.

"Jamal, you think you can keep running for the rest of your life? Hide out forever?"

Jamal looks at me because he's willing to take that chance.

"Tell me what happened at the Pike," Steve says.

I'm expecting Jamal to jump up, resist. But he doesn't. He's been waiting to tell his story.

Jamal repeats what he's already told me. Except now he definitely thinks Chris killed Angela. I'm not so sure. Steve takes notes feverishly, hanging at the edge of his seat, listening to Jamal, and asking more questions.

Steve glances at me as I fidget. He takes a long pause and gestures at me to share my suspicions.

"But you don't think the boyfriend killed her, Tracy?" Steve asks.

"Ex." Jamal's jaws clench a bit, and his voice goes tight. His eyes dull. I know that memory from the Pike must be flashing through his head. The night he lost Angela.

"Chris said he suspected Scott, but that doesn't mean he knows. Chris's uncle is still sketchy." I play the audio I recorded. It's hard to hear, so I turn it all the way up. We huddle around my phone.

Steve rubs his hands over his freshly cut fade. "I wonder if Chris shared that in his police report."

"When I confronted Chris at the cemetery, his thoughts were scattered, but he didn't claim he saw Jamal kill Angela—he just blamed Jamal. With the gun, Mandy's story, Chris blaming

Scott, Jamal could get his story out there and convince people it's the truth."

"I'm not going in until I'm confident I can prove I'm innocent." Jamal's about ready to jump out of his seat right now and run back to the shack.

The front door slams open. Mama hollers for me by the entrance as she steps into the house with Corinne. I look at the clock above the mantel. Nine. Mama's back from visiting Daddy and gone to Monday choir practice already? Steve's biting the inside of his cheek when Mama zeroes in on Jamal on the couch. She rushes Jamal like she's trying to tackle him.

Jamal can't speak because Mama has him all tangled up in her arms—kissing him and hugging him.

It takes me too long to notice that Mama's not alone.

ALL OUT OF OPTIONS

Beverly's hands are filled with grocery bags. Quincy stands, holds steady by me as he studies his sister. She stays standing in her police uniform, watching Mama hug Jamal. For a moment, there's joy in her eyes. She keeps the bags in her hands and goes to meet him, too.

"Jamal. You're safe." She side hugs him. Jamal is tense, overwhelmed.

Beverly pauses, catching herself from being lost in the moment. She's back on duty. She can't drive away and pretend she didn't see Jamal. The law doesn't work that way.

Mama looks to me, then Steve. Jamal checks Beverly out; she's between him and the door. His gaze moves to Corinne, who's watching shyly. Like she's not certain what to do. The room goes quiet when Mama sees our expressions.

A prickle runs up my neck. Jamal breaks the stillness to take a small bag from Corinne and lift her up.

"You're back." Corinne hugs around his neck.

"I been here this whole time, Bighead. Where you been?"

My eyes water. I inch closer to Mama and Corinne all loving on Jamal. Warming myself with their happiness. It doesn't seem to matter that this moment won't last. We fool ourselves into thinking that as long as we're huddled together and Beverly holds those bags, we can go on like this forever. I eye Steve, willing him to fix things. He gives me a nod. He's going to try.

Steve approaches Beverly. "I'm from Innocence X and will be representing James Beaumont. Jamal is my newest client, though. Did they find the gun?"

"Jamal also?" Beverly's heard about Steve, but for Daddy, not Jamal. We all know this is big. She's too shocked to speak. She nods, confirming they found the gun.

Beverly turns to us.

"I have to take Jamal in." She puts the grocery bags down. "I came by to question Tracy about the gun, but I can't walk away after seeing Jamal."

The room changes the moment Beverly's hands are free.

"Beverly, let's listen to what Jamal has to say." Mama has her arms wrapped around Jamal, pleading.

"I ain't going in!" Jamal raises his voice for the first time, and that quietness that kept everything calm vanishes.

"I've known you forever." Beverly extends her free hand to

Jamal. "I'd never want to hurt you, but I took an oath. You know you can trust me."

"Like my pops? Like how yours went down? I ain't going in. You're gonna have to shoot me."

I can't help a gasp escaping.

Beverly shakes her head. "It doesn't need to be like that. I'll call in some of my guys I trust. Newer ones. Have enough people to—"

"No." Jamal stays firm. "I ain't going in. I don't trust your people, Bev."

"If you won't come with me, I've got to call it in."

"Then call it in, Officer Ridges. Because I ain't leaving this house."

Beverly winces at Jamal's formality. Corinne clutches Jamal as we all watch in disbelief. It's like the world is ending right in front of me. Jamal trusted me, and I failed him.

"But what about that gun? Chris and Justin at the Pike." Quincy waves her off. "Now what's he gonna do? Every officer out there's looking for him. You think they're going to bring him in alive, like they did Dad?"

"Don't talk about Dad." Beverly grimaces.

"I know exactly what officers do when they think somebody's guilty. Even if it means taking down everyone around them." Quincy taps his leg.

"I'm not doing this with you right now, Quincy. I know you don't like it, but I'm trying to do better. Be better. Change things my way."

"How's taking him in bring justice to Angela?" I say. "What happened at the Pike?"

"Chris still claims Jamal killed Angela," Beverly says. "Says he was out at the Pike looking for evidence. Angela wasn't murdered with a gun, so they don't think it means anything. They're . . . they're still convinced it's Jamal."

"Spinning it." I give Beverly a scowl. "The last time this happened to us, my daddy was dragged, jailed, sentenced, and sent to death row in less than a year. What should Jamal have done?"

"Damn, Tracy," Beverly says. "I don't know."

"Do you think Jamal's guilty?"

Beverly doesn't answer me.

"You're supposed to be a cop. To protect and to serve." I pause, deciding if I should say more. I can't hold it in. "It doesn't mean you can't think for yourself."

"You think I don't?"

"What about your dad? Do you think he deserved to die? That he was guilty?" I can see how much the memory pains her. Quincy winces as her eyes begin to tear.

"He first taught me how to shoot, right there on that field." Beverly points down the road from the thicket of trees toward Tasha's neighborhood. "I'm a cop because of what happened to my dad. He wouldn't want fear to control me. I couldn't think of anything else that would make him prouder than to protect our family. I don't know what happened with your dad or Jamal, but they deserve justice like everyone else. If I can help be a part of bringing justice, the right way, I want that."

Jamal unwraps Corinne's arms from gripping him and hands her to Mama.

"So, this how you want it to go down?"

"You gotta go in," Beverly says.

"Or what? You gonna shoot me? Drag me? I can't believe you'd be the one to do that, too."

In the distance is the faint sound of police cars. They reach closer, overwhelming, pulsing loud and echoing across the fields. I can feel Jamal panicking inside.

Because I'm panicking, too.

IT GETS WORSE

Beverly steps outside to talk to the officers. When she comes back, her face looks drained. Officer Clyde follows her, stepping cautiously inside our home. He has his hand by his gun. Beverly motions for him to ease up, and he relaxes his hand.

"Sheriff Brighton's here now, Jamal," Beverly says. "Let's bring you in before things get complicated."

"I'm not going in," Jamal says.

"I'll be representing Jamal." Steve cuts between Jamal and Officer Clyde. "Give me and my client a minute."

Quincy's body shakes next to mine. I touch his arm and he's ice-cold. I see him reliving the trauma he went through as a child. I clutch his hand, but it's like I'm not here.

"He's going to need to make a decision," Officer Clyde says. "Sheriff's not going to let him get away again."

"We have to go. The sooner we can get you in the car, Jamal, the better," Beverly says.

Steve goes to Jamal. "Come on, trust me, let's go together. I'm your legal representation getting out of here."

Jamal nods, but his eyes are wide, his mouth a thin line. He's scared to death. Just like me.

Sheriff Brighton approaches the house, his eyes steady on Jamal when he sees him. My stomach sinks because I don't know what this means for Jamal. Guilt that I made Jamal come home to talk to Steve takes over.

"We got things under control, Sheriff," Beverly says.

"Is that true?" Sheriff Brighton looks to Officer Clyde.

"We'll be out shortly," Officer Clyde says.

Steve whispers to Beverly.

"He'd like his interview to happen here," Beverly says.

I look to Steve and hope this is possible.

"We don't need to manage it that way." Officer Clyde intercedes. "I'll bring him in."

"We need to get him on the record right away," Beverly says.

"That's what the station is for," Sheriff Brighton says. "We're following protocol on this. We can't allow your family connection to rule how we do this."

"Your son was at the scene of the crime," Beverly says. "And there are claims your brother's gun was the one we found. A gun that Angela was allegedly returning to your son that may have been used in the death of that girl at the march two months back."

My chest swells at Beverly holding her ground. Sheriff Brighton takes a step back, his face contorted, puzzled. This is new information to him.

"Let's do this right on both accounts so we won't have issues charging," Officer Clyde intervenes.

"I'll secure the perimeter. We do this by the book." Sheriff Brighton nods and folds his arms across his chest, eventually turning toward the police cars.

The officers spread around the house. No option for Jamal to run away now.

A white SUV pulls up to the field. The lighting is poor, but I can tell this is no cop car. My stomach twists as I wait to see who it is. The car slows when it reaches our driveway and stops behind the police cars. A man gets out; the flashing blue and red lights bounce off his pale skin.

Richard Brighton.

My throat catches, and Quincy locks eyes with me. I can see his body going weak. Like the lights are giving him flashbacks to the night he was shot. Sweat beads on his face, and his eyes look glassy. He's going to pass out if more cops follow. He leans on me; I help him take a seat. My chest is tight and my head is spinning. Quincy has always looked out for us, and I don't want him near any of this, but I have to focus on family first.

I go to Jamal.

"Jamal." I point to Quincy, who's struggling. "We know what happens next. We've lived through it. We don't have options. The best way to de-escalate is to not put up a fight. They're ready for battle out there. Don't let their fear grow so all they see is war."

I don't know if that's the right answer, but I also know I can't control police responses. I can only follow what I've been preaching in Know Your Rights workshops.

Jamal's biting his lip, trying to hold it together. I wrap my arms around him. "They gotta take you in. Walk out with Beverly and a lawyer—that's the best we gonna get."

Jamal holds on to me. His fingers dig into my shoulders. My throat aches. I got him back, and now I'm losing him. It hurts to be the one to convince Jamal to step out that door into a situation I know I can't control.

Jamal hugs Mama, then lifts up Corinne and gives her a kiss. She clings to his neck, won't let go. He has to pry her off, because he would never use her as a shield, as much as she's trying to make that happen. She's sobbing.

"Let's go." Jamal closes his eyes.

Steve joins him; Beverly flanks the other side.

"I gotta cuff you, Jamal," she says. "I won't do it tight. It's just to settle the officers outside so they can relax, okay? Take a breath now."

Jamal takes a long breath. A tear slides down his cheek. When he squares his shoulders, my heart bursts with pride. He won't let them break him.

Officer Clyde leads all of us out of the house, leaving Jamal, Beverly, and Steve inside.

Eventually, Beverly walks out with Jamal and Steve. My throat constricts because I want Jamal to be seen clear as day. Unarmed. Not a threat. Jackson's death replays in my mind as if it's all happening again.

As soon as I think about the past repeating, Quincy puts his hand on my shoulder and holds me tight. He shook himself out of his fear and is now looking at me to calm down. I don't have the words to speak. I hate that I have this thought that history is going to replay itself. It paralyzes me.

I swallow hard and focus on watching Jamal. He walks out in a T-shirt and pants, leaving his thin hoodie inside. He's so hesitant, moving slowly. He makes his way down the steps. Sheriff Brighton approaches Beverly, but she waves him off. Jamal's not going to be calm if he thinks the sheriff won't listen. We all watch helplessly because we know once Jamal's in the police car, there's little we can do.

I glance at Steve, trying to keep Jamal calm.

"Tracy." Quincy takes my attention away. "Jamal will be okay." His eyes are sure. He's convinced. I try to nod, but I notice a movement beyond the police line.

Richard Brighton is edging forward. No one seems concerned as he approaches his brother.

I look over at Jamal, then at Richard. This isn't good.

Sheriff Brighton sees his brother, and his face turns firm. I'm stuck between running closer and fear that if I cause a distraction, it will create an aggressive response.

I can't hear what Sheriff Brighton says, but he seems to be trying to control the situation, explaining to Richard what's going on. Richard goes from excited to furious. He must have been asked about the gun.

Sheriff Brighton is now talking sternly; he puts his hand on his brother, directing him to his car, but Richard's not listening. He's getting more and more agitated.

"He killed a white girl—my nephew's girlfriend," Richard yells. "I have a right to be here."

Beverly notices the commotion and hurries to move Jamal into the police car. Richard pivots around the sheriff and steps toward Jamal, like he's going to tackle him.

Jamal shifts; he's getting ready to run with hands cuffed behind his back. Anything to protect himself from Richard.

Richard yells, "Gun!"

I hear it before I see it.

A gun goes off.

Someone is screaming.

Beverly and Jamal drop to the ground. Steve crouches, hands over his head. Mama's wail freezes my blood.

Sheriff Brighton tackles his brother.

Beverly is lying over Jamal's body.

Officer Clyde yells, "Halt!"

The chaos is a cacophony in my ears. I'm the one screaming. Jamal's been shot.

RELIEF AND PAIN

I can't stay frozen any longer. I have to move closer.

"Jamal!" I scream, pushing my way toward him.

"He's fine. He's fine. He's fine." Quincy got there first and rushes back to my side to stop me.

I have to see for myself. Because all I see is black on the ground, in the darkness.

When I get closer, Jamal is sitting up. Steve's next to him. He's reaching for Beverly, who's slumped over.

No, no, no, no.

"Call a bus!" Officer Clyde waves wildly for everyone to put their weapons away. "Officer down! Officer down!"

He immediately begins to administer aid to Beverly. I realize I'm rocking in place, mumbling "no" over and over again and yet feeling relief at seeing Jamal unhurt at the same time. It's all too much. Beverly is one of the best of us.

"She was taking him in," Officer Clyde shouts at no one in particular.

There's chaos among the officers, guns drawn, but I can't tell who fired the shot.

Sheriff Brighton has cuffed Richard and is waving another officer to take him into a police car. Then the sheriff orders everyone, "Weapons down! Weapons down!"

Quincy is frozen, watching Beverly. I hold him while Officer Clyde continues to administer aid, trying to stop the bleeding.

Officers join in helping Beverly and clear out space for when the ambulance arrives. Jamal's been placed in the back of a police car, cuffed, leaning on the glass, watching them help her. Our gazes meet. What does this mean?

An officer moves out of the way, and I can finally make out Beverly talking while she lies on the ground.

"It's her shoulder," I say to Quincy. He steps closer, but an officer pushes him back. Mama and Corinne join us. I pull Corinne close. Curve my body over hers like a protective shell. Mama puts her hand over Quincy, who's at my side.

Pain pushes out of my chest and up through my throat, like rocks are filling me up until I can't breathe. Helpless watching Beverly.

I expect to see relief in Sheriff Brighton's face now that Jamal is under arrest, but he's frantically looking between Beverly on the ground and his brother in another police car. He barely seems to register when an officer drives away with Jamal. His face looks anything but relieved.

THE TRUTH SHALL SET US FREE

Mama, Corinne, and I are huddled in a cold conference room. Across the way is Jamal in a smaller interview room. He's still handcuffed, but at least not in a holding cell. I feel like I'm turning sideways.

I had the same disoriented feeling seeing Quincy ride in the ambulance with Beverly: the ground pulling at me, so I don't know what's up or down. It didn't help that the officers seemed just as confused.

Sheriff Brighton walks down the hallway, stopping at Jamal's door. I stand, until I see he's stopped by a man in a gray suit who isn't dressed like the rest of the Galveston County police force. The sheriff insists on speaking with Jamal. He's turned away. My body shakes with relief, hoping this is one step closer to clearing Jamal's name.

Steve enters our conference room. Mama clutches her shirt and stands.

"Sit." Steve gestures with his hand. "This is going to be a while."

"Are they gonna let us talk to Jamal?" I ask.

"No." Steve points to Jamal's room. "Once they complete his paperwork, they'll let me join him."

I clear my throat. "What's next?" I sip lukewarm water from a Styrofoam cup.

"Outside investigators have been called in. They've given approval for the ballistics on the gun found at the Pike to be done by an external unit."

I exhale. My biggest fear was that Jamal's fingerprints would be planted on the gun or they'd use it against him without any real evidence.

Corinne smiles, even though I know she doesn't know what that means to us. She just knows we're happy about it.

The plainclothes officer in gray, I realize, is from internal affairs. Not Galveston County police. I still don't know who to trust. What kind of involvement Sheriff Brighton had. Did he know? Was he part of a cover-up? Or just couldn't—didn't want to—see the truth?

I rub my temples, then glance down at my phone for an update from Quincy. I want to be at the hospital for him and Beverly. As usual, I'm pulled in two places at once.

No news yet.

Mama brushes her forehead, the strain showing in her red eyes.

"You got any answers?" Corinne whispers to me.

"Jamal's safe." I squeeze Corinne's arm, gentle. "That's all that matters now."

Corinne rests her head on Mama and fidgets with her shirt.

I take a long breath. Jamal's under arrest, but Richard's actions might have put the focus on his guilt. I only hope Beverly won't have long-term injuries. By the time the ambulance pulled away, she was alert. Talking. Her shoulder was hit, but the other cops said she'd survive.

Out the window, I see Dean enter the police station with his parents. Mama glances at me, and I shrug. I didn't contact him.

A few minutes later, Officer Clyde appears from the back of the station, his face ashen. He's changed his uniform, the blood on his shirt now gone. I'm relieved. The front-desk officer points toward Mrs. Evans, and Officer Clyde meets her. They talk close, in hushed words. Dean and I catch glances, but he doesn't move toward me.

Officer Clyde enters our conference room. His silver hair is disheveled, stress on his face.

"Mrs. Evans is here to make a statement, and she'd like your family to be there. It's unusual, but we'll allow it if you agree."

Mama and I exchange glances. Lost at what she could possibly say to us when we got bigger things going on. Mama nods at Officer Clyde.

Steve motions for Officer Clyde to step out to talk to him before the Evanses enter.

Mr. Evans holds one arm around a rigid Mrs. Evans, whispering what must be words of comfort when they finally enter with Officer Clyde and another plainclothes officer. Dean doesn't meet my eyes and takes a seat next to his dad.

Mrs. Evans puts down a photo. The photo. The one from the lynching. She closes her eyes as tears form. A coldness settles in my chest.

I study Dean's mom. Whatever she's been through has been ingrained in her since she was a kid. Her father left imprints of his beliefs on her. How much she's held on to is a mystery. Still, it's a choice.

"When I was ten years old, I witnessed a murder. One that my father, Charles Greene, Grand Wizard of the Galveston County chapter of the Ku Klux Klan, was involved in. They murdered a man named Minh Nguyen."

I expect her to stop, but she chokes through several more names from the photo that she thinks we should know about, those who witnessed the murder like her. Two names jump out. "Cathy Marcom Davidson. Richard Brighton."

"Wait. As in Cathy Davidson, Mark Davidson's wife?" I ask.

Steve hushes me. I bite my cheek, holding back questions I'm dying to get answered.

Mrs. Evans stares down at the table, as if looking at us will make her stop talking. She begins with the night of the lynching.

"I couldn't sleep after what I saw. It was so brutal. My father said that the man was nothing. Not to be so upset. But I couldn't stop thinking about him . . . hanging there . . . wondering if his family knew . . . In the middle of the night, I snuck to the phone and called the police to leave a tip about the body. I didn't think they'd trace the phone and show up at our house like they did."

Mrs. Evans had called about the lynching, but the story on the news was only about Minh Nguyen disappearing. Not about a body being found. The cops did nothing.

"The officers arrived." Mrs. Evans's voice is strangled. "My dad joked with them. He knew them all. It's no secret most probably knew who he was. Some were members. He told them I had a nightmare, and they believed him. I had defied my dad, and they left me there. Left me to suffer his wrath. After that night, I knew I could never speak a word about it again."

Her admission strikes hard. The moment I saw the photo of the body, the way they posed around it. Proud. They all kept that secret. And as a girl Mrs. Evans reported it, but she was shut down by the police. Her father was protected. I'm still confused about why she wants us to hear this.

"Cathy Marcom and I became close friends years later. The secret we kept—that terrible secret—tormented us both. Cathy had dated Richard until he became abusive, too, so she left him for Mark Davidson."

Mrs. Evans gulps hard, then looks to Mr. Evans. He strokes her arm, and she refocuses on the center of the table. She rubs her fingers over a scar on her arm. She paid physically for going against her father. That fear to speak out beaten into her. Dean's face is red; he's gulping for air to keep from breaking. I look away. I need to focus on the truth she's finally speaking.

"In the weeks before the night of the Davidsons' murder, I'd been speaking to Cathy often. Our store is just a few blocks away. Cathy was scared because Richard kept threatening Mark, telling him not to work with James or Jackson."

I do a double take at Mrs. Evans. Mama takes my hand under the table, and we hold on for the truth that must be coming. Her legs are quivering next to me.

"Mark wasn't having it. He refused to be threatened like that. He . . . he was a good man. Mark called Richard to let him know he was a businessman, and he wasn't getting caught up in Richard's personal beliefs. Cathy grew up with Richard. She knew he was violent. That he wouldn't let it go. That's why I stayed late that night at the store, to keep an eye on Cathy. In case she wanted to ride back with me."

I'm staring at Mrs. Evans with my mouth open. She knew Richard was threatening the Davidsons. All these years acting above us when she knew the truth. Richard had all the motive in the world, not Daddy. And then Richard went after Angela because she got ahold of his gun. The same one Scott used in the mob at the Black Lives Matter rally.

"I called the police station, even let the prosecution know about Richard during James's trial, but they didn't call me back. Said they wouldn't need my testimony. They had evidence that it was James and Jackson."

Mrs. Evans is distracted. Lost in thought. Like she's holding back more. "It never went anywhere. When Jackson Ridges faced off with the police, it was clear he was guilty. I let it go."

"Jackson was scared his family would be hurt," I blurt out. "You should have told the defense, not the prosecution. How could you do that?"

My hands grip the table. I feel my face go hot as I hold back the pain of betrayal that flashes through my body. A white witness—silent all these years—who could have freed my daddy. Someone I knew and saw all the time.

"Let's hear the full story," Officer Clyde says. "She's making a statement here."

But I can't stop. "You knew they were innocent. Why don't you say it? Tell us the truth! For the first time, say it!"

"I did what I was supposed to do. I saw Richard leave the office after seven-thirty, waited an hour to hear from Cathy, but she wouldn't answer my calls, so I dialed 911. I did. Got someone to check on them at their office."

"Why didn't you say something?" Mama finally breaks her silence. She's holding Corinne now, who's lying over her, crying.

"Everyone was so convinced the case was closed. I called the police to check on her. I was interviewed and shared my doubts. Wasn't that enough? If I accused Richard directly, he'd hurt *me,* threaten to disclose things about my father."

"But your father's been dead five years now," Mr. Evans says.

"I . . . Things were settled. James had a trial. They found him guilty." Mrs. Evans rocks in place, sobbing. "My God. What did I do?"

She's facing reality—the truth she's always known.

I can't take it any longer. I stand up. Seven years we suffered because she was afraid to get involved. Passive enough to watch this happen because it wasn't her responsibility. All this time, Mrs. Evans held the answers to my daddy's freedom.

And she said nothing.

"I made myself believe that Richard had nothing to do with it. It was easier to think James and Jackson did it. The police already arrested them." Her eyes are bloodshot. Like she's cried it all out of her and has nothing left to tell but the truth.

I look away. She's upset. Scared. Wants to justify her choice, but I can't accept it.

My father didn't do anything wrong, and Jackson Ridges paid with his life.

Mama lifts her head, looking at Mrs. Evans with betrayal flitting in her eyes. But triumphant, too. The truth is finally confirmed: Daddy and Jackson were innocent.

X FACTOR

Stephen Jones Sr. enters the police station the following morning. My hand covers my mouth—because it's not my regular old Steve—it's the living legend. Tall, with a gray beard, but same bald head, dark skin, and wide smile. A Black woman trails behind, dressed in all black and wearing cop-looking sunglasses. She smiles, but it's a hard one.

"Mr. Jones," I croak out from the hallway behind the desk.

"Yes," his voice booms. He's got an aura of importance. I can see why he stands out in court.

"I . . . I'm Tracy Beaumont," I fumble out.

The desk officer immediately lets him pass through.

Mr. Jones slaps my shoulder. "It is a pleasure to finally meet you, Ms. Beaumont. This is Dom, my lead investigator."

My hands tremble as I show them to the conference room we've taken over since last night. Mama's home resting after dropping off Corinne at Tasha's, where she'll be staying for a few days. My chest swells with pride thinking about the moment Mama will meet the founder of Innocence X.

Steve soon enters, but it's clear who's taken over as alpha dog here. Mr. Jones has officers delivering him coffee and getting access to a computer in the conference room.

Over the next hour, we fill them in on everything we know. Including new suspicions that Daddy's and Jamal's cases are connected. Stephen Jones writes notes furiously. He makes calls and researches the story about the girl who was killed in the crowd by a gunshot.

"You think the gun is the same one?" Mr. Jones asks Steve.

"Sheriff brought in his son, Chris, last night," Steve says. "He revised his statement. He was the first to find Angela, not Jamal. Richard is now suspected of attacking Angela, which led to her death. He needed that gun. May be the same one used in the Davidsons' murder. Chris admitted his uncle knew about the meetup, delayed his arrival. He's now spilling on the underground hate group and confirms his friend Scott stole his uncle's gun and shot at the crowd at the Black Lives Matter march in April. Thought it would be funny. Suspects and witnesses have been filing in all morning."

Mr. Jones lets out a long whistle. "This will be one hell of a story."

I've gone over all the possible headlines in my story, too.

CORRUPTION IN CROWNING and JUSTICE FOR THE BEAUMONTS are my favorites.

"What's this mean for our young client, Jamal Beaumont?" Mr. Jones looks to me.

"Steve said the charges are dropped." I touch my hands to my face, still in disbelief.

"A few more official loopholes to go through," Steve says. "But the DA's receptive to dropping charges. He may need to serve some community service for running with a warrant."

"Under these circumstances, I would hope that's all. And even that feels unnecessary." Mr. Jones nods at Dom. A secret language between the two. She's already up and out, calling the district attorney's office.

"Now, to complicated matters," Mr. Jones says to me. "Has Steve told you that while we might have evidence to prove your father's innocence, there are more hoops to go through?"

I hesitate before speaking, fold my hands in my lap.

"How long?"

"I've read enough of your letters to know you're a relentless advocate. That's why I can't in good faith give you a date. This will still be a fight, although we have a lot going for us already."

I rub my hands over my mouth in frustration.

"Gun ballistics have changed over time," Mr. Jones says. "It's not exactly a science anymore. I've seen things fall apart with this. We don't know if the gun is tied to the Davidson murders, but we do know there's a connection to an affiliated member of a hate group and the death of two young women. We'll need to press hard on the evidence and get more witnesses who might be willing to come forward, or get an admission. Mrs. Evans's statement will be key, but I want more."

Dom returns, taking down names of people to interview and asking how we came to certain conclusions. I wait for more questions from Mr. Jones, but he's done. He jumps on his phone, emailing and texting.

I look up when I hear a familiar voice.

Quincy.

My heart melts. I move to the door, open it, and flash a wide smile. Behind him is Beverly. An overwhelming joy fills me when I see her. She's moving slow, her shoulder bandaged and her arm in a brace. She winces with each step. There's a crowd of her fellow officers around, but her focus is on us.

Beverly took a bullet for my brother, risked her life when another officer was quick to take a shot when Richard yelled, *"Gun!"* She protects and serves.

We'd given Beverly a hard time about trusting the law, but we were mistaken: she is what the law was always supposed to be.

I hesitate, then reach out to hold Quincy. I'm worried that somehow if I look him in the eye, he'll be able to see my guilt about his sister being shot. He doesn't give me another second to question. He flings his arms around me and lifts me up. I let go of my fear and hold him tight. Quincy puts me down. I reach for Beverly but stop because she looks too fragile.

"You should be resting," I say.

"Had to see it through, make sure Jamal gets released." She turns to Mr. Jones. "And shake this man's hand."

Mr. Jones opts for a fist bump, then Beverly smiles at Steve. He shakes her hand—the one not in a sling—and I notice how their touch lingers. I look to Quincy to see if he notices. He shakes his head at me, then chuckles.

"I'm assuming you haven't been watching the news?" Quincy asks.

I shake my head.

"It's all over," he says. "Turn on the television."

I flick it on in the conference room and turn up the volume, flooded by news pouring in. The red BREAKING NEWS headlines scroll across the bottom of the screen:

Breaking News: Innocence X founder Stephen Jones takes high-profile case. Inquiries into Davidson murders and new witnesses.

Breaking News: Jamal Beaumont to be released as suspect in murder of eighteen-year-old Angela Herron.

A Black female reporter stands at the steps of the county jail.

"In a strange turn of events, local white nationalist Richard Brighton will be charged with the murder of Angela Herron. A reliable witness has also come forward with evidence that would connect Brighton to the murders of Mark and Cathy Davidson more than seven years ago, claiming that prosecutors hid the crucial evidence at the time. We'll be following these cases closely."

I cover my mouth. I used to dream about this day for Daddy. Replay all the ways that his story would finally be told, but I never thought it would be like this.

"News travels fast." Mr. Jones turns to Steve. "Good job, son. You went with your gut in taking this case. Tracy, when you get to college, let me know if you're looking for an internship."

I nod, still in shock.

"What does this mean now that it's on the news like this?" I ask.

"It means they can't hide this story," Steve says. "It's on every channel."

Each moment I've held in—twisted up for years of prayer, hope, anguish—all unwind as I let out a cry.

"Daddy's coming home," I say. "Daddy's coming home." Each time I say the words, they feel more real.

I flick through a few news stations to catch the coverage. All are on Daddy's case, highlighting Innocence X, who have been working on exoneration cases for decades. Daddy's story is their most visible case to date.

My fists unclench. How long have I been holding myself ready to fight? I look at the clock on the wall. Time shifting to our side.

TWO MONTHS LATER

Jamal is suited up in the same outfit from *The Susan Touric Show.* He holds on to Corinne's hand, who's shaking next to him. Mama's got her hand on Jamal's shoulder. I'm wearing yellow today. A bright-colored dress for what I'm hoping is the best day of my life. My hair blown out, even took the time for makeup.

We take the courthouse steps as a family, fighting through a swarm of news media.

We enter and go through security for the Court of Criminal Appeals, courtroom 8. Judge Vandyne is the presiding judge among the nine judges who have been reviewing Daddy's appeal. My footsteps make the familiar sound of walking on the marble floors.

As I reach the door, I suck in air to balance the rushing feeling of blood pumping through my body. I've learned over time that you have to control yourself in a courtroom. But this one will be like none we've faced before. Instead of a row for the jury, it'll be the judges lined up in two rows. We've all been warned not to let it intimidate us. That our focus should be on Daddy. On Judge Vandyne. Jamal, Corinne, and Mama go before me. I wave them ahead as they're cleared to enter. I need a moment. I've dreamed of this day, and I don't want to forget a second of it.

Once I'm settled, I partially open the left door and slide into the courtroom.

Tasha and her family are seated on the defense side, right behind our row. Daddy Greg's arms are around Tasha and Monica.

The courtroom is packed. I show my wristband to indicate I've got a seat reserved. Near the front of the courtroom, I see the people closest to Daddy's trial: my family, the Evanses, Mrs. Ridges and Quincy, even Sheriff Brighton and Officer Clyde. It warms my heart to see *our* community members seated like a shield of protection, with the church members led by Pastor Jenkins and the community center regulars that Dr. Scott gathered. This time we're not leaving without justice. You can smell it in the air.

This time will be different.

Judge Vandyne's glasses hang at the tip of his nose; he's focused on the papers in front of him, not on the eight other judges. He barely looks up at the prosecution or the defense. The courtroom is silent when the side door opens.

Daddy. Not in a white jumper, but in a suit.

Two correction officers at his side, but this time no cuffs. They joke with him, maybe trying to get him to relax, but Daddy is stone-cold serious. His eyes searching for his family. I can see him scanning for me. I slip into the front row behind the defense, where Quincy joins me at the end of the row.

I make sure Daddy knows I'm here before he's seated. He's got his long, dark fingers wrapped together to keep from shaking. Stephen Jones Sr. greets him; they shake hands. I watch Daddy glance back every few moments at Mama, then us. He finally lets a smile peek out when Mama mouths, *Don't look so guilty.*

The bailiff calls us to rise. It's starting.

My eyes begin to well as I think about how much time we've lost with Daddy. I look back out to the courtroom. Dean catches my eye and he mouths, *You got this.* I smile. Our friendship took a hit, but we're strong. Something in me knows it will be able to survive.

The judge calls the attorneys to the front to review the appeal. He and Stephen Jones Sr. talk back and forth, and then the prosecutor answers some questions.

"Your Honor, we'd like to submit an oral argument to go with our appeal," Mr. Jones says.

"Objection," the prosecutor says.

"I'll allow it," Judge Vandyne says.

The prosecution looks frustrated, but they weren't expected to object. Especially being under scrutiny for their approach to the first trial since the media made Mrs. Evans's statement public.

We should've known the district attorney's team would try to pull something; they've never been fair to us before.

The room is silent when Stephen Jones Sr. begins to speak. He commands the courtroom with his words.

"A rush to judgment took this innocent man's freedom from him." He points to Daddy, and the courtroom hangs on every word. "His family has suffered seven long years knowing that, at the time of the murder, he had the best witnesses you could ask for—his arm around his pregnant wife, children playing at his feet—but their truth was unable to stand in the court of law because their voices were silenced. Overpowered by a desperate attempt to close a case. Now another family suffers. All because the prosecution charged the wrong man, and the real killer was free to murder again. Free to spread hate through racist organizations. Your Honor, let us end this injustice here and now with the Beaumont family and start to heal our community. Grant justice for James Beaumont."

I watch Judge Vandyne as he takes in the argument, knowing that the other eight judges have already weighed in. They've had time to consider. To feel the weight of the personal impact this has had on our family. And front-row seats to the injustices throughout the entire process, all leading to Angela's murder.

Ultimately, this decision comes down to whether the judges will affirm Daddy's conviction or reverse it, forcing us to go to the Supreme Court. We hope it won't go that way. We want Daddy home. Today.

I'm nervous. My heart is sinking. Judge Vandyne has the

same expression Judge Williams had years ago when he confirmed what the jury's decision would mean for Daddy. Death. His matter-of-fact demeanor always rubbed me the wrong way.

He thought he was being just, but what I've learned is you can't separate humanity from the legal system. That's what Mrs. Evans did. She didn't think about our family. The real people affected. She closed that door years ago when the trial started. Now that she's opened it up again, I wonder if she'll ever be the same. The guilt eats at her. I hope Judge Williams lies restless at night, thinking about Daddy's case.

Daddy looks at Mr. Jones, hoping for a sign, then turns to us. Our eyes are misty. The ache inside takes over again. Nothing here that I can control. I squeeze Jamal's hand.

I just want the prosecution to make this easy, but I look over at them and they appear stubborn as ever. This feels too familiar. Tasha touches my shoulder as I clutch the bench with my free hand. The thought overwhelms me. I'm paralyzed by the realization that if we don't win today, time might run out before we can even make it to the Supreme Court.

The prosecutor stands to make his oral argument.

"Let me review it," the judge says.

The prosecutor hesitates, then hands over his brief and argument. He remains standing, waiting.

"Sit."

"Your Honor?"

"Sit."

Murmurs take over the crowd. The edge in the judge's voice is harsh. He hits his gavel, and the court is silent. Mr. Jones puts his hand on Daddy's to calm him.

Daddy whispers to Mr. Jones, who shakes his head slowly. He doesn't seem to know where this is going. I squeeze Jamal's hand.

"We have reviewed a signed affidavit from a Sheriff Brighton," the judge says. "An official report filed by two witnesses stating that Richard Brighton was in the vicinity at the time of the crime, found by Officer Beverly Ridges in a sealed evidence bag, that was *not* turned over to the defense at trial. We have a ballistics report from a gun owned by Richard Brighton that matches the gun used in the killings of Mark and Cathy Davidson, and we have reviewed DNA samples never tested during the trial that are a match for Richard Brighton. Witnesses who previously testified they saw Jackson Ridges and James Beaumont in town close to the time that the Davidsons were murdered now say they were pressured to make false statements. One witness is named outright as a known repeat witness for the police."

"Your Honor—" the prosecutor begins.

The judge doesn't even acknowledge him.

"The prosecution does not object to a review of the appeal and wrote a statement to support the case. But as I read the statement, there are no apologies to the court. To Mr. James Beaumont. No statement regarding the police's and the prosecution's tampering with evidence, with witnesses."

The courtroom starts buzzing. We can feel the judge moving

toward a decision that has already been carefully considered by the other judges. Judge Vandyne has been given authority to continue presiding without more review.

The judge sets down his papers and removes his glasses.

"Mr. James Beaumont, please stand."

Daddy lifts his body up with help from Mr. Jones. I can tell he doesn't know how to process what's happening. It's fear and hope all mixed into one body. I rub my thumb inside my palms to settle my nerves.

"Mr. Beaumont, do you still claim to be not guilty of the murders of Mark and Cathy Davidson?"

"Your Honor, I'm not guilty."

"Then on behalf of the Court of Criminal Appeals, with regret and sorrow for the trials you have been through, and the seven years you have served, may God forgive us all for what we know now, you are a free man. I hereby reverse your conviction for the murder of Mark and Cathy Davidson."

The room explodes in applause. Daddy turns to us immediately, Mama falling to her knees, but this time praising God. I cover my mouth with my hands. Jamal can't get to Daddy on his side so he just puts his arms around Quincy and me, Corinne squishing in the middle. Crying out in joy. Unbelievable joy that it's all finally over. I'm bursting so much my chest feels like it's exploding. Buzzing and zipping inside.

It's over. The clock has stopped. We can stop living our life counting the days, counting the time between Saturday and Monday visits.

Jamal takes Corinne to see Daddy. Quincy places his hands on either side of my face and kisses me.

"You did it." Quincy presses in closer to me, resting his forehead against mine.

I flick my eyes at him but don't move.

"Completely platonic, don't get excited." Quincy's voice is soft, but there's a shakiness behind it because we've been inseparable ever since Jamal's been free.

"Maybe it should be more," I whisper.

Quincy stops joking and kisses me again. Each time I kiss him, I'm lost in us. He places his hand by my ear and kisses my lips once more. Quincy gives a halfway grin. I hold on to his hand until it's time for Daddy to speak.

We follow Daddy through an exit that leads to the front steps of the court, where the media has been gathering, waiting for him to speak. Before he goes to the mic, Daddy extends his arm to grab my hand and pull me up next to him. I look out at the crowd. The courtroom catching up to us and surrounding the cameras. Across the street, the sidewalk is filled with people who weren't able to come to the courtroom but wanted to make sure there was justice. I'm taken aback by the swarms of people here to see my daddy free.

Daddy whispers, "Baby girl, this is all because of you."

He gets on the mic, going down the list of everything he's thankful for. He sticks to the speech he wrote because he didn't want to miss a name or a moment. The crowd is overflowing, growing. I breathe out slowly, take pride at being able to stand next to my daddy. No longer in Polunsky Prison, a free man, for the first time in seven years.

Daddy finishes to cheers.

Cameras clicking, reporters yelling questions, but they're overtaken by the shouts of people chanting, *Justice. Justice. Justice.*

I'm soaring inside. The word rattles through my body. Daddy lifts my hands up with his. Then Mr. Jones and Steve take the mic. We drop back, and our security guards escort us away as Innocence X takes more questions, holding court with the media now, so we can escape without anyone following. Mr. Jones has them captivated.

I hold my breath, waiting until Daddy sees our surprise.

He stumbles toward it, speechless. Mama passes me a knowing glance. All my comments over the years, I swallow up because she was right. The look on Daddy's face to see his old Buick, just like the last day he drove it—it's priceless.

Daddy's car is polished clean, parked on the side of the courthouse in a private spot.

Mama hands the keys over to him. He shakes his head. "I haven't driven in years."

He hands me the keys. I refuse. So does Jamal.

Seeing Daddy drive us home is just as meaningful to us. Daddy clears his throat as he sits in the driver's seat and we all pile in, waiting for him to turn the ignition. I can feel he's nervous that it might not work, that the moment will fall apart. Like everything else.

Daddy waits another minute, then turns the key. The engine

revs, then starts purring. Daddy starts out slow, cautious. When we reach the highway toward Crowning Heights, we can see him relax. No longer looking over his shoulder. He lets out a laugh, a great belting laugh as he grips the steering wheel at ten and two, like he's just learning how to drive again. Corinne is giggling watching him. He looks in the rearview mirror, and our eyes meet. I don't say anything when I see that Daddy's laughing, but tears are running down his face.

It's all real. We can let it out. We're holding on to each other, windows rolled down, letting the wind whip on us as Daddy drives us home.

For the first time, I allow myself to shut the worrying away. There're still some uncertainties, for sure, but the most deadly countdown has ended. With justice secured for my father, I'm finally free, too.

Monday, September 27

Stephen Jones, Jr.
Innocence X Headquarters
1111 Justice Road
Birmingham, Alabama 35005
Re: Death Penalty—Intake Department

Dear Steve,

You thought I'd stop, huh? This is going to be my last letter. I bet you wonder what I'm going to be doing. I'm starting my senior year with my own podcast: Corner for Justice. I decided I didn't need to be the editor of the school newspaper if I can reach a larger audience with social media. I have just over 100,000 followers already! It's all about highlighting injustice. Would you be willing to do an interview? I've got a lot of people lined up, so time's ticking. I don't plan to wait seven years for a response.

Thank you again for everything you've done. Congratulations on your recent case. Don't forget us when you're big-time. I've got a couple of cases you might be interested in.

Peace and solidarity,
Tracy Beaumont

AUTHOR'S NOTE

While *This Is My America* is a work of fiction, it is rooted in US history and fueled by my decades of work in education and advocacy for diversity, equity, and inclusion. Growing up, I was an activist in my community as much as a daydreamer in the library. At the time, I had trouble finding books with characters who looked like me: the gap of diverse literature from diverse writers was (and still is) staggering. Nowadays, I write the stories I wanted to read, to fill the space in between those worlds.

Racism in the criminal justice system was imprinted on me at twelve years old when Los Angeles police officers violently beat Rodney King. I was shocked at the inhumanity of his treatment, and when the video aired on national television, I thought surely justice would finally be served. But it wasn't. When a jury acquitted the police, the Black community exploded and rioted in anger. I felt their rage. Their pain was my pain.

In 1997, I marched against police brutality for the first time at a youth rally in Pittsburgh during the NAACP national conference. The city was still rife with tension in the Black community from a few years earlier, when Jonny Gammage, a Black motorist, died of suffocation after he was pinned to the pavement by white officers. Those officers were charged with involuntary manslaughter; none were convicted.

With no books to turn to for Black protagonists, I found that rap became my life's soundtrack, from Lauryn Hill's lyrical prose influences through Public Enemy, Ice-T, and N.W.A teaching me that art can be used to express discontent. Rap was my generation's tool for expression, and it was this music, not high school English classes, that taught me how to be a writer.

I wrote *This Is My America* to tackle serious topics and give hope to the next generation. For my son and daughter, who will one day need to find meaning. In 2014, my then-six-year-old son burst into uncontrollable tears in public after seeing video footage of Eric Garner take his last breath, held down by police officers, with no one attempting to resuscitate him. "He couldn't breathe," my son cried. "He couldn't breathe, and they didn't stop." He worried, what if someone called the police on me because he was crying? What if the police held me down, his asthmatic mother? Then I wouldn't be able to breathe. In that moment, I knew my son's days of innocence were over. Corinne Beaumont's character represents my children's fragile innocence on the line.

This Is My America seeks to expand the now very public conversation on police brutality that the Black Lives Matter movement made possible through activism. One in three Black boys born today will be incarcerated in their lifetime. After the 1960s War on Crime, the 1970s War on Drugs, and the Crime Bill of 1994, mass incarceration skyrocketed. The prison-industrial complex is a $182 billion industry that feeds off the lives of Black, brown, and poor people caught up in its vicious cycle.*

While mass incarceration is a complex problem, I wanted to simply (*ha ha*) focus on how it's almost impossible to prove someone is innocent without adequate representation. Bryan Stevenson's incredible legacy, *Just Mercy*, was the first nonfiction work that made me realize I could explore topics I care most deeply about in my young adult stories. I based my character Steve Jones on Bryan Stevenson, and the fictional Innocence X on the incredible organizations Equal Justice Initiative and the Innocence Project.

Tracy Beaumont was written in honor of all the Black girls and womxn leading movements and the young womxn I advise and mentor, who are powerful beyond measure. I envision "Tracy's Corner" as a way I would call other students to action if I were in high school today. I was a lot like Tracy, full of idealism and a desire to make the world a better place. I was president of my multicultural club and the local youth NAACP chapter in high school, and we held many meetings in the NAACP's downtown office. In college, as a student organizer and co-president of the Black student union, I worked to bring my peers together to talk about important issues and try to effect change. Now I work on a college campus as an ally and advocate, and I bear witness to my students' active engagement.

---

* prisonpolicy.org/reports/money.html

This Is My America is a piece of fiction; if this story were true, there wouldn't be an immediate happy ending for the Beaumonts. They would continue to live in the same society, combating racial prejudice and inequality—with all the disadvantages and stains of post-prison survival and recovery. I wanted to leave my readers with hope but nevertheless reflect real-life struggles, which is why Tracy's friend Tasha and her family are still on an uphill journey of life after prison at the end of the novel.

This Is My America's DNA is embedded from beginning to end with complex topics that impact Black Americans today. The Beaumonts' story showcases how generational trauma caused by mass incarceration reverberates throughout the Black American experience today. The story weaves past and present. It is based as much on Thurgood Marshall's story told in *Devil in the Grove* as it is on *Just Mercy.* The present is still a reflection of the past.

The death penalty is one of today's most horrifying examples of the legacy of slavery. This is why I selected the topic of the death penalty out of many issues of mass incarceration. This history began as early as 1619, when African slaves were brought to the British colony of Jamestown, Virginia, as part of the transatlantic slave trade. Legal bondage of those enslaved and their descendants continued until the ratification of the Thirteenth Amendment ended de jure slavery in 1865. During the Reconstruction era, Southern whites rebelled against the end of slavery, and a terrorist group, the Ku Klux Klan, was born. By 1870, Klan representation had expanded to almost every state. Slavery had ended, except as a punishment for a crime. So former slaves found themselves being charged with vague crimes like "loitering." The country had profited from slavery, and prisoners became a viable exception for use of free labor.

Equality wasn't realized for those who were freed. In 1896, the US Supreme Court upheld the constitutionality of racial segregation with the *Plessy v. Ferguson* decision. This "separate but equal" doctrine permitted separate public facilities as long as they were of "equal quality." It was not until 1954 that the Supreme Court revisited the doctrine. In the landmark case *Brown v. Board of Education,* the Court found "separate but equal" to be unconstitutional in public schools. Major legislation followed in the next decade: the 1964 Civil Rights Act, the 1965 Voting Rights Act, and the 1968 Fair Housing Act.

Some declared the United States a post-racial society upon the election of Barack Obama, the forty-fourth president. This declaration is refuted by the rise of white supremacists since the election of the forty-fifth president. The stain of racism also rears its ugly head each time a viral video reveals police brutality or racial disparities in arrests and convictions. Worse, Black people are regularly viewed as threats in public establishments throughout the country simply because they are Black. In 2018, two Black café patrons in Philadelphia were arrested while waiting for a white colleague—*New York* magazine titled its story "Black Loiterers, White Lingerers, and Starbucks." In Oakland, a white woman called the police because someone was Barbecuing While

Black in a public park. In Dallas, a police officer shot an unarmed Black man in his home, where she claimed to have mistaken him for an intruder after erroneously entering his apartment, thinking it was her own.

I share these viral stories as examples because the victims weren't believed when they told their stories. Our larger society doesn't accept that the horrors of racism persist until they view bodily trauma on television or, more recently, cell phone or police video of these heinous crimes.

Another authorial decision I made was to adapt the real visitation practices in Texas. To better humanize James Beaumont, I decided to not place him shackled behind a glass wall during interactions with his children and wife. I want readers to know James as his family does and to feel his loving presence without barriers as he interacts with them.

The appeal process for death penalty cases is complex and differs by state. The Court of Criminal Appeals is Texas's highest state court for criminal cases, consisting of nine justices (including a presiding judge). I provided a simplified version of an expedited appellate process so as not to bog down the story with criminal appeal procedures that are specific to the state of Texas. With this challenge, I chose to depict an appeal proceeding that could include James Beaumont and his family. My ultimate goal was to show elements of an arduous process while also infusing hope and leaving space for the reader to ponder the next chapter for the Beaumont family.

I also wanted to portray the continuing legacy of white supremacy and terror that persists today. During the late 1970s and early 1980s, Vietnamese fishermen clashed with the KKK in Galveston Bay. For years they faced harassment and were forced to defend their livelihood despite intimidation and violence from the Klan. This story informed my selection of the lynching of a non-Black person to further highlight the widespread fear and targeting of the KKK. But we cannot forget that of the almost five thousand lynchings in US history, over 70 percent were of African Americans. I urge you to see the National Memorial for Peace and Justice, located in Montgomery, Alabama. The memorial, which can also be viewed online, is dedicated to the memory of enslaved Black people, people terrorized by lynchings, and African Americans shunned by racial segregation.

Lynchings and capital punishment draw many comparisons as inhumane and unequal treatment largely applied on the basis of race. As of April 1, 2019, there were 2,637 inmates in prison who had been sentenced to death, across thirty-two states. African Americans make up about 13 percent of the US population but are 42 percent of the people on death row. It's important to acknowledge that, nationally, 95 percent of prosecutors are white, according to a 2014 study by the Reflective Democracy Campaign. This lack of diverse representation leaves more room for implicit (and explicit) bias against defendants of color.

Evidence of disparity is most egregious in the state of Louisiana, where the odds of a death sentence are 97 percent higher in cases where the victim was white. Slavery was abolished, but the economics of the prison-industrial complex serves as an exception. Take, for example, the comments of a Louisiana sheriff, Steve Prator, who in 2017 railed against the move to release prisoners, citing their ability to provide free labor. I hope the reader will ponder the application of the death penalty as it relates to the legacy of slavery.

As I wrote this story, I was cautious not to add any details for voyeuristic purposes while also recognizing the trauma behind real-life incidents. To omit some aspects in this story would be to deny this reality. However, the Black American experience is not a story limited to pain; it is one that is joyous, remarkable, filled with possibility. I also celebrate the amazing voices and stories of other authors who are working to expand representation on stories we have yet to fully tell.

Knowledge (and representation) is power, and I truly believe movements are made by the next generation. The legacy of racism runs deep in our society, but we can stop this cycle if we all are involved. We can let the world know enough is enough. You can make a difference. Your voice matters. Demand justice and equality. I hope I leave my readers with empathy, awareness, and agency.

In solidarity and respect,
Black Lives Matter.
Kim Johnson

ADDITIONAL RESOURCES

Criminal Justice Organizations

Innocence X is fictional and not grounded in the operations and practices of actual organizations that are dedicated to this work. The websites of the following organizations provide information about work in criminal justice reform:

The **Innocence Project** focuses on DNA testing for exonerations and criminal justice reform. innocenceproject.org

The **Equal Justice Initiative** was founded by Bryan Stevenson. The first book you should pick up is *Just Mercy*, Mr. Stevenson's memoir. eji.org

The **Death Penalty Information Center,** a nonprofit organization, provides facts and analysis for the media and the public. deathpenaltyinfo.org/documents/FactSheet.pdf

Prison Policy Initiative is a nonprofit and nonpartisan group that researches the harm caused by mass incarceration. prisonpolicy.org/reports/money.html

Suggested References

The topics of racism, injustices in criminal prosecution, and police brutality are unfortunately controversial issues. Some people may resist or even attack efforts to shine a spotlight on American law enforcement and our justice system. But it is this critical juncture that must be examined, as it sits at the crossroads of racial equality. Below are some references that I would suggest if you are interested in the topic and want to learn more.

Alexander, Michelle. *The New Jim Crow: Mass Incarceration in the Age of Colorblindness*. New York: New Press, 2010.

Coates, Ta-Nehisi. *Between the World and Me*. New York: Spiegel & Grau, 2015.

Crenshaw, Kimberlé W. "From Private Violence to Mass Incarceration: Thinking Intersectionally About Women, Race, and Social Control," 59 *UCLA Law Review* 1418 (2012).

Du Bois, W. E. B. (William Edward Burghardt). *The Souls of Black Folk*. The Oxford W. E. B. Du Bois series. New York: Oxford University Press, 2007.

DuVernay, Ava, director. *13th*. Forward Movement, Kandoo Films, Netflix, 2016. netflix.com/title/80091741.

Goffman, Alice. *On the Run: Fugitive Life in an American City*. Chicago: University of Chicago Press, 2014.

Kendi, Ibram X. *Stamped from the Beginning: The Definitive History of Racist Ideas in America*. New York: Nation Books, 2016.

King, Gilbert. *Devil in the Grove: Thurgood Marshall, the Groveland Boys, and the Dawn of a New America*. New York: Harper, 2012.

Kuklin, Susan. *No Choirboy: Murder, Violence, and Teenagers on Death Row*. New York: Henry Holt, 2008.

Moore, Wes. *The Other Wes Moore: One Name, Two Fates*. New York: Spiegel & Grau, 2010.

Rothstein, Richard. *The Color of Law: A Forgotten History of How Our Government Segregated America*. New York: Liveright Publishing, 2017.

Stevenson, Bryan. *Just Mercy: A Story of Justice and Redemption*. New York: Spiegel & Grau, 2014.

Thompson, Heather Ann. *Blood in the Water: The Attica Prison Uprising of 1971 and Its Legacy*. New York: Pantheon Books, 2016.

Wytsma, Ken. *The Myth of Equality: Uncovering the Roots of Injustice and Privilege*. Downers Grove, Illinois: IVP Books, 2017.

ACKNOWLEDGMENTS

First and foremost, thank you, God, for leading me in a purpose-driven life.

Kevin and my littles, J and W: I love you to the depths of the earth and the heights of our universe. May the world never rob you of your innocence. It's your love that drives me, and I always try to be everything to you. J—I know you love me the absolute most (I tell myself this when you follow me to the bathroom). W—I'm so proud of who you've become. One day, when you're older, your comics and moviemaking skills will dazzle the world. Kevin— Thank you to my loving husband for giving me space to write. I know I'm a lot! Zipping and running everywhere, taking on new things, and being *called* to serve. I'm so fortunate to have you and know there is a lot you sacrifice also for this to happen. Thank you to the Johnson extended family for all your support and the stacks of books and conversations on race, justice, and politics.

Thank you to my mother, who cultivated greatness in all her children (and our extended immigrant and African family). We might not always do everything the way you like, but you raised God-fearing children who are grounded in your values. You taught us the meaning of hard work. Your daughters are purposed to touch the world in different ways. Thank you for taking me to the public library, which was my reading foundation. To my dad, who loved to read. It planted a seed.

To my sisters, the real AQs—Kawezya, Kalizya, Kanyanta, and the ones who are the true Ks—we should be the ones with a reality show. *WE* grinding all day, every day. To Kal and KK: You're my biggest fans, always pushing love and greatness. You make my cheeks blush when you share with the world how proud you are of me. To my brilliant baby sis, Kawezya: You were the first person I let read my stories. You answered my legal questions, shared your experiences with a death penalty pro bono case, and made countless connections to attorneys working pro bono to appeal death penalty sentences. Thank you for responding to all those last-minute requests and rambling emails and texts. I can't wait for you to begin your writer journey. We have to have another brainstorm session at our faves, either Calabash or BusBoys and Poets in DC, so we can begin that co-writing project we've been mulling.

To my extraordinary agent, Jennifer March Soloway: Thank you for finding me in the query trenches and taking a huge chance by signing me. You gave me confidence to share an unfinished project. You offered a few weeks later, and I'll never forget that moment. You have taught me so much, and your incredible support means everything to me. Our author-agent relationship is magic. Thank you for all that you do.

Thank you to Chelsea Eberly, my first editor at Random House. Once we spoke on the phone, I was convinced you would be my greatest cheerleader and would care for my project with the utmost respect. I'm so grateful we were able to see the project all the way through the copyedit. I wish you the best in your new journey. I feel incredibly blessed to have worked with you. Your insight, thoughtfulness, and support have been amazing with this delicate and important subject. You left me in incredible hands with my current editor, Caroline Abbey, who has been just as lovely and supportive. Caroline continues to protect my voice and ensure that my story stays true to its intent. What an honor.

To every single person at Random House Children's and the entire Random House team that helped make this book possible: special thank-yous to Barbara Bakowski, Anne Heausler, Alison Kolani, and Jules Kelly. Ray Shappell, for your amazing design detail that made the book perfection. The marketing team, designers, school and library team, digital and social media, you are all just incredible. Kathy Dunn, my wonderful publicist, who has worked tirelessly to connect me and my book to readers.

To Chuck Styles for the amazing cover. I feel so blessed that my love of art has also found itself in a cover from a true Black artist. May you continue to shine.

Thank you to those who were essential to my writing journey for *This Is My America,* as far back to when it was called *Just Mercy.* I'm forever thankful for Raechelle Garrett, Jennifer Dugan, Janae Marks, Cass Newbould, Sarah Darer Littman, Ely Azure, Gail de la Cruz-Villanueva, Rena Baron, Ronni Davis, Maura Jortner, Judi Lauren, Bethany Morrow, Kim Rogers, Jen Ung, and Matt de la Peña.

Thank you to the many people who shared various experiences

with law enforcement, the legal system, incarceration, and the death penalty in the United States. Thank you for opening up your world to me and trusting me. In addition, I am especially grateful to the police officers who actively work to break down implicit and explicit bias and systems of oppression in their policing. Officer Beverly Ridges's character and the evolution of the characters Officer Clyde and Sheriff Brighton represent the varying changes in policing that can build bridges of justice if people actively work to transform it. A special thank-you to Samson Asiyanbi, trial attorney and former fellow with the Equal Justice Initiative. You gave me incredible context on exoneration work and research to follow up. Any inaccuracies are mine and not a reflection of the expertise or opinions of those interviewed.

I began writing in 2011, at thirty-two years old. I'd never thought of myself as a writer. I had terrible grammar (okay, still have). I want to thank the following people who at some point helped me grow as a writer—I am a better writer for their efforts. Thank you to Lindsey Alexander, Rachel Solomon, Suja Sukumar, Kiki Nguyen, Wade White, Laura VP, Aften Brooks Szymanski, PCC Crew, Jenny Chou, Cindy Rodriguez, Kara Taylor. And to my Willamette Writers/SCBWI Oregon family, who made me feel welcome in a space where there were only a couple of Black attendees each year: Fonda Lee (we pitched together years ago, and you were my first real-life writer friend), Christine Mitchell (one day I will write a script! You are a joy!), Joanna Bartlett (my roomie), Jennie Komp (write that book, it needs to be told), Cindy Swanson, and Heather Penn. And to the recent years' WilWrite conference planners, who have made the effort to bring diverse speakers to Oregon. It matters and I appreciate it.

To the sponsors of all the writing contests I was successful at and those I wasn't: I gained something through all of it. To all the people who create communities through social media: You make it a better place. Especially Brenda Drake, Kellye Garrett, and Beth Phelan.

To my first online writing and publishing communities: PCC for life, Write Pack, and the #Roaring20sdebutgroup. To all those who made voice and space for my book to even exist, such as the diversity kidlit groups, We Need Diverse Books, and Justina Ireland for Write in the Margins. Thank you.

To the people who tried to crush my dreams: You didn't. I'm ten times stronger now.

To the Sigma Delta chapter of Alpha Kappa Alpha Sorority, Inc.: As your graduate advisor, I hope you learn from me as much as I learn from you. To Zeta Sigma Omega chapter of Alpha Kappa Alpha Sorority, Inc.: You continue to fill my tank of sisterhood and inspiration. Every day you hold your heads up and aspire to the highest standard. Be supreme in service to ALL mankind.

To all the Black student leaders I've been blessed to support and learn from, past and present: Your sacrifice to be an activist and leader will teach you lessons that will take you far in life, personally and professionally. You don't sit back and watch, you move for change. Shout-out to BSU, BWA, BMA, BSTF, and whatever iteration of groups you turn into; keep trying to work together.

To Doneka, my bestie/boss: Thank you for pushing and supporting me. We don't have easy positions, but you always have my back and make sure to tell me to "WRITE, so we can get up outta here." I wouldn't be able to manage writing, family, service, and work if I didn't have people in my life like you who make it okay to do this.

Thank you to my readers.

If I forgot you, please charge it to my head and not my heart.

ABOUT THE AUTHOR

KIM JOHNSON held leadership positions in social justice organizations as a teen. She's now a college administrator who maintains civic engagement throughout the community while also mentoring Black student activists and leaders. *This Is My America* is her debut novel. It explores racial injustice against innocent Black men who are criminally sentenced and the families left behind to pick up the pieces. She holds degrees from the University of Oregon and the University of Maryland, College Park. Kim lives her best life in Oregon with her husband and two kids.

KCJOHNSONWRITES.COM